TALES

of

G12

*Many thanks and
Best wishes to Jan
from Nancie*

TALES

of

G12

NANZIE MCLEOD

First published in the United Kingdom by
Nanzie McLeod, Glasgow

The author has asserted her moral rights.

British Library Cataloguing-in Publication Data.
A catalogue record for this book is available from
the British Library.

ISBN 0 9529527 7 7

Origination by McCulloch, Glasgow
Printed by Bell & Bain Limited, Glasgow

Contents

6

DEDICATION

I should like to dedicate this book to the skilled tradesmen, masons, carpenters, glaziers, plumbers, blacksmiths and many others who turned the ambitious dreams of architects into reality and built the luxurious mansions, gracious terraces and tall splendid tenements which are to be found in G12. We also owe a debt of gratitude to those countless, magnificently strong and hairy Clydesdale horses who dragged vast quantities of red and grey sandstone, bricks, timber and all the other necessary building materials, to the area.

Thanks to
Jak, Jean, Eleanor and Robin
for their valuable assistance.

Thanks also to my four daughters
Kate, Esther, Sarah and Alice
for their support and encouragement.

INTRODUCTION

*"Despairing of literal and absolute truth, I have not scrupled
to make such further changes as seemed conducive to the
reader's profit and delight."*

Nathaniel Hawthorn

I echo this statement and, as with my other short stories,
I have used facts, personal experience and a lot of
imagination. The postcode G12 (previously designated
W2) covers a large leafy area to the west of Glasgow. It has
been considered a desirable part of the city in which to live
since Victoria's reign, when the magnificent terraces and
mansions which line Great Western Road were built. Not
every suburb of G12 is so splendidly luxurious, though the
dense residential projects of the twentieth century were of a
high standard and provided homes for the various ranks of
the emerging middle class. Many of my stories are set in
Hyndland which is one of those suburbs and which has been
my home for most of my life.

I hope that my memories may awaken some forgotten
facts for the Hyndland resident and also interest those who
are unfamiliar with the splendid tenements of Glasgow. No
one need fear that they will discover anything unpleasant
about themselves. Some short factual articles in this book
have appeared in *Hyndland Heart*, an interesting little magazine produced by the Hyndland Residents' Association. Other
small pieces are personal musings which I hope will be
excused, or skipped.

As well as the nineteenth century magnificence of Great
Western Road and Kelvinside, G12 includes the less grand but
still impressive suburbs of Dowanhill, Hillhead, Hyndland,
Kelvindale, Partick and part of Anniesland. All areas are
densely populated for each tenement provides eight flats and
many of the mansions have been subdivided to provide two
or three apartments, each one spacious by modern standards.
The west end tenements are four or five storeys high and

generally built of red sandstone, though not always. The flats range in size from two rooms and kitchen to seven rooms and kitchen. Even the smallest and most modest are well designed with high ceilings, large windows and fine details. The common entry hall of the building, known as the close, is usually tiled and these are often beautifully decorated with Art Nouveau designs. The standard of the various dwellings demonstrates the wealth that was Glasgow's.

G12 homes are in great demand and fetch large sums. Unfortunately, as in all cities, the proliferation of the motor car creates problems. A tenement with eight homes in it is likely to own at least eight cars but command only forty or fifty yards of frontage in which to park them. Many of the streets are busy main roads with daytime restrictions. With vehicles becoming larger, the problem seems insurmountable.

Also falling within the G12 boundary is the campus of Glasgow University with its various museums and departments, much of Kelvingrove park (though not Kelvingrove Art Gallery and Museum, which is in G3, on the other side of the River Kelvin) the Botanic Gardens, the Western Infirmary, Gartnavel Hospitals and until recently, the BBC. Naturally there are many shopping areas to service the needs of the G12 population. Great Western Road, Byres Road and Dumbarton Road are lined with shops and various small shopping centres have developed in pockets of spare ground in the last thirty years.

Apart from a few years in Canada and six months in Hamburg, I have lived in Hyndland for most of my long life and have always been glad to return to it. It is a very convenient area, close to the city, yet not far from the mountains or the sea. There are shops and a good school but more than that, it shares that friendliness and democracy that Glasgow folk bring to everyday living. The residents are mainly, though not all, professional and business people, comfortably 'well-heeled' rather than truly wealthy. Probably the older people, like myself, must struggle a little to pay the large council tax and the fuel bills required for the high-ceilinged rooms, but I cannot imagine living anywhere else.

Recently I heard the story of a woman from Sri Lanka who came to study in Glasgow. Before she left home she was strongly advised that she must try to stay in G12 if she possibly could. So we may consider it a post code of *world renown* and I am happy to say she was successful in locating herself here.

I should like to thank Ann Laird, author of the book *Hyndland - Edwardian Glasgow Tenement Suburb* for the excellent facts and illustrations in her book which have greatly helped and inspired me. The first edition now being out of print, Ann is currently working on an enlarged second edition.

For many years Ann has been tireless in her work to awaken interest in and appreciation of the astonishing heritage here in Glasgow's west end. Even the youngest of the tenements, terraces and villas is now over 100 years old and best practice by co-owners and property managers is more crucial than ever in securing the long-term care and maintenance of these buildings. To this end, Ann Laird's Scottish Tenement Group campaigned at Holyrood to promote the new Scottish Tenement Law of 2004.

As convenor of Friends of Glasgow West and chairman of the local Community Council, Ann continues to invest her energy in helping to protect our environment and improve our awareness of it, and we are grateful to her.

WEST END

Each one who studies cities finds,
    that the elite avoid prevailing winds.

And will always do their best,
    to build their homes out to the west.

Finding *that* the easiest solution,
    to avoid industrial pollution.

In London, Knightsbridge and Maidavale
    with elegance the eye avail,

Assuring each who therein dwells,
    that there's no chance of nasty smells.

We have Edinburgh architects to thank
    for Stockbridge and Comelybank,

And though grim and grey, to be sure,
    their atmosphere is very pure.

In Glasgow the ambitious bride
    will look to Hyndland or Kelvinside,

Where red sandstone tenements stand supreme
    and represent her dearest dream.

But those aspiring to the occidental
    must be prepared for sky-high rental,

Or perhaps a mortgage
    which will make their banker's knees begin to quake.

And Council tax is quite obscene
    for those who live where air is clean.

But Luxury is never free
    and the west end's where *one must just be!*

That's where the intelligentsia meet
    for conversation and viands sweet,

Polishing up their cultural skills,
    indulging esoteric thrills.

✧◆✧

AN AMBITIOUS PROJECT

Hyndland was farmland and countryside until the end of the nineteenth century when the scheme for the Hyndland tenements was born. It probably started as just an idea that was kicked around in some comfortable club, perhaps a few remarks exchanged when several whiskies inspired imagination. The excitement of the approach of the new century may have helped. Later, at a more sober time the project would be considered seriously. Next, the bare bones would be sketched by an ambitious young architect and finally the necessary financial details would be discussed. I would guess that is pretty much the scenario which attends every architectural achievement, great or small, since long before the Pyramids or the Parthenon.

The suburb would be built to the west to make sure that prevailing winds would chase away every shred of industrial smoke or smell and unlike the repetitive housing schemes of today, where each house mirrors its neighbour, those brave speculators decided to offer a wide range of dwellings. Taking into consideration the fact that families of different size, aspiration and income might want to locate in this smart new area, they set out to provide a variety of suitable accommodation. It was a clever and democratic idea and ensured that Hyndland acquired the personality of a village rather than a suburb. A very select village, for the magnificent dwellings of Kelvinside, Great Western Road and Dowanhill, where the very wealthy lived, were near neighbours. I wonder if those affluent home-owners were unhappy to hear about the projected encroachment of tenements on the countryside?

Hyndland was a logical design, with the largest flats built at the top of the hill and gradually diminishing in size as they moved downhill. Each block of tenements was built to enclose a rectangle of backyards, with the back of each building overlooking its own small drying green, where a wash house and a bin shelter were located. A service lane lay between the back greens, dividing the rectangle and giving access to the Corporation lorry which uplifted the copious, ash-laden rubbish

three times a week, in the middle of the night. Larger flats had
more generous drying greens and some provided a coal cellar for
each tenant.

The main thoroughfare, Clarence Drive was, or was likely to
become, very busy and so the more luxurious flats were located a
block away in Queensborough Gardens, which runs parallel to
Clarence Drive, and also in the quieter side streets, Falkland,
Lauderdale, Polwarth. There was decorative ironwork round the
gardens and fine tiles in the closes, the stone work was restrained
but elegant with simple decoration, columns and pillars and
charming conical towers marked each corner building. There was
a great deal of very beautiful stained glass, much of it sadly
destroyed in the war.

Falkland Mansions was built as the *crème de la crème* and
offered a few very luxurious four-bedroomed flats, some with
three fine public rooms, each of the latter brightly lit with
windows (often four forming a bay) extending across one wall.
Floor areas average sixteen square yards and ceilings are eleven
feet high with an intricate, decorative cornice. With maid's room,
butler's pantry, cloakroom, impressive stained glass windows,
over mantles, even a fireplace in the large hall, these flats were
for the wealthy and successful Edwardian. Some had a main door
to the street and made no use of the close, others had a main
door and also a tradesman's entrance in the close.

Other large flats are more modest in detail though they still
offer a great deal of space. On the south side of Clarence Drive at
the top, all ground floor flats were built with a sunny basement
to the rear of the flat, providing room for a larger family. My
own flat falls into this category but most of these two-level flats
have now been split into two more practical homes and mine was
divided in 1996.

I know of at least one other two-floored flat, though there
may be others. It is in Hyndland Road and rather than the basement, uses the ground and first floor with a splendid staircase
joining them. It is like a small mansion unexpectedly tucked
away in a tenement and has a beautiful outlook south through
the trees of Queensborough Gardens. But the Hyndland scheme
offered flats of all sizes to choose from and each flat, even the
smallest bachelor apartment, had a pleasant sitting room with a
bay window and a spacious kitchen with a bed recess for the

live-in domestic.

Towards the foot of the hill were modest one- and two-bed roomed flats for the bachelor or the young couple starting out, modified in proportion to the requirements of the prospective tenant. Outwardly the four storey tenements are coherent, with lofty generous windows in every room, but several different architects were involved and the interiors vary interestingly. Some flats echo a Victorian influence, while others embrace the Arts and Crafts style.

Shops were incorporated in the earliest Hyndland Road tenements. They had beautiful frontages, now destroyed, alas, by modernisation.

A few shops were included at the foot of Clarence Drive but the main group in that street were not built until 1926. The school was built in 1912.

The suburb of Hyndland was a social experiment, made long before the days of those inquisitive questionnaires which try to pinpoint exactly what we need. It must have been an impressive sight when all those towering red sandstone tenements were spanking new, built by speculators for the ever-growing range of middle classes of our wonderfully successful city.

I wonder how those businessmen got it so right without any market research?

No doubt there would be mud, rubble and workman's huts still lying untidily around for the several years that building was in hand. The red sandstone would still be harsh and raw before years of coal fires cast a sooty veil across it. There would be little greenery to add poetry to the streets.

In 1907, when my grandparents, in the early days of their marriage, were looking for a Glasgow flat to rent, they would never have considered living in Hyndland. For them this mushroom suburb would have been too distant from the centre of town. Difficult enough, as an up-and-coming artist, to attract clients and sitters, without expecting them to trail out of the city. Though there was a local railway station, Hyndland was two miles distant from Charing Cross and still further from the city centre. It would be 1910 before tramlines were extended and the yellow tram, number 24, would service the area and trundle along Hyndland Road before hurtling down Clarence Drive on its way to Anniesland.

Although the rent for those luxurious and pristine flats with their 'up-to-date kitchens and bathrooms' was modest, probably many Glasgow professional people shared my grandparents' reluctance. The splendid flats were 'slow' to be tenanted. Too slow for the businessmen who had invested in this venture. At times, high standards had to be modified, sometimes building stopped altogether, leaving some strange gap sites which would not be filled for the next seventy or eighty years, some more successfully than others. Of course Hyndland did eventually succeed wonderfully well and I wonder what the reaction of those long-ago businessmen would be to the immense wealth represented nowadays by their entrepreneurial genius.

Recently our building has had the mullions replaced in the impressive tower of bay windows. As I watched the workmen wrestle with the weighty pieces of red sandstone, I was again reminded of what an immense undertaking it was to build these massive tenements, around 200 of them, without the benefit of modern machinery or transport, or modern communications to help manage the sheer logistics of the enterprise.

Peter the Great of Russia used his great wealth to buy countless treasures. One of these was a giant lapidary vase of enormous weight which was dragged to the St Petersburg palace by one hundred and sixty horses. The procession was watched by thousands of citizens. That monstrous Russian vase, though no doubt admired by millions for its size and breath-taking value, has lain useless for centuries. But, for me, this extravagance pales in comparison with the building of G12 where tens of thousands of people have worked, reared their families and made their homes. And there should be a memorial to the noble Clydesdale horses that dragged the endless supply of heavy building materials to the site, uphill and over cobblestones Without their strength our beautiful buildings could never have been created.

The only thing that Hyndland was lacking in 1905 was history. These streets of varied human habitations were without yesterdays. The atmosphere must have been thin and clear with no shared anecdotes, no ancient grumbles or feuds and no possibility of referring to last year's scandals.

Hyndland was a tabula rasa with its future yet to be written.

Though given time, it would produce its own joys, mysteries and murders.

✧◆✧

LET'S ASK DR. JUNG

It was almost the last week of the Rennie Mackintosh exhibition in the McLellan Galleries but, as is so often the way with something on your doorstep, I had not yet managed to visit it. There were rave reviews and people returning for the fourth and fifth time but I think it was the sound of the technology that put me off. I dislike headsets and the idea of a strange voice whispering in my ear as I view an exhibition revolts me, no matter how fascinating the detail. Art is subjective and I may not agree with their opinions or I may not want to give the same amount of attention to every item on display. What happens when I decide to skip a few objects because they do not interest me? Or perhaps because it is too crowded around them? Chaos, with the tape describing furniture as I look at paintings. No, a headset echoes the inflexibility of unhappy schooldays. Besides, I understand and retain information more successfully if I read it. That's why I had problems at University. Some lecturers were more entertaining than others but that did not mean that I remembered what they told me. Give me text any day. The spoken word can be very boring.

Soon the wonderful Mackintosh models, paintings and artefacts would be carefully packed and fly off to New York, Chicago and half a dozen other places around the world. Only ten days were left and I certainly wanted to see it. I look back with great affection on the two winters that I attended an evening pottery class in the amazing Glasgow School of Art. It was thrilling each week to climb that punishing hill and then glide up the elegant front steps to slip through the first and then the second swing door and find oneself in an entirely different world. I swear I became a different person in that beautifully proportioned warmth as I filled my lungs with the aromatic smells of linseed oil and copal varnish. I would descend to the humid basement which was crowded with other subtle perfumes, as well as immense, intimidating plaster casts. There I would forget my banal

everyday life and delve my hands into the yielding clay.
After a few satisfying minutes of bashing it with ferocity, I
would centre it on the wheel and impose my will on it... ah,
such sensuous pleasure and power! What matter that the end
result was often an ashtray. I shall be eternally grateful to
CRM. His building has such beauty and ambience and I
found happiness and a sort of ecstasy there. But this is not a
story about those far off days.

On Saturday evening Gertrude phoned to suggest that,
before it was too late, we should visit the exhibition.

"I have heard that there are tree*mend*ous queues going
right along and up Hill Street by *midday!*" she said in her
deep dramatic voice. She studied elocution as a child and her
simplest statement is full of portent.

"I think we must get there *early*. Before the *crowds
gather.*"

She might have been arranging the start of a bloody
revolution.

"Suits me fine." I replied.

"Shall we ask Fiona? She has been *going through a bad
time.*"

"Isn't she always? I've got a bit fed up with her and her
bad times, you know. I suppose I've been more frank with
her recently and we're not so friendly just now."

"Oh dear, *I'm sorry to hear that*. Perhaps an nice little
outing is just what's needed to *set things right* between you
again."

I had no desire to "set things right". That vulgar phrase
which links speech with an unhappy bodily function was
invented for Fiona. She talks non-stop and is a bore of the
first water, always full of moans and sensational problems. If
she does not have her own problem, she will burden you
with her neighbour's. Failing that she will find some
unknown person in the newspaper and bemoan their hardship. Then when she has looked at the tragedy from all
angles she will start to speculate about how much worse
everything might become in the near future. Speculation is
such a useless occupation. I am afraid that I have decided
that, though we have known each other from schooldays,
Fiona is a useless friend. And selfish, for the result of her

bewailings is that she hogs every conversation. Politeness makes it difficult, if not impossible to interrupt a tale of great hardship or travail. While the rest of the company is limited to head-shakings and tut-tuttings, Fiona, with her staring eyes and her little quiet voice of exaggerated gentility, talks and talks interminably. Nobody else gets to say a word. She becomes the centre of attention and achieves a power which would be denied her were she dependent on her wit or attraction. If she golfed or played bridge or embroidered or *something* it might help, but since she took early retirement, and I mean really early, she is in her mid-fifties like the rest of us, she does very little with her time. I don't know how she puts in her day, she never cooks and hates housework. I think she is lazy and, if the truth must be known, rather too sure that a glass of wine will make everything seem better. No I did not care to "set things right".

"I suppose, yes we could do that. If you want to," I must have sounded unenthusiastic because Gertrude immediately said,

"Just a cake and a *coffee*, you know. *Not lunch.*"

"Fine, can we make it Tuesday? You're free that day aren't you and my time is my own this week."

My job has flexible hours, which suits me as I work well in the early morning and late at night. I should have been a Bohemian, as Roland always used to say.

Gertrude is a primary teacher, but job shares as she also cares for her very elderly mother, who, I may say is a lot jollier than her daughter.

✧✦✧

On Tuesday morning I had such a vivid dream just before I awakened. As often happens, my dream included a staircase. Dr Jung would have something to say about that for he developed some of his most important theories from his dreams of staircases, where each flight descended and took him deeper and deeper into his primitive race consciousness, or something like that. But I do not attach much significance to my flights of stairs, indeed it might be strange if they were not part of my sleeping thoughts. I have lived in tenement flats all my life as have most of my friends and relatives. At present I live in a main-door flat where one

climbs seven steps from pavement level to enter the front
door. It is a two-storey flat and two flights of stairs lead to
the basement. A great deal of the first twenty-five years of
my life was spent in my grandparents' top floor flat which,
unusually, made use of the attic space. After negotiating the
long marble-faced flights of the close, the interior of the flat
contained *two* staircases. The main public room was two
storeys high with an elegant black wooden staircase which
was more than a little reminiscent of the work of Mackintosh
although the architect was Burnet and pre-dated the Art
School. A workaday back stair was situated near the kitchen
and much of the imaginative play of my youth was enacted
on or under one or other of those stairways. It would
certainly be strange if staircases did not feature in my
dreams. More incredible for an Eskimo or a nomadic Mongol
to dream of staircases, igloos and yurts having no such
structures. I could write for hours of the varied staircases
which have appeared in my dreams throughout my life but
only that Tuesday dream concerns this story. In it I was
upstairs on an old-fashioned Glasgow bus. Just before
descending to the open platform, I noticed that Roland was
sitting at the back and I nodded to him. When I alighted at
the stop outside my own flat, I immediately realised that I
had left something on the bus. It seemed like a tremendous
moment of decision for me. Should I return to the bus to
retrieve the lost object, whatever it was? The bus still stood
there and yet I hesitated. I knew that the forgotten object
was important but I was reluctant to reboard the bus. The
bus slowly pulled away then almost immediately stopped at
the red traffic light before turning the corner into Clarence
Drive. It was only yards from me and I had a second chance
to jump aboard and reclaim my goods. I gave it great consideration, time seemed to stand still, but "No" I turned away,
deciding to go to the lost property office later in the day, in
spite of the inconvenience. Then I wakened up but found it
difficult to shake off the tension that I had felt. I lay in bed
considering what the dream might mean, if anything. I
smiled at yet another powerful dream containing a staircase.
What was the reason for my unwillingness to reboard the
bus? Was it Roland whom I did not wish to confront or was

it some mental 'baggage' which I wished to discard? What was it that was forgotten, or deliberately left, on the top deck? Was the stair symbolic or was it just an integral part of my life, a prop which furnished every scene? And why think of Roland after four and a half years? It was an interesting puzzle and I found it hard to relinquish the thoughts that the dream had generated.

Gertrude, Fiona and I arrived at the gallery early and hardly had to queue outside at all, though we made slow progress up the massive curving marble staircases -*more stairs*! The building evoked happy memories of the annual Art Institute and the Chamber Music Society and also the marvellous Children's Ball held each year by Margaret Hopkins, that unsung heroine who taught so many generations of Glasgow children to dance. Painting, music and dance, these various aspects of Glasgow culture had all inhabited these gracious galleries throughout my life. I stood apart from the others and visualised long-ago little girls in puffball ballet dresses skipping about in excitement. As a senior student, I had faced the problems of marshalling the correct groups for the polka or waltz. The interval was even more stressful as I tried to protect pristine tulle and satin from meat paste sandwiches, jam tarts, ice cream and jelly. It was a wonderful orgy. I expect those little girls, only ten years or so younger than myself, are matrons nowadays. Although Miss Hopkins seemed old to me at the time, perhaps she was still teaching when those pupils brought their own little girls to polka and guzzle ice cream. I sometimes regret that I never had a miniature ballerina of my own or a little chap in a kilt and sparkling shirt, but that's the way life goes. I wasted so many years with Andrew, such subterfuges, such secrecy and lots of lies, which I hated. Always hoping, hoping. Ironic that when his wife finally left him, he immediately dumped me. I was nearly forty then so no tiny kilts or tutus. And by the time that Roland came along I was too old and anyway, who could imagine Roland as a father?

Gertrude opted for the headset and Fiona and I donned our specs to study the copious notes hanging beside each exhibit. It was certainly a massive and impressive exhibition. Hard for us to appreciate just how impressive, as we were familiar with much of it, although there were also wonderful pieces which I had not seen before. The models were magnificent. Not completely convinced of his now acclaimed genius, I certainly found his story unbearably sad with the lack of recognition in Britain in his lifetime. How terrible that in his final days of poverty, an old client bought a delightful painting for thirty pounds *as a favour*. One wonders if the present mass adulation stems from a guilty conscience.

After circling an exquisite model of Hill House many times and bending to view it from all angles, I made a mental note to visit the real thing again soon, having been there only once in all my fifty five years.

We left without having quite seen every item and in desperate need of a coffee. Crowds and the concentration had made it a strenuous morning, almost too much for one visit. As we stood outside the Galleries, Fiona's plaintive voice stabbed through the noise of Sauchiehall Street with the threatening whine of a mosquito.

"What I could not understand was why the people with headsets were standing in front of the written explanations, making it difficult for those without headsets to read. It made me very angry."

"I adored the re-creation of Miss Cranston's tearoom." I said, "I wish we could go somewhere like that for our morning coffee. Such style and such a lovely space."

The others agreed enthusiastically

"We could go to the Willow Tearooms." said Gertrude.

"It makes me awfully sad as I remember outings with Mother," whispered Fiona.

"I'm never sure how authentic it is anyway," I put in hurriedly before she launched into another tale of misery. "I think the colours are pretty suspect."

Being an accountant does not stop me from having aesthetic sensibility.

"Let us just *go across the road*. It is *near* and it is *very well spoken* of... and I think, yes." Gertrude added the meaningless coda in order to avoid the sin of finishing her sentence with a preposition.

An imposing entrance of rich dark wood and shining brass led to a large shop filled with what must be the most comprehensive selection of cakes and dainties in the western world. Cakes iced and decorated or loaded with whipped cream, pastries with fruit, nuts and jams, multi-coloured meringues, petit fours, rum babas, marzipan fruits and gingerbread men. Liberal applications of coconut, angelica, chocolate buttons and marshmallows guaranteed a limitless variety of subdivisions. Recreated in fondant were those ikons of the nineties, the Lion King, Pocahontas, Wallace and Gromit and occupying a side-table were vast gateaux like Victorian architecture. I hurriedly averted my eyes from an obscene chocolate structure. In spite of the variety behind the curved glass of the counters which ran the length of the shop on either side, the colour most in evidence was pink. Much of the icing and nearly all the fondant was pink. The gateaux were particularly pink. Pink, pink, pink. There was a preponderance of pink and I did not find it attractive. Pink is a colour that I have never cared for. Even the wood of the shop fittings glowed with a dark pink sheen.

The opulence of the shop was not continued with the staircase. I expect that architects consider a staircase as so much wasted space, a means to an end, but I believe a gracious stairway adds nobility and atmosphere to a building. Struggling up steep stairs and bumping against people coming down can destroy other more positive aspects of any building. The Burrell Museum is a sad example of mean stairways.

Please forgive me, it is now obvious that stairways are not only an obsession of my dreams.

On the upper floor was the pink tearoom, predictably pink tablecloths, two pink carnations per table in a small pink china receptacle and on the walls pictures of pink flowers or pretty pink girls. I suddenly remembered that Roland was awfully fond of pink with an excruciating pink bathroom, although his pink pyjamas and shirts really suited him. He was very handsome when I first met him with his dark hair and deep blue eyes and swift nervous movements. He was as slight and graceful as a boy, though seven years of my cooking changed that.

Fancy dreaming about Roland this morning after all these years. Did I have any regrets?

I slumped disconsolately in my seat. That magnificent showpiece of Miss Cranston's had made me very dissatisfied with these roseate surroundings.

"No, no pink cake for me thank you, Gertrude, just a coffee, a very black one."

I suppose I was being churlish but Fiona was in full flood about the really absolutely scandalous thing that had happened to her neighbour and Gertrude was listening to her carefully, ready to act as Greek chorus when the correct dramatic moment arrived.

Why was I here with these two women? I had lots of other friends that were more fun. Was it because we had gone to school together? But I had little in common with them then and even less now. Fiona in her shabby anorak and woolly hat looked ready for a day of hill-walking rather than a visit to town. If only she *would* do some hill-walking and shut up. Gertrude with her Marks and Spencers pleated skirt and bow-at-the-neck polyester blouse was the archetypal unmarried lady in her fifties. Oh dear I was becoming more and more bitchy and why had I not gone home after the exhibition? I could have pondered on that dream.

Roland had a highly developed bitchiness and was a keen theatre-goer. We used to make each other laugh in extremes of unkindness about the people around us in the auditorium. That dream had certainly brought him to the forefront of my mind. Or was he there already? Why had I resisted meeting him in my dream? Would I avoid him in a similar situation on a real bus? Would he avoid me? Supposing he were to climb upstairs to this pink tearoom this moment, should I be glad to see him?

Roland entered my life three years after Andrew left it, when I still considered myself broken-hearted and resigned to a life with no romantic future. Roland quickly changed that. We fell madly in love and soon a delightfully full-blown affair was in progress. As we were both well-known in the district and as we never actually lived in the same house together, there was always an element of intrigue and mystery in those years. Unlike the deceit of the relationship with Andrew, our love affair was more of a game in which there were no losers. A charming game that lasted seven years. I always knew it was a game which would end and eventually I ended it. Why? Perhaps because he liked pink, or because he was bitchy or extravagant. Or perhaps because he, like Fiona, was an indefatigable talker. He was not boring, often very witty, but *relentless*, leaving little space in the conversation for others. Strange, I had almost forgotten that characteristic but remembering helps, for perhaps guilt explains my reluctance to return to the bus?

In the background I was aware of Fiona's tragic voice trundling along with occasional, deep and sympathetic inter-jections from Gertrude. I had no idea what they were talking about.

Laying two pound coins on the pink cloth, I stood up and with what I hope was a kindly nod, headed for the narrow stairs.

BYRES ROAD

Where would G12 be without Byres Road? It is not an imposing street and hardly quarter of a mile long but it has been the shopping and entertainment centre of the west end all my life. A pleasant walk from Hyndland, it has always provided a cinema (once upon a time there were two) subway station, library, many food outlets and at least one good shoe shop. The pubs have also remained, though they were never of much interest to me. Changing fashions have forced Byres Road to re-invent itself many times. Nowadays there are innumerable coffee shops where there were only a few elegant tearooms in my childhood. (It was before WW2 that I was introduced to hot buttered pikelets in a Byres Road tearoom. I liked them very much and it would be many years before I learned that this was the same delicacy as English crumpets.) Those tearooms offered light lunches or high teas, though I did not ever sample them. Nowadays Byres Road offers a wide range of eating from haute cuisine in silver service restaurants like the Ubiquitous Chip to sandwiches, pizzas and hamburgers, from exotic Asian food to fish and chips. Even pubs offer modestly priced food. Three major supermarkets battle it out with ready-to-eat meals at bargain prices, often with the added attraction of a bottle of wine. There are delicatessens, charming fruit shops, a chocolatier and an excellent fish shop full of tempting piscine luxuries. Elaborate cakes and pastries give a Parisian touch to some windows and pavement tables tempt patrons outside to brave the traffic fumes in order to emulate our French cousins. Food seems almost to have overtaken every other interest, though there are several estate agents showing photographs of des. res. in the area and also quite a few travel shops. Of course vintage and charity shops proliferate, exposing our need to rid ourselves of unnecessary articles before we buy more of them, though the splendid OXFAM book store, sadly the only present outlet for books in Byres Road, is a wonderful facility which I appreciate.

What do I miss? What has changed?

There are no butchers in Byres Road. First the beef scare, then the supermarkets have chased them away. Few will remember long-gone McKeans, the pork butchers, who were able to offer interesting titbits in the lean years immediately following the war. The jellied veal and the liver sausage, a spreading paste which we would now term paté, were delicious, or seemed so at the time. Occasionally we would have lightly salted pigsfeet.

Incredibly, Woolworths has gone and is much missed. I also mourn the loss of John Smith's book shop. Bargain Books, which continually threatened us with its imminent closure for many years, has finally disappeared

Tullys, a wonderful hardware store of the past is another great loss. It sold every item of household goods and every screw and gadget required by the DIY enthusiast and was there for most of my life. To buy a hammer or a teapot now, means a trip into town. Also simple things like thread and elastic require a bus journey, though it is not so many years since a wonderful fabric shop (which was my delight and temptation) removed its premises elsewhere.

Byres Road now has fewer outlets selling clothes than previously, if one does not count the charity shops. There used to be several outfitters for both sexes and forty years ago the Greenock Wool Shop was only one of several small drapers that sold not only knitting necessities, but stockings and underwear, even swimsuits. And I can remember a hat shop in my youth.

One thing that still exists in this short, fairly narrow, fiercely busy street, is style, though of course much altered throughout the years. At different times, my contemporaries and I have walked along its pavements in flowing New Look skirts requiring five yards of fabric, in close fitting tartan trews, in shapeless 'sacks' with swingback coats, in smart tweed suits, in mini-dresses worn above the knee with the newly available tights and in ankle-length flowered dresses with scarves and ponchos. I find it depressing that the omnipresent jeans, anoraks and hoodies have taken over in the last thirty years. However, today I saw some fashion excitement in Byres Road. I saw many women, young and not so young, in thick black tights worn with a short, very short, tunic or jacket. Some were jaunty in black velvet shorts. This 'principal boy' look seems to be the *dernier cri* these days and for those blessed with good legs and a nice figure, it is stunning, no matter what the age. However, it should probably be avoided by those who have indulged too enthusiastically in the Byres Road plethora of foods.

Then there is the vintage look which, though not always successful, can be magnificent. Unfortunately last week I saw one that I considered disastrous. Quite a pretty young woman, not exactly obese, but certainly very fat, wore a short denim jacket and many gold chains over a long tightly-fitted black T-shirt. Teamed with this was a knee-length layered skirt of very limp tulle frills, which she constantly smoothed and adjusted. Black tights and silver shoes completed her outfit. I found it a little sad that she had been so led astray by some wildly stylised model in a magazine. However, she was speaking vivaciously to a young man with purple hair and seemed happy, if self-conscious.

Many on the crowded pavements of Byres Road are students of Glasgow University where, quite properly, the demands of the intellect have always taken precedence over the lure of fashion. For these young people, denim is usually the preferred fabric for nether garments, jackets and incredible, raw-edged, miniscule skirts.

A fair proportion of the Byres Road pedestrians are of course conventional G12 residents and less *outré*. They will present themselves in clothes which are well-made and respectable, having been purchased in one of the large fashion chain stores. Sadly, in spite of wealth and maturity, some of them also believe that jeans, that uniform designed for navvies and cowboys, are a suitable garment for most occasions. And I will not speak of mid-calf shorts!

Just as Byres Road meets Great Western Road there is a very fine church, now no longer in sacred use. It is known as the Oran Mhor and it has been recreated as part restaurant, part pub, part theatre. It offers many exciting cultural opportunities, exhibitions, book launches, storytelling and charity events. Perhaps the most interesting is the self-explanatory *A Play, A Pie and a Pint*, a season of lunchtime performances.

Each production lasts for a week and offers an amazing variety of work. Some are monologues, some use several actors. One of my favourites was a small opera which was visually marvellous, with excellent singers and music ranging from classical to jazz and folk. Some of the writers are established and some have their first chance to see their work performed on the small stage, while the audience decorously drink their beer and munch their excellent pie.

I am writing this in 2010 and even five years ago it would have been a very different article for Byres Road reflects the wider society. Last year, when it seemed that our economy was tumbling about our ears, I walked along to Byres Road to buy fish. I had been away for three or four weeks and was thunderstruck at what had changed in that short time. I was aware that Woolworths had gone forever but standing on one spot, I could see that a large, long established chemist, a travel agent, a camera shop, Bargain Books and at least two other premises had also all closed down in my absence. It was frightening. Fortunately the climate has changed a little and Byres Road looks as thriving as ever, though it will always be a chameleon indicator of G12 society.

A GREAT WEE JOB

Ah'm lucky tae hiv a job, Ah know that an' it's a great wee job. Ah work in RS McColl's the newsagent and sweetie shop an' thur a post office therr too, jist a wee wan. The shop's in the snobby bit o' Glasgow so thur a lotta posh folk tae deal wi' maistly, but thur an awful lot o' nice people comin' in as weel, like home helps an' the bin men an' blokes makin' deliveries an' that. Och an' Ah like the auld yins that come in fur thur papers in the moarnin' wi thoan pernickety wey o' speakin'. Itsa same faces ivry day, same time ivry day an' the same paper. S'funny, ye'd think they'd like a chinge but no, it's aye the same thing thur lookin' fur.

"A Glasgow Herald and twenty Silk-Cut, please."

or

"The Scotsman and the Radio Times please, if it's in."

Or mebbe,

"The Record and a packet of peppermints today, please."

Jist as though it wisnae that ivry day. I hiv tae smile.

Thur one wee wifie aye gets a Mars bar the day she buys her People's Freend. Noo wid ye no' think that if she liked a Mars bar she wid hiv one mair nor once a week? They've plenty cash, a' they Hyndland toffs.

Sometimes thur's an auld geyser coughin' an' splutterin' an' Ah'll say,

"That's an awfy cauld wind the day." An' that seems tae cheer 'im up an' Ah might say,

"How aboot a packet o' Tunes fur yer throat, surr?" They like the "surr" an' he'll buy them an' thank me. An' Ah'm fair chuffed at makin' a sale an' mebbe he's just needin' a wee fuss made o' him.

Ma Mammy liked a wee fuss made o' her but she didnae get much o' that. Except mebbe from ma auntie in Port Glasgow.

Ma poor wee Mammy.

✧◆✧

Ah really like the shoape in the mornin' though it's an awfy early stert. Ye see, Ah've aye tae be in tae get the paper boys an' girls organised an' oot on thur roonds *an' Ah'm the boss then*. Ah'm *really* in chairge an' it's great! An' Ah don't take any snash from they snotty-nosed wee west-enders. Ye should hear the wey they talk, they must practise fur 'oors tae talk like that.

"Does Mr Lombard in Falkland Mansions still want the Scotsman as well as the London Times, Cameron?" some wee nosey-wax'll ask in thon voice.

Ah don't know how they fund oot ma name wis Cameron because ah've aye been ca'ed Ronnie. Cameron's a queer-like name an' Ah think they jist say it tae annoy me. Ah jist wrinkle ma brow an' talk louder an more natral,

"It's a' wrote doon fur ye. Ye jist hiv tae use yer eyes."

Then anither yin'll squeak oot,

"And is Mrs Smith-Talbot in Lauderdale Gardens still on holiday do you know?"

"If the papers are no' therr in the bundle, yous'll no' be able tae pit thim thro' her letter-box, wull ye!"

Ye hiv tae assert yersel wi' thae wee snobs, ye know. They're worse'n the grown-ups. Ah could sack them, ye know, if they were cheeky or late or onythin'. Ah've goat the power. Ah don't know whit thae wee kids is workin' fur anyway. They're no needin' the money. They a' live in big hooses an' thur faithers drive big caurs. They've got the Reebok trainers an' the fancy anoraks an' the Iphones an' it's daft if ye ask me, weans still at school an' gaun oot in the dark lonely streets deliverin' papers. Ah wisnae much younger than them whin Ah wis picked up by the polis fur bein' oot in dark lonely streets. An' then Ah wis sent awa tae the residential school at Cardross. It doesnae seem fair does it? An' Ah wisnae even tryin' tae earn money nor nuthin'.

Ah wis niver a crim or onythin' bad. Ah jist liked gaun oot at night. It wis the excitement, ye know. Ma Mammy wid be sittin' at the TV wi' her fags an' a can. She wis aye awfy tired, ma Mammy. It wis the early mornin' cleanin' that wore her oot like, an' at night she jist watched the telly. Well efter the cartoons wis finished, Ah wisnae interested. A' thae men an wimmin kissin' an' lassies dancin' an sodgers fightin' an' who's wantin' tae watch that? The wee shop shut at eight, so aboot hauf past seeven Ah'd stert tae whine fur crisps an' ginger an'

usually Mammy wid gie me the money an' enough tae get a
Dime bar fur hersel'. She aye liked the Dime bar because she said
it remindit her o' the stories ma Granny used tae tell aboot
dancin' wi' the Yanks at the Locarno. Ma Granny's awfy frail
noo but mebbe she cud dance in the aulden days. She still has
blondie-like hair an' wears thae peerie heels. S'funny but ma
Mammy niver seemed tae suspect Ah wouldnae come hame.
She must hiv hid a short memory 'cos Ah always scarpered wi'
the cash. Aye, Ah wiz goin' up the town reg'lar fur a while therr
an' Ah used tae feel bad aboot her sittin' waitin' fur her Dime
bar but mebbe the Tennants made her furget, 'cos she niver said.

     She wis mair nor half asleep an' Ah suppose she had other
things tae worry aboot, like whit ma Dad wid be like when he
cam in.

     S'funny Ah wis niver feared when Ah nipped oot the close
at Hamiltonhill, just kinda jumpy an' excited. It wis nae
distance tae Sauchiehall Street an' Ah'd soon meet some ither
guys. Nothin' really bad iver happened tae me. Things happened
that Ah didnae like, but Ah niver think aboot that noo.

     Up the town wis great, wi' a' the lights an' shops an' clubs
an' cinemas an' the crowds o' folk dressed real smart. The
Polis seen me aften enough but Ah aye jooked awa up a close,
til wan nicht a spry wee polisman grabbed me an' tuk me
hame tae Hamiltonhill. Ma faither wis in that night, fur a
chinge, an' efter the polisman left, Ah goat a right doin' an ma
mammy got a wallop when she tried tae stop ma faither. Ah
didnae get tae the school fur a coupla days an' Ah wis lonely
so Ah sneaked oot an' skedaddled up the toon an' here the
same smert wee polis picked me up an' when he saw the scabs
an' bruises, he took me tae the station. Mind you, they were
awfy kind tae me therr an' Ah had a cuppa tea an' a pie an a
piece o' jam-roll. It's jist what Ah told ye. Ah'm a lucky devil.

     But Ah niver went home that night an' the next day Ah wis
moved tae Cardross residential school an' Ah niver stayed in
Hamiltonhill again. Ah saw ma Mammy toothry times after
that, right enough, but Ah niver steyed wi' her again. Ye're
better no' tae think o' they bad times in yer life.

     That's whit they used tae tell us in Cardross onywey.

It's a long day here in the shoape, but it's busy an' Ah niver feel tired. Thur's aye somethin happenin' an' Ah've made a few wee chinges to make it work better, ye know. Ah thought at first the manager might no' like what Ah done, but either he didnae mind or he didnae notice. Ah shifted that crisp display round the ither wey so the wee weans would see it an' greet tae thur mammy fur a packet. An' Ah brought the Birthday cards lower doon because the wee auld wifies buy the maist o' the them an' they couldnae reach them that high. Then thur wis a' they porny mags spread oot on the top shelf an' it wisnae richt ye know. A' they bare bums an' tits'n stuff starin' doon at you because thurs auld folk an' teachers come in here a' the time, an' they shouldnae hiv tae look at that sort o' thing. Ah mean Ah'm all for a laugh in private, but no spread across the top shelf, so Ah tidied them into a bundle an' Ah brought the Gardenin' Times along a bit on wan side and the Engineerin' News along on the ither side an' Ah like it better now an' so do some o' the auld yins. You wouldnae think they would like tae talk about it would ye, but one auld man even congratlated me. He said Ah wis a hero. Mind you Ah don't know if the manager's even noticed it yet.

The Post Office opens at nine. It's like Fort Knox wi' the steel shutters and the burglar alarms gaun aff. Ah suppose thur's quite a lot o' cash in a Post Office. Even a wee wan like oors. Ah niver thought aboot that before. Thur's a' the giros an' the pensions fur auld folk an' young mithers an' thur's stamps an' parcels bein paid for. Aye, thur a lot o' cash comes an' goes in a Post Office. Mair like a bank really. Whin Ah wis in Cardross, they wad aye be talkin' aboot robbin' banks an' gettin' thoosands. It was a' talk an' no one ever thought o' Post Offices but mebbe a Post Office doesnae sound so darin'. Ye niver seen a movie wi' Billy the Kid robbin' a Post Office, didya.

We a' talked big oot at Cardross. It was jist a kinda game an' Ah wis as bad as the next yin but ye see Ah wis different too because Ah didnae *believe* whit Ah said. Ah knew it wis a' rubbish. Like a kinda fairy story. Some o' the lads really believed that they wid get rich some day by robbin' or kidnappin' or marryin' a millionaire popstar. Daft buggers, so they wur. But ye huv tae be soarry fur thim.

They wur quite good tae us at Cardross but we would all talk aboot daein' a runner, an' some o' them did break oot an' cam back boastin' o' all the wickedness they'd been up tae. A lot o' that wis jist mair fairy stories. Ah niver done a runner from Cardross. Ah thought aboot it but naw, Ah couldnae. S'funny innit, Ah wis never feart when Ah wis oot on the streets in Glesga, niver oncet. But the hostel see, that wis different. The hostel wis up on a hill wi' big dark trees a' aroond aboot it, an' tae get tae the road ye hid tae walk doon through they trees an Ah wid look oot the big windaes at the trees an' sometimes they wis far awa an sometimes they wis nearer tae the windaes an' if the wind wis blowin' thur wis a funny kishin' an' wooin' in the branches an' Ah knew Ah could niver do a runner 'cos Ah could niver walk past they trees in the dark. No way. Even when ye got tae the road, ye were that far from the town an' it wis reelly, reelly dark. An' Ah've niver fancied hitchin' lifts. Nae fear.

But Ah liked the hostel fine, an' the staff wur a good laugh. It wis warm and the grub wis good and there wis green an' blue doovies on the beds an' TV an' table tennis an' snooker an' sometimes at night they let ye make pancakes wi'thick syrup. They wur great an' the place wis a' modern, ye know, like in a magazine, bright colours an' carpets an' big windaes. It wisnae like home, but they wur quite kind.

But see the place doon the hill? Whaur we had wur lessons. Ma Goad, it wis different. Oh it wis different right enough. It wis a great big hoose, auld creepy like somethin' oot a horror film. Mebbe it wis swell in aulden times but the pent wis peelin' an' the ceilin's wur crumblin' doon an' the flairs a' creaked an' thur were pails tae catch drips in when it rained. An' doon the Clyde therr it rains maist days. It would hiv been a rerr place fur playin' hide'n seek but they kept thur eyes on us a' the time an' we were marched from wan place tae anither jist like jailbirds.

We niver hud mair nor six in a class and thur were aye two teachers. That wiz in case anyone cut up rough, Ah suppose, but Ah niver seen that happen. We didnae learn much but the teachers were kind. Ivry day we had tae answer a wee daft questionnaire askin' things like,

"Have you learned something interesting today?"

"Are you happy?"

"What would make you happy?"

Near everyone said they'd be happy tae get back hame wi' thur Mammy. Even when thur Mammy had been real bad to them, honest, that's what they said. Honest tae Goad. Some faithers wiz worse even than ma Dad, the things they done, but Ah niver knew before that a Mammy wid be bad tae her wean. Ah cud hardly believe it, but it wis true an' yit they still wanted hame tae hur. Funny that, intit?

Ah quite liked fillin' in the questions an' Ah always done wee designs roond the edge o' the form an' the teacher smiled when she seen them.

If ye'll believe it, thur wis kids at Cardross had tried tae top thersels an some were slicin' thur airms an sniffin' glue, an ithers were crims or runaways. Ah suppose Ah wis a runaway too, but when Ah wis aye back in ma bed before breakfast Ah don't think that should count. Ah niver really knew why Ah wis in Cardross a' that time away from ma mammy an' her so ill an' Ah don't even know if ma mammy knew aither. Ah don't suppose ma dad cared.

People didnae really talk much aboot the bad things that hid happened tae them but sometimes ye heard stories an' at night ye often heard folk greetin'. But maistly, it was boastin' an' big talk an' cuttin' up rough jist tae keep yer end up.

Ah niver cut up rough but we had craft oncet a week an' wan time Ah refused tae dae it. The rest o' the class wis girls an' they were makin' somethin' ca'ed love-herts out o' bright pink furry nylon. Some daft thing tae hing up in thur bedroom. An' they were cuttin' up the fur intae wee pieces tae push inside the hearts tae make them look fat an' they wur *gross* an Ah said Ah widnae dae it. Mebbe the girls liked them but Ah didnae so Ah said in a big loud voice,

"NAW, AH'M NO' DAEIN' THAT."

Ah said it real loud 'cos Ah thought the love-herts wur *disgustin'*. Ma heart wis bangin' when Ah spoke up an' Ah wis surprised at bein' so brave.

The main teacher wis frownin' an' screwin' up her face at me but the ither yin wis aulder an' she said Ah cud draw if Ah wantit an' she showed me how tae draw a sidey-oan view o' a face. Ah think it was ca'ed a profeel or somethin' like that an' it wisnae difficult an' Ah still draw faces that wey an' Ah don't think the auld teacher liked the love-herts any better'n Ah did, the way she looked sideyweys at them wi' her mooth tight an' her brew wrinkled.

Right enuff we hid some rerr outin's from Cardross. We went tae a Sports Centre every week and hid tennis an' swimmin' an' football an' Ah loved a' that. Ither days we went tae a ferm an' got tae feed the hens an' clap the coos an' horses. Wan boy wis mad to mulk the coos. He wis aye mulkin' the coos. An' wan night we went up the toon tae a pantymime but Ah niver thought o' daein' a runner. They wis a' talkin' about doin' a runner oot the back o' the wee bus but it didnae happen. The pantymime wis a'right an' we hud icecream.

When ye looked out the hostel windaes, ye could see right across the Clyde tae Port Glasgow where ma Auntie an' ma two wee cuzzins stay. Long ago ma Mammy took me therr oan a veesit. We went oan the train and whit a grand day we hud. Ma two wee cuzzins took me oot a walk tae see thur school an' they hud me runnin' up an' up an' up a big high hill, it wis mair like a mountain. It wis really high up. Ma cuzzins wur bonny wee sturdy lassies wi' curly hair and wee muscly legs. They cud run up the hill that fast an' Ah wis aye pechin' an' pantin' behind them an' Ah can remember them lookin' back ower thur shoulders an' gigglin' an' shoutin' through thur curls,

"Hurry up Slowcoach. Ye're awfy slow! Ye're like an auld man." an' laughin' harder than iver. They wis aye laughin'.

Half way up the mountain thur wis like a wee forest beside the road an' thur wis a lovely wee waterfa' fa'in' doon away ben the trees jist like in a calendur. It wis that unexpected beside a' they coonsil hooses. An' Ah stood an' watched it fur a long while an' Ah liked the sound it made, too. It wis jist magic.

We had a rare big fried tea that night too an' Ah wis that hungry efter a' the mountaineering. Ah'd niver hud black pudden before an' it wis awfy tasty.

Ah used tae sit at the windae in the hostel, before it got dark, an' look oot at the river Clyde an' jist wish Ah could flee ower the watter tae Port Glasgow an' see ma wee cuzzins again.

An' it's years since Ah wis in that hostel and Ah've been oot on my own fur mair nor a year noo an' it's funny tho' cos Ah've niver been back tae Port Glasgow but Ah still feel happy when Ah think o' that waterfa' an' ma two wee girl cuzzins.

Ah might go back soon an' see if thur still livin' at the foot o' yon mountain. Ah cud take the train doon.

But Ah hiv tae tell ye sumpn'. See me, Ah've really fallen on ma feet. Ah'm a dead lucky guy, Ah know that. The place Ah'm stayin' is mebbe no great shakes but Ah've got this rerr wee job an' Ah'm on the up 'n up. Ah'm goin' places! Ah know it! An' Ah've made a great new friend who says he'll help me. He cam in the ither day tae let me know he's the new assistant area manager an' his name is Georgie an' he's reelly, *reelly* friendly an' we get on just great. He's a reel smart dresser an' whit a *joker*, he's a laugh a minute.

Georgie comes from Lanarkshire an' he hasnae fund digs in Glasgow yet but he's due tae visit this branch next Tuesday tho he sez Ah've no' tae let oan tae the manager, cos it's a surprise veesit. An' he's gaun tae bring in a sleepin' bag an' kip doon in the back shop an' he sez if Ah could keep the place open late an' borrow a sleepin' bag we cud bring in some cans an' hiv a wee perty an' thur plenty nuts an' crisps oan the shelves. An' Ah sez mebbe ma two wee cuzzins would like an invite but Georgie sez he knows two ither girls, mair fun nor cuzzins so Ah'm really lookin' forward tae Tuesday.

Anither thing he sez tae me wis it didnae maiter if ye took some cash oot the till at the beginnin' o' the week, as long as it wis put back for the till-check on Friday an' Ah didnae know about that 'cos when Ah sterted the job, they niver said. But that's handy intit?

An' Ah know where Ah can get a sleepin' bag an' Ah'm really lookin' forward to meetin these two nice girls.

D'ye unnerstaun how Ah feel Ah'm on the up an' up now? An' mebbe Ah'll soon be an area manager jist like Georgie an' Ah'll kin take ma two wee cuzzins oot tae a swell restrong in Port Glasgow for Ah think they'd like that fine.

Ah jist wish ma wee Mammy wis still allve an' Ah could give her a Dime bar ivry day.

✧◆✧

CHRISTMAS DISASTER

On 17th December 2006, a disaster occurred at 17 Clarence Drive. After an hour or two of ominous rattling of small débris behind the walls and at the kitchen windows of the tenement, there was a collapse of masonry at the back of the building, leaving the kitchens on the second and third floor open to the elements. A cupboard and a boiler fell to the ground. Luckily there were no fatalities or injuries, though one resident and his little boy had just been to the bins in the back court with rubbish. Structural engineers rushed to the scene and finding that load-bearing joists on two floors were affected, judged the building unsafe. With very little time to plan or think, the residents were evacuated and Clarence Drive was closed to normal traffic. By three thirty the street was filled to the brim with police cars, fire engines, ambulances and a Serious Incident truck. The last was the size of a small house. A policeman manfully tried to re-route the Hyndland Road traffic but, in spite of his energetic directions and generous swags of red and white plastic tape everywhere, some motorists seemed unwilling to accept that such a main thoroughfare could possibly be closed.

Every day we read with sympathy of those poor people all over the world who are homeless for one reason or another, but it makes it particularly real when the people affected are neighbours and friends and the building only a few doors away. Officials from Glasgow Council held a residents' meeting in the school the following day, Monday, which I attended. It was a miserable affair and I was terribly saddened by the havoc which this accident had caused. The people affected included one man who had recently recovered from a heart attack; (he was back in hospital that night), a wonderful old lady in her nineties, now safely living with a son; a family with five children (and a houseful of Christmas presents); an elderly couple, the husband taking it all philosophically "Just like the Blitz again" he joked, but his wife was very distressed. Another couple had been away for the day and returned at 11pm to find they would not be allowed into their home and their two hungry cats must wait until morning to be rescued.

The officials were very sympathetic and seemed anxious to help in any way they might. Unfortunately the residents would only be allowed to visit their homes for one hour the following day, Tuesday, and they would not be allowed to enter any of the rooms at the back of the building. There was a general gasp of horror and the faces around me were blank and hopeless. No one could yet tell the amount of work necessary and the time of year made it difficult to obtain the requisite building materials. It was impossible to put a time limit on their state of homelessness. It could be months.

My flat is only a few hundred yards distant from number 17. When I returned home, I was terribly aware of missing that special atmosphere of safety which normally envelopes you as soon as you step over your own threshhold. Something was different and I realised that my confidence had received a blow.

That night, before I went to sleep, I struggled with an impossible task. If I had been given only minutes to leave my home, which articles might I have deemed irreplaceable and grabbed?

STRANGERS ON THE DOORSTEP

I suppose that the first house in any street is liable to requests for directions or information regarding the area. Especially if that house is a main door flat near a bus stop, at the top of a hill and in the middle of many tenement closes.

Mary Doune, who had moved with her husband Dick and their two little girls, to such a house in 1965 would never have guessed at this particular drawback for she had lived in a top floor flat previously.

At first she was indignant at such regular interruptions. It seemed as though every week someone stood on her doorstep and took it for granted that she would be able and willing to solve their particular problem. She was an organised young woman herself, made sure of details in advance and disliked asking help from strangers.

"You would think I was the guardian of Clarence Drive," she would grumble, "I should get a salary for running the local information bureau."

Eight years later, she had more personal problems to deal with when Dick moved out, having decided that he no longer wanted to be a husband and father. It was the fashion then to "find oneself" and quite a lot of men set off on that search in the seventies. There were four little girls by this time but Mary rolled up her sleeves and dealt with it as best she could.

As Mary matured, she started to feel more sympathy for those tired folk on her doorstep that had perhaps trailed around several streets, searching in vain for the right address. They might be old and forgetful or just misinformed.

Mary's flat had previously belonged to a doctor and a surprising number of the callers had been his patients in the past. As five, ten, fifteen years rolled past, these ex-patients became fewer and frailer, but still one or two came each year in search of that long gone physician. He must have been a very charismatic doctor, Mary reckoned. He had seemed as old as Methuselah when he showed them round the house in 1965 and must be nearly a hundred by now, if he still survived. She would kindly suggest this possibility to the enquirer, who would shake his or her head in disbelief or perhaps incredulous sadness at the passage of time, before tottering unsafely down the five front steps, their white knuckles gripping the railing for support.

To further confuse the issue, another doctor practised just around the corner in Hyndland Road, until he retired in 1980. Mary was used to discussions about whether the old person on her doorstep was mistaken and it was perhaps the other doctor that was sought. These deliberations could last for quite ten minutes and Mary would be unable to help in any way except by listening sympathetically.

As the years passed her patience grew and also her sense of humour.

Sometimes the callers were younger and thought that they knocked at the dentist's house for the dentist's house was three doors along from Mary's. When she redirected them, they often looked questioningly at her as if she might be mistaken.

She would joke that, as well as ailing travellers, all the lost cats in the neighbourhood knew that they would get a welcome if they came to her door and would be returned safely to their owners. If they were genuine strays quite probably they might have a nice home found for them.

"The word goes around in the feline world, you know."

It did seem as though her home was a well-known cat refuge.

A most beautiful black cat was sitting on the front steps one day. He was friendly but muddy, thin and worn and had obviously travelled a long way. After making enquiries locally and advertising for an owner, Mary persuaded her best friend to adopt him and for many years, Black Magic was a handsome Hyndland character.

Another time a pure bred brown Burmese cat was found at the back door of the flat.

"Goodness they've discovered I have a back door as well as a front!"

It was a mystery where this valuable cat could have come from, for in spite of many phone calls to vets in the area and also to the Burmese Cat Club there was no trace of an owner making a frantic search. Perhaps he had climbed aboard some vehicle in Manchester or Birmingham for a snooze and awakened far from home in Glasgow.

This Asian aristocrat was also suitably homed with one of Mary's friends.

One night at eight o'clock in the seventies, when her daughters were still young children, the blue eyes of a Siamese cat peered through the glass panel of the front door. When Mary opened the door, he walked in purposefully, handsome and dominant. As there were already two female cats in residence, there was a hurried rushing around and shutting of doors. Those of the family already settled in bed, jumped up and joined the excitement. Mary sighed for she was particularly tired that night and had been looking forward to that brief hour of respite that the single parent enjoys when the children are at last settled in bed.

A little food was offered to this visiting cat, who ate daintily and allowed himself to be petted, before starting to explore the house, commenting favourably on each room in his strange hoarse voice.

When the girls were finally all shuffled into bed, Mary searched for the stranger to shut him into the kitchen, as she did not quite trust him not to wander around all night.

He had disappeared!

She looked for him upstairs and downstairs in the large flat, under beds, behind furniture, inside every cupboard, beguiling him with soft words and tasty treats. Not a sign. Her two older girls left their beds to help her. Mary was feeling completely exhausted when Celia, her second oldest. voiced her fears.

"Mummy, I saw a film once about a devil cat and it looked a bit like this one... it had blue eyes and in fact it looked *awful* like this one."

"Absolute nonsense, darling. There is certainly *no such thing* as a devil cat."

"Well where's this one gone, Mummy? He's disappeared into thin air. That devil cat in the film, he could disappear into thin air and when he appeared again, his eyes were..."

"I don't want to hear any more of that idiotic supernatural rubbish, Celia. You know I hate you watching those silly frightening films. I suppose you watched it at grandma's."

"Yes, but she said not to tell you. She likes films like that. And so do I."

"I can't think why."

"Well if I hadn't seen it, I wouldn't know about devil cats."

"There's *no such thing as* devil cats and this is certainly NOT a devil cat we're looking for. It is a scared, nervous little pussycat, hiding in a strange house."

Even as she spoke, Mary knew this was an inadequate and very wrong description of the large confident animal who had walked through her front door. Fear is infectious and even mothers of thirty-nine, especially when they are very tired, can become superstitious.

"Really girls, I don't know where he is and I'm too tired to look any more. I think we should just all go to bed."

"Can we all sleep in the same room, mummy?"

"Celia, that would be ridiculous and far too squashed."

Anne, her oldest daughter who had been very quiet so far, now whispered,

"I would like us all to sleep in the same room, mummy."

Mary nodded wearily and blankets and pillows were quickly collected and they piled into the two beds beside the younger girls. Shamefacedly, Mary had made sure that the bedroom door was closed but Celia, after peering carefully under the beds, wedged a chair under the door handle. Mary was too tired to remonstrate.

In the morning light, the Siamese cat emerged from a cupboard which had been thoroughly searched the previous night. There was no real mystery for on the highest shelf, a luxurious folded rug, still slightly warm, proclaimed his sleeping place.

Mary mentioned in the grocer's that morning that she had found a lost Siamese and within an hour, the grateful owner came to collect her darling, bringing half a pound of chocolates as a reward. Later, Mary was somewhat put out to find that Mr Main, the grocer, had received a bottle of whisky for his part in relaying the good news. Though Mary would not have welcomed whisky, it seemed unfair that the grocer, who had neither provided feline sustenance nor suffered the uncomfortable night, had been more generously recompensed.

One morning, many years later, another cat, an extremely

fat tabby sat mewing disconsolately on the doormat and Mary exclaimed,

"Don't tell me that you are homeless! You are an *obese* cat and should be ashamed of yourself. Come in at once and let me see what is written on your collar."

She read "*Pirrelli*" and Hayshaw, also a mobile number but no address.

"You're certainly well named, for you're just like a collection of spare tyres and *I won't be feeding you!*"

Hayshaw's address in the phone book was half way along Falkland Street.

"Well that was a bit dangerous for you to be crossing Clarence Drive. What were you thinking about, crazy cat? You had better stay here until you're collected and taken home safely."

Pirrelli seemed quite content to do so, but looked quizzically at the empty saucers which the resident cats had left. Mary phoned the mobile number but was told Mr Hayshaw was in a meeting at the moment. Would she phone at midday? She was informed the second time, that Mr Hayshaw was out to lunch. Could he call her back?

Pirrelli settled into the kitchen nicely and was given a few biscuits to stave off the pangs of hunger. By four o'clock there was no word from Mr H, and as Mary wanted to go out, she phoned again and was lucky this time.

"Pirrelli? In your house?" the voice sounded unsure. "He goes out all the time and I don't think he would get lost. Just put him out and he'll find his way home."

"But he's on the wrong side of Clarence Drive and I wouldn't put him out just now. It's the rush hour."

"I'm sure he'd be fine,"

Mr Hayshaw sounded very unfeeling.

"Actually," he continued "I am away from home at present and a friend is looking after the cat. In fact I should tell you that I am in Switzerland just now."

Mary hung up and sighed deeply.

Three long distance calls to Switzerland!

Later she struggled across the road with the heavy and unwilling cat, only to have him leap from her arms into a garden on the other side of Clarence Drive. She tried unsuc-

cessfully to entice him from the shrubbery but finally gave up.
At least Pirrelli was on the safe side of the road and unlikely to
perish from malnutrition for a week or two.

Sometimes the claims on Mary's kindness were human
rather than feline and she was very happy to be there on the
spot. Over the years several older people fell or collapsed on the
pavement and Mary was quick to rush out with a chair and a
glass of water or even to phone for an ambulance if required. If
there was an accident at the busy corner, she might summon
the police and an ambulance.

One day, an agitated man, almost unintelligible and with
blood streaming down his face, came to her door. He had been
knocked off his bicycle by a careless passing motorist who had
not stopped. She brought him in and dressed his cuts, which
were fortunately superficial and made him tea. As he spoke, his
anger boiled over and he became even more difficult to understand. When he calmed down, Mary realised his fury was
directed not so much against the motorist, as against her neighbour in the next main door flat. This other, admittedly elderly,
lady, had immediately closed her door on him when he had
applied to her for help. Mary was glad she had not acted similarly, although at first sight he had been alarming.

The most dramatic incident happened in the early eighties.
Mary answered the door about seven o'clock one night in early
October, to find a teenage Asian girl standing on the doorstep.
She was nicely dressed and well spoken and when she asked if
Mary knew of any nearby hotel where she might stay that
night, Mary named a few local places but when the teenager
asked how much it might cost, Mary was unsure.

"Do you think that it would be more than ten pounds,
Miss?"

"I am afraid it would be quite a lot more than ten pounds in
those west end places."

The girl's dark anxious eyes melted Mary's heart. This child
was about fifteen, not much older than her own daughter
Margaret and she was obviously in some sort of trouble.

"Why don't you come in and have a cup of tea and we
could phone around and enquire."

The girl smiled a lovely smile and accepted the invitation.

Without much difficulty, Mary found that the girl had left home because of a row with her father. He wanted her to leave school and work in his shop, while she wanted to continue her studies and escape the slavery of menial work. It was perhaps not the whole story but it was a familiar one and Mary accepted it at face value.

She said she was called Priya but would give no other name

"First of all, Priya, I think we should phone your mother..."

"No, no they mustn't know where I am. He'd take me back home again right away. I know he would."

"But just think how worried your mother will be. I know how desperate I should be if my daughter ran away. Let's just phone and tell your mum that you are safe."

"No, he would come for me."

By this time Margaret and her younger sister Janet had joined them in the kitchen and Priya was looking more relaxed and happy, though any mention of her father brought a terrified look to her face.

Mary left the girls together and phoned her friend Doris, an educational psychologist, who suggested that a hostel for young homeless women in Wilton Street might take Priya in and she very kindly offered to arrange it and drive the girl there.

Priya insisted that she wanted Mary to come too.

As they drove along Great Western Road, Priya in the back seat with Mary, became more and more nervous. When the car turned off the main road, Mary was astonished when Priya suddenly dropped to her knees on the floor, hiding her head in her hands.

"Priya, what is the matter? Get up my dear!"

Coincidentally, the car was about to drive past Priya's own house.

Priya was calmer when they reached the hostel and it seemed a pleasant place. The warden was kind and welcoming. However there was a problem. Priya refused to give her name and the warden would not accept her without it being declared. Mary and Doris pleaded, explained, cajoled and the warden became cross but Priya was adamant. She would not divulge her name.

It was all very awkward and they left the hostel in silence. Just as they were about to get into the car, Priya stepped backwards and said,

"I'm not coming with you."

And she turned and walked quickly down the street.

"Perhaps she will just go home now, as it is nearby," said Doris hopefully.

"I doubt it and I am worried about her but I don't think we should chase after her. There's not much more we can do, really."

At home Margaret and Janet were waiting to see what had happened. It was an adventure on a boring Friday night. Mary had to tell them of the failure of the plan.

After the usual delays and procrastinations they went off to bed in the basement flat.

At ten o'clock, Margaret came upstairs again.

"What's the excuse this time?" said Mary, trying to look fierce.

"Mummy, that girl's back here again. She must have walked home from where you left her and she's lying down on the ground outside our window. She's going to be sleeping there all night and it's getting awfully cold. Should I ask her in to sleep with us?"

"No I don't quite think you should do that. I don't know what to do. If it's really cold I expect she won't stay there long."

"Oh mummy you couldn't let her sleep there all night, could you!"

"Doris and I gave up most of our evening to help her find somewhere to sleep and she was too stubborn to make the best of it. I feel I've done quite enough already and I'm not a bit happy about you sharing your room with a stranger."

"She could have the extra mattress on the floor and there's plenty blankets..."

Mary still said no to the proposition while realising she was unlikely to win.

Half an hour later, Margaret came up again.

"I'm going to make her some cocoa to warm her up. Is that all right? Janet and I will have some too."

"Is she in the house now?"

"She's sitting on the window sill with her legs inside... please, I really think she should just come in and sleep with us."

Holding on to the last shreds of her authority, Mary said,

"She can come in then but I do not want to know anything about it. *I am ignorant of the fact that she is sleeping in my basement.* Do you understand? She might be in trouble with the police for all we know. She seems very nice but we know nothing about her. I'm not at all happy about it."

"Oh thank you mummy, that's great."

Margaret disappeared with the three mugs of cocoa and a wide smile and Mary was left rather troubled.

At eight o'clock the next morning Mary answered the door to a tall and handsome young policeman. Priya stood beside him.

"Good morning, madam. Do you know anything about this young woman? We found her in the lane at the back of the house early this morning and she says she slept in your house last night."

Mary nodded.

"That's correct. Please come in."

Mary told the whole story and the policeman listened and wrote quickly, sometimes giving a kindly smile to Priya. Mary was pleased to see that he was so well disposed towards the girl. Then he asked,

"Now, Priya, perhaps you'll tell me why you were standing around in the cold at six o'clock this morning."

She hesitated and looked at Mary then at the policeman.

"Well you see there's a boy I know, we were at school together and he's an apprentice plumber and he's working at the back of these buildings just now and I know he'd help me and I might even go and stay with his Mum, and I know he'd give me money if I needed it and I was there early to catch him before he started work, but maybe he wouldn't be working on a Saturday."

Then she wept a little and the policeman looked at Mary with raised eyebrows.

There was a silence then the policeman spoke in a more official way than previously.

"You see we have been told to look out for a young runaway girl of your age whose father says that she's stolen jewellery worth twelve pounds..."

"*That's not true,*" Priya burst out, "It's all my own jewellery that I got for my birthday. Look!"

And she displayed three slender golden bangles.

"And," the policeman continued, "money was taken as well. The exact amount is stated here as six pounds fifty pence."

"That was my *wages* for the week. I didn't steal a penny. That's what I always get on a Friday. He gave it me out the till! I work late every night and that's my *wages*. That's so unfair, I didn't steal *anything* at all."

The policeman looked at Mary with slight shrug and a very meaning look and smiled even more kindly to Priya and patted her shoulder.

"Now you're not to worry. Dry your eyes and I'm going to take you to a very nice lady who'll give you a tasty breakfast, for I bet you're hungry and then we'll try and get these mistakes all sorted out and I'm sure you would like to say thank you to this lady for her hospitality before you go."

Priya dried her eyes and Mary gave her a hug and whispered to her not to worry.

Mary was very much impressed at the sympathetic way that the policeman had dealt with the case. He was so young too! He would go far.

Mary was touched when Priya phoned her later in the morning.

"They're so kind to me here and they'll find me somewhere to live so I don't need to go back home again and I can stay on at school and do my Highers. Isn't that great. And thank you so much for your help and give my love to Margaret and Janet. I promise to phone again soon."

Mary was delighted, though she would never hear from Priya again.

It was evening before Margaret told her mother that Priya had many large bruises on her back and what looked like cigarette burns on her legs.

"How horrifying! Awful! Well, Margaret darling you are a bit of a heroine. I'm afraid I must have seemed hard-hearted and I'm glad you were so persistent."

"Well I knew she couldn't sleep on the ground all night, could she."

Margaret was always a practical girl with a kind heart.

✧◆✧

HYNDLAND SHOPS

I recently read a short piece by Charles Dickens about his favourite seaside resort. In describing all the different shops in the little town, he gave a wonderful picture of that particular time and place. It set me thinking of the Clarence Drive shops as I had known them in my childhood and how they had changed through the years. There were one or two blanks in my memory and perhaps someone will help me out or correct me.

Before Peckham's established their excellent delicatessen on the corner, we had a wonderful toy shop for a few years. But from the thirties, and before, to the mid sixties, it was a fish shop. The old fashioned open window where the several different fish were displayed must have made it a bitterly cold workplace and the shop girls were bundled and booted to deal with this. We were modest but regular customers and the firm sent me a nice bouquet on the birth of each of my daughters.

Next to that was the ice cream shop and cafe, which was gathered into Peckham's premises in the nineties.

What a tempest was stirred in 1949 when the idea of a cafe was suggested! Though it would close at nine pm and would not open on Sunday, yet there were very strong feelings against it. All trading had previously shut down at 6pm in Hyndland and late night premises such as cafes and pubs were safely at a distance in Byres Road. It seemed self evident to many residents that a cafe would be a *bad thing* for the local young people. It might well attract gangs of undesirable youths who would almost certainly loiter with criminal intent. In spite of forebodings, a charming Italian family took over the cafe and ran it for over forty years, becoming an important part of the community. The residents learned to meet for coffee in the shop and my daughters and I enjoyed many a slider on a hot summer evening. I still miss that excellent ice cream.

I cannot remember what that little shop was before it became a cafe. Can anyone help?

The newsagent, with its Post Office, has remained very stable throughout my life, although the layout has changed. In the thirties, forties and fifties, there was only one door and the deep counter to the left was stacked with newspapers and journals, some magazines even hung from the ceiling. Behind the counter were school supplies, rubbers, rulers, notebooks and compasses. I was always fascinated by those articles. I cannot remember sweets on sale, probably not as there were at least four sweet shops in Hyndland.

The post office counter was at the back of the shop and if one wanted to write a telegram or fill in a form, one disappeared round the corner to a rickety little table where a dipping pen with a dreadful nib and a meagre supply of ink made the task difficult. The post office staff behind their wire screen always seemed rather grumpy and unhelpful, very different from the present friendly folk who are separated from the public by bullet-proof glass. I wonder what those long gone officials would have thought of the immense sums that pass over the counter nowadays.

The entire west wall of the shop was shelved to display the Lending Library. I suspect that most of the books were well read murder mysteries or romances, though I only remember borrowing the *Tarzan* series. I soon graduated to the larger and superior lending library on Hyndland Road, where my maturing tastes could borrow and enjoy *Just William*, the *Chalet School* and *P G Wodehouse*. That shop is now a trendy dress shop.

Next to the newsagent, in what is now the smart pizza takeaway, was the sort of little drapers' shop which no longer exists. It was run by two old souls who fascinated me. One had a distinct moustache which I thought unsuitable for a woman. I was convinced that they lived in the back shop. Pretty well anything could be bought in that cave of glass-fronted cupboards, hats, scarves, stockings, gloves, underwear, nightwear, wool, thread, zip fasteners, elastic, hair-nets, kirby grips and a good choice of ribbons, all colours, broad and narrow. No doubt ladies could buy corsets or girdles there. It was probably an excellent little business. I can remember my mother buying me a liberty bodice with suspenders to hold up my stockings when I was six. It was soft and white and the buttons were made of rubber and I liked it very much. I cannot remember when that shop closed, but I wish we had one like it now in Hyndland! It metamorphosed into a 24 hour laundrette in the seventies, which I found wonderfully convenient at a time when I had a large family laundry to deal with. I could have the daily wash drying on my pulleys by eight o'clock each morning. It was quite a social hub and friends met there regularly, perhaps some romances blossomed.

The next shop is a now a well-stocked grocery but I have a complete blank about its use in my childhood. It sold foreign artefacts in the sixties. I seem to remember it, though perhaps wrongly, as a hat shop after that.

The fish and chip shop which opened in 1971 was previously a grocer, a real old-fashioned one. Thomson was the name for many years. The butter and cheese were cut from large blocks, sugar was weighed into brown bags as were the biscuits which were in display boxes with glass tops. A broken biscuit was usually available for a well-behaved child. It was a small crowded shop, what with customers, goods and several assistants. Before the war, Mr Thomson kept a full time accountant and a message boy, as many customers phoned in their order, sometimes at almost closing time, and expected immediate delivery. The bill, though it might be only a shilling or two, was often charged 'to account'. The war put a stop to these unnecessary luxuries.

Where we now have a herbal health shop, R S McColl's sold their sweets and chocolates. Their Russian toffees were particularly good, though liable to search out any dental defect.

The shop which sells gorgeously exotic flowers was once an elegant baby linen shop. It was run by a Belgian lady who had come here after the first world war. The tiny smocked dresses, pastel cord dungarees and soft woollen jackets were hardly practical though no doubt a temptation for affluent grand-mamas. That business lasted well into the sixties.

The hairdresser has always been a hairdressing establishment as far as I can remember, although the firm has changed through the years.

Bradford's bakery was a butcher's shop until the sixties. When I married in 1959, the butcher gave me a splendid

carving knife. He had known me since I was a young child
and no doubt expected me to continue my custom. In the
mid sixties my four year old daughter was greatly entertained by the sausage-making machine. After the extruding
process was completed the handsome young apprentice
would deftly twist the sausages into a neat bundle, much as I
would have dealt with a hank of wool.

Peckham's Wine was a dairy for many years before it was
taken over as a grocer's by Mr Gilliland. Dairies were the
only shops to open on a Sunday at that time, and then only
till 10 30am, very handy if one had run out of milk or bread
and they generally kept a few groceries. In those days before
the introduction of late night or Sunday shopping, one had
to plan ahead concerning food supplies, for many stores
were closed from one pm Saturday until Monday morning.
We are so very spoiled nowadays.

Mr Gilliland had been the manager of Thomson's before he
set up on his own in the dairy in the sixties. He had been in
the trade all his life and told me of the tough times of the thirties, when employment safety hung by a thread. At eighteen
he was unexpectedly asked to take over as manager of a
Maypole dairy, when his superior, 'a wonderful boss who
taught me everything' as Mr Gilliland described him, was
suddenly fired for a very minor fault. As the women on the
staff were older, the teenager was urged to "grow a moustache
as quickly as possible". Perhaps the sixties were as difficult for
business as the thirties, for though Mr Gilliland and his wife
and son worked hard, the shop closed suddenly one night in
1971. Mr and Mrs Main took the shop over and ran a very fine
grocery and delicatessen for many years but they did not
succeed in acquiring a liquor licence though they tried repeatedly. The west end had not yet acquired its taste for wine.

On the other side of Clarence Drive were a group of
wooden huts. Behind them was a large grassy gap site which
I have heard was used as a POW camp during the war,
though I was out of Glasgow at that time and have no
memory of it. Nowadays a block of flats and shops, built in
the sixties, stands in this location at the corner of Lauderdale
Gardens. The wooden huts were erected for administration
when Hyndland was in the process of being built and

remained as offices for the payment of rents, I believe. No doubt they were considered temporary in the 1900s, but they were still in use as adhoc business premises in the mid sixties. One housed an electrical business, another tiny one did boot and shoe repairs, while the largest structure was the successful fruit and flower shop belonging to Mr Smith. In the sixties, his son would move across the road to Thomson's old premises and for several years would provide first class fruit and vegetables of more exotic varieties than most greengrocers offered at that time. Now we can unthinkingly pick up garlic, peppers, aubergines, pineapples, kiwi fruit or asparagus in our supermarkets but in those days people drove from all over Glasgow to buy them in Smiths. This old family business was eventually defeated by the larger firms and Peckham's took it over as a fruit shop.

Nevertheless I loved and had many happy memories of the little wooden shop on the other side of the street. It had a rural atmosphere and there was always a cloud of delicious aroma in the street for they boiled beetroot and made jam and pickles on the premises.

One of the first home movies that I ever made was in 1957. Two ginger kittens were fighting in Smith's flower-filled window, chasing, leaping and struggling with each other, knocking jars of marigolds and anemones flying, creating devastation as I kept my camera rolling for as long as the wind-up mechanism lasted. It was a splendid film.

In 1971, the Chipchik Inn opened. Fast food had started to invade Hyndland. Theresa and her mother and husband Carmen made excellent fish suppers which were much appreciated. I no longer used my deep fryer for we could have chips from the shop once a week as a treat.

Sadly, both Carmen and Mr Main died, comparatively young men.

✧◆✧

Mrs Caledon's Hobby

It was nearly the end of the twentieth century and Mrs Jane Caledon had lived in her large corner flat near the top of the hill for more than thirty years. Although a tenement flat, it had a 'main door' and had no access to the close. Seven marble faced steps led from the pavement to her front door. It was a two-storey flat, like several others in Hyndland, and spacious enough for a large family with four rooms, kitchen and bathroom opening from an unnecessarily impressive T-shaped entrance hall upstairs with another two rooms and bathroom and an only slightly smaller hallway downstairs, where the back door opened to a large sunny walled garden. Because of the hilly terrain, the lower flat was only half the size of the upper.

When Captain Caledon, a determined and dominant husband, had first considered buying this desirable residence in 1967, all those years ago, Jane was aghast. Speechless. Though she had happily lived "up a close" all her life, this place was enormous, and seemed to embody all the drawbacks of tenement life with none of the benefits.

The flat had been neglected and required a lot of improvements but as Jim Caledon, a large man with an imposing beard, strode through the empty rooms, he chuckled triumphantly.

"It's a *marvellous* bargain. And with a main door, we won't have any more problems with gossipy neighbours or that stair woman needing hot water at an awkward time."

His wife remained speechless, for with her husband at sea for weeks at a time, meeting neighbours seemed more of a comfort and a pleasure than a chore. The previous owners had been heavy smokers and the dark walls, ceiling and woodwork were impregnated with nicotine. She wondered how they would ever rid themselves of the smell. Also it was likely that she must deal with those cold marble front steps herself.

The first six years of their marriage had been spent in a modest but charming three room and kitchen flat in Novar

Drive. It had sold for three thousand pounds and this one, almost twice the size, was a bargain at four thousand, although it would need around two thousand spent on improvements.

In Novar Drive, Jane's neighbour upstairs, Meg Brown, had been Jane's best friend and Meg's pretty teenage daughter loved to baby-sit Jane's two little girls. Old Mrs Albert on the ground floor often baked scones and pancakes to hand in for the children, while Jane was happy to shop for her occasionally. Mrs A. was an old lady with the unusual habit (for old ladies) of always being the first to end a conversation. Then there was Tommy McCann and his wife Marjorie on the top floor, a charming and attractive couple who took a lot of responsibility for the maintenance of the building. Tommy seemed more able to negotiate with the factor and the tradesmen than anyone else in the block. Yes, all those people were important in Jane's life when her husband was at sea and she dreaded losing them. And there would certainly be more cleaning in this new flat, nearly twice the size of the previous one and in a cold winter the fuel bills might be startling. Jane had been very content with the smaller house and would never have chosen such a large place herself, however she smothered her reservations and assured Jim he had made an excellent decision.

She was an adaptable girl and once the work and decoration were completed, she quickly fell in love with their new home and their lives expanded to fill the extra space.

Six tall windows made the sitting room bright throughout the day and though traffic constantly rushed past, the well fitted windows kept it surprisingly silent. At the back of the house the large sunny kitchen overlooked an almost rural scene of shrubs and trees filled with birds. Jane loved the contrast. Her sewing machine was permanently set up downstairs and with the playroom for the children, their toys were less in evidence upstairs. In fine weather Jane drank her coffee in the garden while the girls skipped and played ball.

An added bonus was that rushing up and downstairs and living her life on two levels kept Jane very fit.

It was not only physically that she lived her life on two

levels. Jane Caledon had a hobby. Throughout her life she had been an ardent film-goer and in the sixties, with television re-runs, she had the joy of once more seeing the films of her youth and even films of her mother's youth that she only knew of by hearsay. It was fascinating. More miraculous was the advent of video. Jane was the first amongst her friends to purchase a VCR and learn how to set it to record at odd times of the day or night. Some of her friends never did learn that skill. Over the years she taped a considerable library of films and at any time could choose to watch the work of Hitchcock, Busby Berkley, Satyajit Ray, Fellini, Ingmar Bergman, Woody Allen or Kurasawa. She adored the cinema and in France would have been recognised as a true *cineaste*. She had the sort of mind that remembered in great detail practically every film she had ever seen. She remembered the director, the actors and the characters they had played. She recalled the plot, the costumes, the locations, much of the dialogue and often the background music and she was able to retrieve those memories with speed and ease. She might have made a great film director herself, but like most women of her generation, her life had been dedicated to caring for people and maintaining property.

She had no regrets, because her hobby had enriched her life for just as she moved between her ground floor and her basement flat balancing the domestic tasks, her mind compared and paralleled her daily experiences and the people she met with those memories of the screen which she could bring to mind so effortlessly. Jane could add excitement to any occasion by referring mentally to some dramatic filmic scenario which mirrored the real life situation. She was quick to spot similarities of feature or voice between acquaintances and obscure film actors and derived much satisfaction from pin-pointing the film in which they had appeared. She did not attempt to share these inner musings or should I say rather that she quickly realised that others did not share her fascination. Jane's friends shared neither the interest nor the necessary mental archives. To explain would have been tedious, perhaps embarrassing. Jane was satisfied to keep these thoughts as private pleasures, although her children had the benefit of the remembered plots of films which she had enjoyed as a child. Her memories were recycled as bedtime stories with Shirley Temple, singing and dancing her way through life's vicissitudes with professional skill and the more abrasive and less famous Jane Withers wisecracking and behaving badly. Her daughters were intrigued by Our Gang, a crowd of ragamuffins, of which one member, Alfalfa, had a hilariously dreadful singing voice which Jane attempted, not very successfully, to reproduce Their favourite story was when Shirley (a neglected little orphan) awakened one morning to find her poverty-stricken garret transformed by a wealthy relative who had suddenly discovered her existence. An exquisite dressing gown, a silken bedspread, rich curtains and rugs had replaced the former poor sticks of furniture.

As the girls grew older, they loved to watch tapes of the Ruritanian romps of Deanna Durbin with her magnificent voice, of Sonja Heine in fur-trimmed skirts, smiling and spinning forever in delightfully frosty scenes, of Esther Williams in a warmer environment, swimming and diving miraculously and of course the teenage romances of Judy Garland and Mickey Rooney. The Andy Hardy series was a special favourite.

Jane considered it a sort of history lesson for her girls.

Jim Caledon knew that his wife loved going to 'the pictures' but was unaware of any more serious involvement. He had no interest in the cinema. When he came home, and after he had divested his mind of the worries and resentments of his recent voyage, he wanted to concentrate on an intense domestic life. For entertainment, he enjoyed dining out, the theatre and golf and Jane was happy to share these. Her lonely hobby was a delicious secret to be enjoyed during his absences and Jane reckoned that she gained twice as much enjoyment out of life as other people did.

After her daughters had grown up, graduated, left home, married and had children of their own, her friends were wont to say,

"Oh, dear! Where has the time gone?"

"All those years, passed in a flash!"

"It seems like only yesterday!"

But Jane could not agree. Now approaching sixty and

still very fit, she felt she had lived a long time and had lived
several lives. Certain films reminded her vividly of her own
experiences at the time she had first seen them as a girl, or
perhaps when she had seen them for the second time as a
young wife or perhaps thirty years later, a grandmother.
Sometimes the several viewings seemed of different films
because of her own changing maturity. She associated films
with the news of the day and was able to remember events
and their approximate date much more clearly than her
contemporaries. She had an unerring eye for style, for her
celluloid studies enabled Jane to pinpoint the year of cars,
clothes, interior design and architecture with astonishing
accuracy.

A comedy which really appealed to Jane was Woody
Allen's "Play it Again Sam", in which the wimpish and
unsuccessful hero, obsessed by the film "Casablanca",
recreates the ending of that film in his own life by
mirroring the self-denial of the hero and in the parallel
setting of an airport at night, complete with departing
plane, relinquishes the girl that he loves just as Bogart does
in Casablanca. Jane adored that film, though less happy
about another of Allen's creations where the actors stepped
off the screen and started to live as real people. Jane was
an escapist rather than a fantasist and her life would have
become just *too* complex if those characters who filled her
mind had started to materialize.

Jane was sixty seven when Captain Caledon died.

Suddenly and very unexpectedly the two-storey flat
started to unnerve her. While not exactly terrified, she
became aware of dangerous possibilities. After brushing her
teeth at night, she was beset with fleeting visions of a dark
figure hovering behind her bedroom door with a heavy
blunt object. Newspapers were full of alarming stories of old
ladies as victims of criminal activity and the downstairs
windows were vulnerable in the quiet back garden.
Returning late from dinner with friends or a midnight show
at the local cinema, she started to consider that someone
might have broken in downstairs and be waiting quietly in
the dark, ready to rush up from the lower flat and confront

her with a knife or a gun. She would tell herself not to be
ridiculous and yet, after unlocking her front door, she would
hesitate on the threshold, struggling to blot out a myriad of
crystal-clear images drawn from "The Cat and the Canary",
"Son of Frankenstein", "Phantom of the Opera" (both the
Lon Chaney and the Claude Rains version), "Psycho",
"Alien" and " The Shining". For the first time her hobby was
proving to be an unpleasant drawback. She despised herself
for allowing her imagination to overtake her common sense.
She had not felt that sort of fear since she was fifteen when
the misery of her first broken love affair had wiped out the
nonsense of childish fears of the Frankenstein monster. She
tried to laugh herself out of what she saw as a humiliating
weakness, but what seemed funny in the early evening
changed when she turned the key in the lock and entered
the vast T-shaped hall of the *apparently* empty flat at night.
Determined not to curtail her outings she kept a stout
walking stick in the umbrella stand and grasped it as soon
as she stepped inside, but on the evening that she felt something was crouching at the shadowy end of her hall and the
small acid-spitting creature in Jurassic Park flickered into
her consciousness, she made her decision. Very quickly she
arranged for planning permission and found architects and
builders to divide the house. It was far too big for one
person anyway. Within the year, the basement flat was sold
at a handsome profit.

Jane was delighted to be living on a single floor once
again and all her fears and imaginings disappeared.
Newspaper accounts of crime left her sympathetic but
untroubled. Acquiring a handsome tabby cat called Matthew
and installing a neat portable TV and state of the art VCR in
her kitchen she decided that the time had come for her to
live more simply. It was cosier in the kitchen and she set
herself a goal of cataloguing all her films on the nights that
she did not go out. For years she had conscientiously taped
films at the annual Christmas celluloid orgy on the small
screen and of course throughout the year. Friday and
Saturday afternoons were a never-ending source of old
films. Jane had shelves specially built in the kitchen to store
her library which was vast and eclectic, ranging from

ancient black and white B movies to videos of the latest successes. As her daughters said, there was never any problem about what to give her for her birthday. If there was not a particular film that she wanted, a box of ten blank tapes was just as acceptable.

"That really is rather a boring present, Mum, so I got you a little something else as well."

But Jane was perfectly pleased with blank tapes. It meant that she need never miss a good movie and she might just eventually track down that elusive movie about teenage romance which had so enthralled her when she was herself a young teenager. There was a boy called Paul in it, or perhaps it was Peter anyway she had always favoured those names. Probably she would have been appalled at the quality of the film if it ever came to light, but it remained always there at the back of her mind, a sort of Holy Grail.

Although there had been lots of different pets when the children were young, Jane had not had a creature to care for since the last of the tropical fish had died nearly twelve years previously. When it had started to float so unhappily on its side that long ago Sunday, Jane had experienced mixed feelings as she wielded the stone and had, as humanely as possible, dashed the Guppy's brains out, but a determination to retire from the responsibilities of pet care was uppermost. However, Matthew had arrived one night on Jane's doorstep, a wet and hungry, lame and lost tabby. She noticed the forlorn sharp-eared silhouette peering through the glass panel of the front door as she passed through the hall to fetch herself a banana. Immersed in the magic of "Singin' in the Rain", she had forgotten to cook dinner. As the cat limped in with that mixture of caution and arrogance which only striped cats can display, Jane realised immediately and without dismay that her pet free days had ended and named him Matthew after a companion of a long ago hot summer.

There is a special understanding which develops when a single human shares a home with a single animal and Jane realised that she had never before given cats proper credit for their intelligence and practical philosophy. She found Matthew the perfect companion, independent, polite and, after proper veterinary care and adequate food, wonderfully handsome. And if unable or unwilling to share her obsession, he certainly appreciated the comfort of a warm lap for long hours of viewing and often displayed an interest in the fast forward or re-wind modes.

Although an indoor cat with a discreet litter box in a cupboard, Matthew occasionally enjoyed a prowl around the shrubbery of the front garden around ten in the evening. It was a busy street with several shops staying open until eleven or midnight and Jane would stand on her front steps for a short time perhaps commenting on the weather to passing acquaintances. Soon Matthew would melt into the groundcover and Jane, leaving the front door slightly ajar, would return to her kitchen. She was quite aware that someone could easily walk into her house and, as was her habit, often visualised that possibility, selecting a variety of characters from her inner list of intruder movies. But with the division of the flat she had lost all her previous nervous fears. She had separated the real from the imaginary and did not believe for a moment that anyone, other than a small damp cat, would walk through the front door at that time of night.

One Sunday night about eleven-thirty, the cat conveyed his wish to go out.

"I think it's rather late, my little dear. And it was very wet just now. You're a silly boy."

The cat was polite but firm and Jane let him out.

The previous week Jane had taped one of the most exquisite and blood curdling horror films of all time, "Onibaba". She had only seen the Japanese film once before and it had made a great impression on her. She determined to watch it late at night, when no telephone or well-meaning visitor might interrupt. As she boiled the kettle for a pot of tea she recalled a moonlit scene where the heroine runs through towering bamboo thickets to meet her lover. The dry rustling sound of the wind in the stalks had reminded Jane strongly of an incident in her own girlhood, when the captain was but an engineer and she smiled as she recalled the memory.

Prolonging the pleasure of anticipation, she labelled one

or two tapes and tidied the kitchen. Then, unwilling to have her film interrupted by Matthew's return, she continued to potter around.

Surely that cat should have returned by now?

As she polished the television screen she felt ridiculously happy and anticipatory. She glanced at herself in the mirror and thought how daft it was for an old body in her sixties to be so bubbling with joy.

Then she heard it. A faint but very recognisable sound.

It was the familiar click of the front door closing!

Matthew was an expert at pushing doors open but, like all other cats, unable or unwilling to close them.

Jane knew she had an intruder.

She felt no fear. She almost felt that she had lived through this situation many times. Standing in front of her TV and VCR, perhaps with some vain hope that she might hide them, she turned to face the kitchen door which had glass panels.

A large shadow approached and the door was slowly pushed open but the thin, red-haired man stayed in the hall. Much smaller than his shadow and smaller than Jane even, he was very young and he carried, inexpertly, what appeared to be a gun in his left hand.

Jane judged him to be an opportunist who had seen the open front door though that hardly explained the gun? With the hall light behind him it was difficult to see his face clearly. His hair was cut *en brosse* and with the light shining through it was certainly very red. His close-set eyes, while not exactly squinting, were unusually interested in his own nose. It seemed as though the boy suffered spasms of pain as a grimace passed across his face repeatedly, but Jane was quick to recognise the famous momentary rictus so typical of Humphrey Bogart.

"Whaur's yer money? Show us whaur ye keep it! Quick!" He spoke high and hurriedly.

"I don't keep any money in the house." Jane's voice was squeakier than she would have liked it to be though not any squeakier than the intruder's.

"Come oan, ye've goat money stashed awa'. Whaur is it? Show me noo!" his voice was slightly gruffer than before.

He's never done this in his life before, thought Jane, and he's useless

"Ah bet ye've a wee nest egg hid awa an' silver and joolery an' a' that. Don't you shake yer heed at me. Ah bet ther a forch'ne in a big hoose like this." He glanced right and left and had probably repeated this script in his head many times before this première performance.

The boy bent his arm above his head and waved the gun about like a bottle of medicine. Both he and Jane knew that he believed he was brandishing it but they both also knew it was unskilful. Jane felt very cool and unconvinced of any personal danger. Through familiarity with similar scenarios, she felt that she too had rehearsed this many times. As the heroine, she was bound to survive, they always did. Especially as the bad guys were always such inexplicably rotten shots. Besides, Jane's sharp eyesight had detected something else which raised her spirits. It was a plastic gun.

"Ah mean, Ah cud bump ye aff... ah mean it"

Jane winced at the old-fashioned slang rather than the menace of the remark. Obviously the lad had watched too many Cagney movies. He would be calling it a gat next. At the same time her heart softened towards a fellow film buff.

"Aye an' then Ah cud strip the hoose an' Ah bet ther plenty in a big hoose like this... Ah'd soon sell *they* in the pub."

His eyes indicated the TV and the VCR. behind Jane.

Jane wondered how those stick-like arms might carry two such heavy items from the house to the nearest pub and the same idea must have occurred to him.

"Whit else have ye goat that's worth a loat? Ye're no' tellin' me that ye live in a big place like this an' ye don't hiv stuff that's worth a loat."

"Well yes, I do own precious things. Some are only precious to me of course."

The boy snorted with a strong echo of Jack Nicholson in "Chinatown".

"Yes, of course there are some things that are worth a lot of money," she continued hurriedly.

"Where? Whit's worth a loat? Show me!"

"There's the piano, it's very valuable..."

"Aw gies a brek, missus!"

She realised how ridiculous she had been, she must be more nervous than she thought and she did not want to antagonise him.

"That rug on the floor there behind you, that's worth over a thousand."

The boy turned and looked at the small Persian carpet in the hall. richly coloured but quite shabby. He gazed at it for a long time. Perhaps he did not believe her or perhaps he was picturing himself attempting and failing to sell an old rolled up rug in a Partick pub for more than a fiver.

"Hiv ye no' goat somethin' Ah cud cairry easy?" his voice was plaintive, but desperation was adding an ugly break to it. "Ye must hiv somethin' *normal*. Somethin' worth *real money.*"

"I have a painting that is worth a few thousand." She was stalling for time. The statement was true but she had not realised the effect it would have. The boy started to laugh very heartily, surprising Jane with a beautiful set of teeth. If this boy had delivered letters or arrived to wash her windows she would have judged him a thoroughly decent fellow. Now with the laughter the scene was almost ended. It was hard for the boy to recover his tough guy attitude. Remembering how important it had been to *act* when her own teen-age daughters had been stroppy, Jane made a swift decision.

"How about some videos? They would be light to carry and you'd sell them easily at a fiver a time. At least. They're the latest. I'll get a poly bag for you."

Businesslike and positive, Jane immediately moved across the kitchen and filled a plastic bag with seven video films, Christmas and birthday presents from her daughters. Unerringly she chose her least favourite movies from the shelves and adding four blank tapes to the bag she put it into his right hand and ushered the astonished young man to the front door, which she opened for him as both his hands were full.

A very wet cat immediately rushed in and pushed past his ankles.

Completely unnerved the red-headed man made one last weak protest.

"Ah hope these arenae from the rental shope."

"Oh, no, no," she laughed, "They're all mine. Ladies in big houses are very honest."

As Jane locked the door firmly behind him, she decided she'd had enough excitement for one night. Tomorrow evening would be soon enough to enjoy the thrilling terror of "Onibaba".

A RARE PLANT IN HYNDLAND

When I moved into my flat forty years ago, a thick layer of red gravel had been laid over the poor, clayey soil of the front garden, in an unsuccessful bid to suppress the weeds, though even the weeds struggled to survive in a soil poisoned by sixty years of Glasgow soot. Three trees were hacked into unattractive little stumps. It was a sad and barren frontage and did nothing to help restore the city air.

My front garden is situated beside one of the busiest corners in the west end. Traffic hurtles around that corner from early morning till late at night, pouring a less visible but perhaps more virulent pollution than soot over my struggling shrubs and ground cover. It is a windy corner too and only partly sunny. Litter is constantly blown into the garden and also deposited by the less conscientious citizens. A considerable amount of bottles and cans are cast over the railings each week. Occasionally I find a returnable bottle and I am pleased to collect my forty pence on that. Schoolchildren leave a surprising number of half eaten apples, chocolate bars and half drunk juice boxes. Some of them do try to make the place look better by hiding their sweetie wrappers and crisp bags deep amongst the ground cover. I appreciate that and consider that a few more litterbins around the streets would turn those children into model citizens. Children are not the worst, it is adults who throw away the small plastic wrappers from cigarettes and also the receipts from cash line machines. These items proliferate and are hard to pick up. I wonder if they realise how much information can be gleaned from one of those little bank slips?

Altogether it is astonishing that anything grows in my garden at all!

However it does grow and I am surprised and grateful that over the years my garden has become green and lush, almost a woodland environment. My philosophy is to encourage any plant that seems to thrive. Several trees have self-seeded, a guelder rose, two hawthorn shrubs, an oak, a white elder and even a chestnut tree have established themselves. The last is still only four feet high, but soon I must find a new home for it.

I was in Hamburg some years ago and the frontage of every house and block of flats was rich with trees, shrubs and groundcover. It made the air of the busy city very sweet and fresh. I wish Glasgow would follow that example. I have done my best.

Last year I received a letter from someone who described herself as a 'keen horticulturist'. Her trained eye had noticed a very unusual plant in my front garden, a rare type of Helleborine. I admit I had never heard of Helleborines! This young lady collected them, but did not have this particular variety and she offered to buy the plant from me for £10.

Naturally I was delighted and later that week I made a new, very interesting friend, Lisa. She is an artist as well as a gardener and lives in the west end. She arrived with all the necessary tools and very, very carefully dug out some of the baby plants which encircled the main flower that she had spotted. She felt the mature plant was too established to risk removing it. She is returning this year to take photographs. You need not search my garden for anything exotic or flamboyant. This Helleborine is not outstanding, very modest in fact and only the searching eye of the enthusiast would have discovered it.

Lisa insisted on paying the promised fee, but as I could take no credit for this famous lodger in my garden and as the seed was almost certainly brought there by a bird, I have donated the money to the RSPB.

This year my garden is once more practically waste ground. For six months, scaffolding for stonework maintenance has adorned the building and several hard-working masons have plodded back and forth, manipulating inhumanly heavy chunks of red sandstone. And of course it has been a particularly long, harsh winter. Shrubs and ground cover appear to be wiped out completely but, perhaps when Spring arrives I shall be pleasantly surprised. The bird population should note that Helleborine or any other interesting seeds are always welcome.

✧◆✧

HORRIBLE EPISODES

I have commented earlier on the fact that Hyndland had no history at the beginning of the century, though that would change in the next fifty years, with two world wars and many local incidents.

Given time, Hyndland would even produce its own murders, one possibly in my own backyard. But that is more than fifty years ago and I shall leave that till last.

I shall refer once more to my young grandparents, as an example of an aspiring young couple who came to Glasgow in 1907. They chose to rent an older flat in the city centre rather than the new west end suburb of Hyndland. The elegant Blythswood Street flat had an excellent view of a piece of history which might not have pleased everyone, but which delighted my grandmother with her somewhat morbid tastes. From her sitting room window, she could see the basement window through which Madeleine Smith had handed the arsenic-laced cup of cocoa, to her importuning ex-lover. It was fifty years since that fatal night but it was a famous and scandalous trial which my grandmother had studied and she now revelled in her ringside seat.

Although the evidence at the time was suspicious and lurid, the verdict was *not proven.*

Strange that there is now a Madeleine Smith Building in Blythswood square, replacing that ancient notoriety with a whiff of respectability.

Two years later, my grandmother was less happy about finding a parcel in the adjacent lane, containing a human skull. However it was not a case for the police. It was a very old skull, probably belonging to a medical or art student.

I should warn you right now that I am not an aficionado of crime. Unlike my grandmother, I neither read books nor watch films concerning that dark side of life. Crime is not easy to avoid, there is a lot of it around and I know many people who delight in police and detective mysteries and who read little else in newspapers. I am not one of them. You will find no well-researched dates, details, clues, nor gruesome descriptions in this article. I think my interest lies mainly in the effect which these happenings have on the people in the neighbourhood. If we think of the murder as if it were a stone dropped into a pond, then it is the ripples which spread out after the event, which fascinate me.

We had a bloody murder in the district very recently. A wealthy, though somewhat mysterious man was bludgeoned to death outside his luxurious home. He seemed a lonely man, uncommunicative with his neighbours and with no known relations. His magnificent car was left unlocked, his private papers were scattered about the street and his briefcase, holding untold wealth, was lying in the gutter. Such were the various newspaper reports at any rate. Then more scandalous rumours were whispered. I do not know if the crime was ever cleared up but it certainly had all the ingredients of a suitable case for an episode of Taggart, that gritty television series which so often features elegant G12 interiors. So often, that one might doubt the safety of living in the area, (though in over sixty years I have suffered no personal injury and only two minor house break-ins).

Two days after this tragedy hit the headlines, I took some cleaning to the laundrette and here I must digress and tell you of the pretty young woman who works in the Hyndland laundrette. Over the years we have had many conversations. Let us call her Michelle, for that is a favourite name in Glasgow and could also belong to one of the Parisian blan-chisseuses that Degas has made so familiar. Michelle takes her responsibilities seriously and in spite of technology, her life is one of constant physical endeavour as she loads dirty linen into the washing machines, transfers heavy bundles of damp clothes to the driers, irons, steams and folds. Her movements are scarcely changed from those nineteenth century workers which Degas depicted, though modern machinery allows her to deal with a larger daily quantity. No doubt Michelle is more educated, better nourished and lives in a more comfort-able and hygienic house than those nineteenth century laundresses, but like them she has dark hair and skin, with heavy mascara emphasising her large eyes. She is vivacious and laughs easily but can become quickly downcast. She adores her little dog and has a ready sympathy for older customers. She is employed for long hours in dealing with the garments which others have soiled, then handed to her to transform to perfect cleanliness once more. Although electricity has taken much of the back-breaking labour away from these necessary chores, the fact remains that she must handle dirty garments and linen which others who are willing to pay rather than deal with, have discarded. Michelle tells me that some of these articles are *very* dirty, She assured me that I would be surprised at what arrived on her counter to be cleaned. Many people seemed to have *no shame* at the state of their intimate garments and as for *restaurants...*

"You should jist see the dish towels that come in here from some of they big swell restrongs. You would wonder what like their kitchens are, *just manky* ! I'm tellin' you, you wouldn't believe it. They must be just really, *really filthy.* *Yeuch*, I would'nae eat there, I'm tellin' you."

Some years ago, on learning that I write, she advised me to write a murder mystery, as that was her mother's favourite type of book. We had fun discussing the clues that might turn up in the laundrette, blood soaked towels, etc. although, aware of my own inadequacies, I never did pursue the project.

The murder victim at the start of this story had been a regular customer at the laundrette and Michelle had spoken to him many times. Now she was emotionally face to face with a real tragedy.

"Whit a shame! I'm that sorry about it. He was such a nice man! An awful nice man. So friendly. I really liked him."

She repeated this several times and wiped away a few discreet tears.

He had brought his linen to wash and his suits to clean for the last eighteen months.

"Such beautiful suits! All hand-stitched and lovely satin linings, too! And his shirts were all made in London too. They had a gold label in them. He was an awful nice man. He was awful generous at Christmas, too. It's jist terrible. I'm awful sorry. Whit a shame!"

Michelle had a sympathetic ear and a keen sense of humour and it may well be that she knew more of that lonely man in Hyndland than anyone else did. What more natural than for him to chat to a pretty, bright-eyed girl.

Perhaps as he spoke to her, he let fall some small item of knowledge that might have provided a vital clue to his murderer. Who knows?

It may well be that Michelle was one of the few people who mourned him.

I was fourteen when my father casually pointed to a flat above the bank at the corner of Byres Road and Highburgh Road and said,

"They'll never find it easy to rent that flat."

When I enquired the reason, he explained that a terrible murder had taken place there some years ago and the premises had been empty ever since.

I remember the surprise I felt at the time. Not fear or horror, just sheer disbelief. It seemed very unlikely to me. A murder! Ten minutes' walk from my house! Just there on the corner that I passed every day on my way to school. Murders were something that happened in films with Humphrey Bogart or James Cagney, films that I found boring and often incomprehensible. Surely a murder could not happen just a few hundred yards from the Grosvenor Cinema.

I did not believe my father was lying deliberately but I suspected he had made a mistake.

And yet as a weekly visitor to Tennants pub, which was just across the road, he should know. Perhaps he was right.

Each day on my way to school, as the number twenty-four tram awkwardly rounded the corner from Highburgh Road into Byres Road, I gazed at that flat, wondering. Certainly for years, it was always dirty and deserted.

Nowadays the bank has been transformed to a coffee shop, joining all those other premises in Byres Road which struggle to satisfy the seemingly insatiable desire of G12 folk for caffeine and the flat looks down on Continental style tables and sunshades ranged on the wide pavement of Highburgh Road. One has to admire the touching optimism which this displays as the sun reaches this corner for only a brief hour in the morning and I believe that Byres Road has the highest traffic pollution problem in Glasgow. Nor would I care to live above a coffee shop named the Tinderbox

Often, when I pass, I still look up at that flat where the murder was committed, but nowadays the windows are well maintained and absolutely normal.

When I was in my early twenties, a sad and terrible thing happened to a young man of the same age. I did not know him, although he lived in the west end.

Whether this particular boy was in banking or accountancy, I am not sure, but the job was to do with finance in some form or other, and like many another young fool, he was tempted. The money was there and somehow he believed it possible that he might help himself to some of it and not be discovered. It is an old story.

With the police in pursuit, he fled and foolishly took a gun with him. Later, cornered in a lane near Westbourne Gardens, he raised the revolver to his head and shot himself, dying immediately.

What terrible sadness and misery must have enshrouded that family. What an unnecessary loss of a young life. Quite possibly his father could well have afforded to replace the paltry sum of money involved. I do not know but I imagined the misery and agony that such a loss would cause to the parents of any of the young men that I knew and I found it terribly sad.

Not far from that fatal lane is an apartment building, cursed with the unfortunate architectural taste of the nineteen fifties, which also has tragic memories.

One winter a glamorous young woman stayed there while performing in a Glasgow pantomime. She was blonde and busty, as was then the fashion for aspiring film and stage personalities. More of a starlet than a star, she would now probably be called a 'media personality'. Perhaps she had more talent than I was aware of or perhaps she had a particularly energetic agent, for her colourful life was often featured in newspapers and magazines.

Some years after she left Glasgow her newsworthiness reached its apogee and tragically granted her a fame which might not otherwise have been hers.

The poor woman was decapitated in a car accident. A fatal car accident is always a strange and horrible thing but somehow a decapitation, with echoes of historic beheadings, seems to add a fearful and gruesome horror to the miserable business and the newspapers certainly made the most of it.

One very hot summer in the fifties, Glasgow Corporation in its wisdom ordered maintenance work done on the tramlines in Clarence Drive. Only ten years later, those same tramlines would be removed forever.

At eleven o'clock each night for a week, a special single decker tram arrived and a jolly, carefree crew of workmen leaped down and joyfully and noisily chucked their various tools and equipment to the ground before starting up the little generator which had been delivered earlier. With double rates for night work, they could afford to be in a good mood. It was not so easy for those of us who were trying to sleep. In the airless summer heat, our bedroom windows were thrown wide open and while the workmen enjoyed a preliminary cup of tea accompanied by gossip and guffaws (no doubt ribald), it seemed to my mother and myself that our ground floor bedroom had been invaded.

Peeping from behind the curtain I saw six of them, sitting on the pavement in a circle, drinking and eating, laughing uproariously. It was a midnight picnic! The generator chugged away loudly, ignored and seemingly unrequired. The refreshments lasted for a couple of hours and sleep was impossible. At two thirty, a lorry arrived and was greeted with enthusiasm. Some replacement tramlines were noisily crashed to the ground with general merriment and chaff. After a short interlude of a pneumatic drill at work, there was another round of tea. When a little tram brought additions to the workforce there was an excuse for yet more tea and laughter. The generator never stopped its maddening beating. At four, another lorry arrived and more tramlines clashed. Perhaps the first ones were collected for it did not seem that any use had been made of them. Finally, at six they threw their tools into another lorry, and with many jaunty quips, the eight men climbed aboard and left us trembling in an unreal silence, with only an hour left before the alarm went off.

The performance was repeated for the next three nights. Though the suffocating heat continued, we closed the window, yet the noise of the workmen absolutely precluded sleep.

On the fifth night they removed their operations and their soirée further down the hill. Though they could still be heard, they no longer seemed to share our bedroom. But certainly some other poor souls must be suffering. It was wonderful to sleep after such deprivation. I have read that sleep deprivation will kill a young animal more quickly that lack of food or drink. It certainly leads to irritability. Following those broken nights, my mother and I, whose lives normally adapted to each other smoothly and happily, had various disagreements and one outright quarrel.

That same week, the experience of another mother and daughter who lived together further down Clarence Drive was more tragic, for the daughter killed her mother with a carving knife.

When I was young teacher, I often met an older teacher, perhaps in her fifties, on the morning bus. She lived just around the corner from me and was very *lady-like* and particularly neat and prim in her dress and hairstyle. We greeted each other but seldom had much conversation on the busy bus. I knew that she lived with her brother, who was much less smart, in fact he looked a dour, shabby old bachelor. I do not know what his work was.

Although they lived in a different street, the tenements were built so that their ground floor kitchen window was in a corner and at right angles and very close to our bathroom window. One night when brushing my teeth, I became aware of loud, angry voices, a phenomenon not impossible, but rather unusual in Hyndland. I admit that curiosity took me to the back door of the close where I made sure it was the teacher and her brother having an 'altercation'.

Over the next few years, rows were a regular occurrence and eventually we shrugged and lost interest. I was quite amused, for no one on the morning bus would have believed that the very correct lady in smart hat and navy suit, might indulge in screaming and shouting matches at night.

Perhaps they mellowed with the years, perhaps we stopped noticing the quarrels, but we were horrified and aghast on the day that she was found dead and her brother was taken into custody by the police. He was later released and we heard nothing more of it.

In spite of our fears, her death was no doubt due to natural causes.

The brother stayed on in the flat for many years, a small, sad-looking lonely man.

MEMORABLE
ENTERTAINMENTS

I have eaten many delicious west end meals in the last forty odd years, mostly dinners, I suppose, and, in spite of changing tastes (and food fashions can pinpoint an era almost as exactly as the style of clothes or architecture), I have almost never eaten a bad one. Certainly some have been better than others, some were perhaps a little too rich, for I consider the balance of a meal more important than each individual dish. At least one was too ambitious, when a delicious fillet steak, that favourite of the 60s, was ruined for me by an unsuccessful brandy flambé. Another friend, a less affluent one, was an excellent cook and in spite of a large young family, she managed to produce the tastiest of meals on her limited budget. Her spaghetti Bolognese, another 60s standby, was absolutely delicious, although it was always a good idea to give her a hand in the kitchen at that last frantic moment when everything needs to be done quickly. I often wished that she had cooked another half packet of pasta but perhaps her purse would not stretch so far. Probably the least successful meal of that era was at the flat of a colleague of my husband. The couple had just moved to Hyndland and I was astonished to be greeted by a hostess who had accessorised her cocktail dress with fluffy pink slippers. Almost immediately she informed us coyly that the first course was packet soup, which was a new and tasteless invention of the time. Home made soup has such an infinity of delectable possibilities. I remember nothing else of that meal.

I have often eaten splendidly in Banavie Road where my far travelled hostess, Liza, matches beautiful table settings to the tasty dishes from some distant country in which she has lived and worked. Those are always elegant, delicious and educational evenings.

Then I have been astonished in Hyndland Road by the charming decor and innovative food of my friend Alison. She has now carved a career for herself in professional catering, producing supreme meals and buffets for special occasions.

More of her later.

Many times have I been entertained royally to dinner in Falkland Mansions by Jak, who also excels in that rare indulgence, a charming old fashioned afternoon tea.

A splendid election night buffet was served by Gaynor in a Kingsborough Gardens town house. Later she moved to a beautifully divided Cleveden Drive mansion in Kelvinside where she provided a perfect wedding breakfast for her son and his bride.

When my friends gathered together at Jenny's house in Victoria Crescent Road to celebrate my birthday, perhaps we drank rather too much Champagne, if that is possible, but it did not spoil our appreciation of a scrumptious meal in an elegant Dowanhill mansion.

In a very fine Lauderdale Gardens flat with a strong Arts and Crafts flavour, I was served a more modest, but important and memorable meal. I was just getting over a bout of pneumonia and two eggs, perfectly poached for me by Margaret, my fellow grandmother, marked the start of my recovery.

Food snob! I hear you say and perhaps you are justified, though I despair of what has happened to food in recent years when the exotic, the extreme and the bizarre have become the norm. When many of the words on a restaurant menu are unfamiliar and when food is arranged in an asymmetric tower which must be dismantled before a properly balanced forkful can be eaten, it just seems daft. For years, every eating establishment has followed this strange impractical fashion. Any idea of a balanced meal also seems to have been discarded. I have been served pork without a green vegetable and with only a smear on the plate of unrecognisable fruit sauce and with potatoes mashed with haggis or some other greasy admixture, I shudder, for I was reared to think that pork without greens, plain potatoes and lashings of apple sauce, was *very bad for you*. Poison almost! For me, the delight of the accompaniments often outweigh the protein, for Britain is perhaps the only country in the world to grow the inexpensive and incomparable Bramley apple which cooks to a tart purée fit for the gods. And what about a wonderful chunk of crisp Yorkshire pudding to accompany roast beef?

But enough of food. Why is it that any conversation, no matter how cultured, philosophic, morbid, witty or gossipy so often veers back to that subject? I want to speak of some other of those entertainments that have happened in G12. For though food, and usually wonderful food, is always in the background, it is not always the *raison d'être* of the assembly.

✧◆✧

It is probably hard for younger generations to realise how little importance was attached to the drinking of alcohol in the fifties. It was not, as it is today, a necessary adjunct of all socialising and was seldom on my shopping list. Nowadays, my friends would feel sadly deprived if no glass of wine accompanied their evening meal and certainly wine is always served when guests are entertained. (Though personally I prefer a glass of sherry before dinner). My grandparents might have a glass of beer with the Sunday roast and my grandmother liked the occasional Martini and Angostura bitters, strange names which fascinated me as a child. My father drank whisky at the club and sometimes met a friend for a beer in Tennants pub in Byres Road. At Christmas, my mother would buy a bottle of whisky and sherry 'just in case of visitors' but we often had some left by October, for most visitors drank tea or coffee. I suspect the greater part of those bottles was used in toddies and trifles. Money was scarce and wines and spirits were a luxury we could happily ignore. Though our family was certainly not teetotal, we were temperate and that was not unusual. No doubt there were other families with more interest in drinking but it was a luxury, and the young people of my acquaintance could not afford it often.

In my far-off student days in the fifties I visited a pub only twice in four student years and was very ignorant about alcohol. It simply did not interest me. I must have been uninhibited enough to enjoy parties and dances thoroughly without it.

When I wanted to throw a party, I was unwilling and financially unable to provide a variety of suitable beverages. The boys in my year would no doubt have welcomed beer and usually visited the pub before a student dance or party, but what would I offer the girls? Wine was not the obvious choice that it is now. It was beyond my budget and also seemed a drink for older people. It was indulged in perhaps only two or three times a year, as a sophisticated accompaniment to an elaborate meal.

To solve my problem I decided to throw a breakfast party with plentiful and unusual food, but no alcohol. Guests would arrive at 9.30am and surely no one would expect to drink at that hour. The morning would be devoted to word games, charades, improvisations and general madness, pretty much an extension of the way we spent our leisure time at Art School. Perhaps, subconsciously, I felt that they could hardly miss alcohol if they were kept busy. More likely I dismissed the subject from my mind. The party finished at two pm with a bowl of soup and seemed to be a success, for I had one each year for three years and no one ever complained of the lack of alcohol.

In the sixties I had a couple of evening parties with games. We were much the same crowd, though ten years older and perhaps less giddy. There was alcohol that evening, vodka and orange, if I remember correctly. I was still financially unable, or perhaps unwilling, to offer guests a wide choice of drink and again concentrated on plenty of good food. The games were more sophisticated. I had a tape-recorder and groups created advertisements for imaginary products, which were all very witty. A wall of unusual photographs invited scurrilous captions. It seemed to be an enjoyable evening for everyone, except my husband, who hated every minute, but of course he had never been an art student.

Sadly, I have only once been invited to this type of creative party. It was twenty years ago in Kingsborough Gardens, again with Gaynor. She advised us on arrival that we were 'putting on a pantomime' and I was the fairy godmother. It was a lot of fun and I think it a shame that so many of the parties I have attended in my life have consisted of sitting, or worse still, standing, while drinking wine and continuing conversations that one might as easily experience at a friend's kitchen table or when shopping in Hyndland Road. Happily I have just received an invitation to a *Thé Dansant*, and once more Gaynor is the imaginative instigator.

I have been invited to some fascinating and unusual, if not proactive, occasions. Occasions which I consider unique to this postcode and I should like to tell you about a few of them.

Paul is a retired musician who lives in Hyndland. Many years ago, he and I started chatting to each other one day, when out shopping. He told me that when hearing difficulties forced him to retire from the orchestra, he returned to his youthful hobby of model making, His first project was ambitious. He decided to make an opera house and the result was featured on television and Glasgow University expressed an interest in it. However it was built on rather a large scale and Paul later destroyed it, for he wanted to create a smaller and more perfect one. Over the next few years, with the industry and dedicated discipline of the musician and a great deal of natural artistry, Paul made several different miniature opera houses, some based on actual buildings and others to his own design. I was fascinated to hear about them for miniatures have always delighted me. My first sight of one of his exquisite creations was at Mairi's house in Cleveden Drive (another beautifully divided mansion) where Paul was giving a charity performance. About twenty-five of us were seated in the room, gazing in admiration at the classical frontage of an opera house only three feet tall. It was lit realistically and there was that breath-taking air of anticipation that enshrouds a theatre before the audience has started to arrive, though one knows that hectic, perhaps panic-stricken, preparations, are taking place behind doors.

There were delighted gasps of astonishment from the audience when the front was removed and a perfect little theatre interior was disclosed. The orchestra pit was crammed with miniature musicians and their instruments and the stalls and side balconies were filled with tiny figures in evening dress waiting for the curtain to rise. Every detail was perfect with the audience supplied with programmes, opera glasses, even a miniscule box of chocolates. How I longed for my grandchildren to share in the marvellous experience. I would have liked to go much closer and examine it all, but the curtain was rising and an unseen source of music played the duet from La Bohème. With skill and the clever use of wires,

Paul moved the two little figures onstage, bringing them close together at the appropriate heart-breaking climax of the song. It was enchanting and unforgettable.

✧◆✧

An even stranger event took place in the eighties, on a Sunday afternoon in Alison's flat in Hyndland Road. An all female group had been invited to watch a performance of belly-dancing, just as ladies of the harem were entertained in Turkey in the not so distant past.

Before the performance started, I remember thinking it could only happen in G12.

The room was large but the ten or twelve guests, plus furniture, left little space for the dancer, a young American girl. As they say nowadays, she was very much 'in your face'. I am sure she was accomplished, but she was incredibly and extremely thin and her diaphanous and scanty clothing seemed to accentuate her knobbly spine and visible ribs. Though she seemed not at all fazed by the propinquity of her audience, I felt myself much too close to such an example of starvation. No doubt she looked good when fashionably clothed in tight jeans and skinny T-shirt, but belly dancing is an art that demands an adequate supply, perhaps a superfluity, of flesh. Sadly, I felt that her figure ruined the performance.

Afterwards the party was more than saved by the buffet where I ate the most delicious smoked salmon that I have ever tasted and also some of Alison's delectable cake.

✧◆✧

Some years later, I was invited to a lovely flat in Buckingham Terrace, which is set back from Great Western Road. I was impressed by the collection of paintings on the walls where many of the important Scottish painters of the last century were represented.

It was a cocktail party, not my favourite sort of entertainment, for I do not care to make conversation while standing, especially when surrounded by comfortable and empty chairs. Though I suppose the benefit of standing is that one can easily move from group to group and communicate with as many as possible in the short duration of the party.

I joined a group where Fiona, a professor of English and a

friend of mine was talking to a tall handsome woman, Pat, who was obviously a powerful personality. Surprisingly, she was dressed very casually, even untidily and looked out of place in that chic company. I gathered she was an author and was writing a play about Margaret Morris, the well known Scottish dancer and wife of the artist, JD Fergusson. Fiona and I were both able to give her quite a lot of information about Morris and I smiled later when I realised that we had saved Pat a lot of research.

When I heard that the resulting play, a one woman show, was to be performed in a private house in Turnberry Road, I was naturally interested. It was a charity affair and would cost twenty pounds, which seemed a modest price for there was to be a supper afterwards, catered by my friend Alison and her suppers should never be missed.

What a spacious and beautiful home Caroline owned, though I must admit it was possibly just outside the G12 border. All around us were interesting antiques and fascinating pieces of furniture, no doubt each one of them with a story attached.

We were seated in an enormous double room, with folding panels to divide it when the larger space was not required. Most of one room would be the 'stage' while the remainder was filled with an eclectic variety of couches, divans, and chairs. Perhaps thirty or forty might be seated.

I arrived early and, like Goldilocks, sampled several chairs before I decided which one was most comfortable *and* gave the best view. Many of the audience were friends and acquaintances and it was pleasant to greet them and exchange the latest family news, as they arrived.

We filled two thirds of the room and looked towards the other third, the 'stage' where a large trunk was an obvious prop amongst the usual furnishings of a west end sitting room. A comfortable little fire burned in the fireplace in that part of the room and when the performance started, a kitten lay sound asleep on the hearthrug. It added a realistic and homely touch and seemed part of the scene, but knowing the unpredictability of sleeping kittens, I hoped it would not prove a disruption.

The actress, Penny Herman Smith, had a long and arduous

part which she played superbly, presenting Margaret Morris
in a more sympathetic light than I had previously viewed her.
Towards the end of the play when the words were particularly
poignant, she moved towards the fireplace and gazed off into
the distance, as sad memories overtook her.

My heart was in my mouth.

Did she remember that her foot was only inches away
from the kitten, still sleeping after more than an hour? Would
she tread on it and have her final speech ruined by a feline
shriek? Perhaps the animal would awaken and start playing
with the trailing hem of her dress, ruining the emotional
atmosphere which she had so cleverly created?

None of these disasters happened. The kitten slept
motionless on the Persian rug and the actress moved back to
centre stage for the final few words. Only when the enthusiastic applause broke out, did the kitten waken, leap up with a
start and race offstage in a panic.

Afterwards, we had the expected magnificent buffet with
savouries and desserts to dream of.

And now the most recent of my memorable entertainments, the *The Dansant* which I have already mentioned. It
happened only yesterday afternoon and was most enjoyable.
We were celebrating the retiral of Alan, Gaynor's husband.
Informality is now so much the fashion, but many of the
guests, myself included, are a lot older than he is and our
generation remembers that dressing well is an important part
of an outing. Everyone wore their best bib and tucker and I
think we looked terrific, in spite of our years. Alan's wife
Gaynor, our hostess, was elegance personified and looked
straight out of Vogue magazine in black and grey silk chiffon.

Benjamin, Alan's son, had put together an astonishing
and amusing selection of photos covering his father's life,
using them to illustrate his witty and eulogistic speech.

In spite of the loud enthusiasm of the trio of musicians,
who were dedicated to the tunes of yesteryear and looked
quite as old as any of us, it was more of a *Thé Parlant,* for
though everyone was on the floor at sometime or other, it
was the conversation which was most enthralling. I found so
many G12 friends and friends of friends, old acquaintances

and some new ones, people one had always heard of, but never met and many who had attended my classes at some time in the last forty years. Fascinating!

There was a fine 'purvey' of wine, juices, tea and coffee, sandwiches, scones and cakes, served, not by waitresses in white apron and cap, but by smartly trousered attendants, for the event was held in the David Lloyd fitness centre. Of course we were not jostled by tennis players, nor was the scent of swimming pool chlorine in our nostrils. It was a spacious and elegant function suite on the upper floor in which our well-dressed crowd mingled and enjoyed themselves, far removed from the energetic and possibly sweaty club members downstairs.

I only danced once all afternoon, but that was certainly memorable, for it was with Campbell, whom I have known since childhood. Strangely, although we have kept in touch at intervals throughout all those years, I last waltzed with him when I was a schoolgirl, sixty years ago.

COINCIDENCE ON THE BUS

It was a drizzly day in March and my friend Clare was going into town. She jumped on a 44 bus and, sitting down in the nearest vacant seat, found herself beside an elderly man who was gazing at papers in his open wallet. He turned to her and smiling wryly, explained,

"Ye know I've got two bus passes here! I found one on the bus yesterday and I took it to the driver, but he wouldn't accept it. Had to hand it in at the main office, he said."

"Fancy!" my friend commiserated, "What a nuisance."

"Och well, I'm not doing anything else and it's no' costing me anything. And that poor soul will be missing his bus pass. I don't really mind."

He continued to shuffle the papers in his wallet and Clare saw that he was looking at a dog-eared photo of two very young men. They were bronzed, wore shorts and open-necked shirts and their hairstyles spoke of many years ago.

Clare ventured,

"Two handsome fellows there. Might one of them be yourself?"

"Aye, ye're right enough. That's George there and me on the left, but poor George didnae get through the war. God, it was hot that day. It was December too. You wouldn't think it, with the sun burnin' like a furnace. Och but the heat was terrible in the desert. I remember that day fine. It was my birthday. I was twenty-one and just fair roastin' in the heat. Aye, it was an experience. Just seems like yesterday."

He sighed.

After a moment, Clare spoke,

"My birthday is in December, too! On the ninth. What date is yours?"

A broad smile creased the old man's face,

"I'm the ninth as well! Fancy that! What a coincidence! Now does that make us twins?" He laughed heartily and turned the photo over.

Written on the back in faded blue ink was the date, 9th December 1943.

Chills ran up and down Clare's spine, for that was the day on which she was born.

THE LANDLADY'S TALE

In the late nineteen seventies and early eighties I was landlady to several students working in the Latin American Institute at Glasgow University. There was an unused room and a small kitchen and bathroom in my basement and with the galloping rate of inflation, I was glad of the extra cash. However the experience brought me much more than money for each of the five mature students who stayed with me was interesting in his own right. It was a rich introduction to distant parts of the world which, and I am now ashamed to admit it, I had taken for granted, hardly considering their vastness, their enormous populations and their differences from the more familiar Europe and North America.

The first lodger was Carmen from Bogota in Columbia. In time, she would become a very dear friend, almost an adopted daughter. She spent some months with me before returning home to do more research for her PhD. She promised to return.

She had passed my name to a young Englishman, Tony, who worked hard and methodically to finish his thesis. At the same time he was able to pop upstairs and take part in the social life in my kitchen, which followed the dance classes I taught. He became part of our crowd, although I could never persuade him to join a class. Tony and my cat Cleo were devoted to each other.

Next came Dora, from Brazil, a tiny girl who felt the Scottish cold terribly. She became great friends with my mother and spent many hours playing cards with her in my kitchen, where the temperature never drops below seventy. At Christmas she went home to Recife for a holiday and returned married to Carlos. I could never feel she was quite serious about completing her doctorate.

Next for a short time I had Yoshido from Tokyo, though Latin American studies seemed a strange choice for a Japanese fellow. His hours of study were also strange for his day started as I was preparing for bed and vice versa. In spite of this we had some charming conversations between eleven pm and midnight.

My cat, Biba, was a very special cat, a retriever cat. Like a dog, she enjoyed having a small toy or crumpled paper thrown for her and she would rush after it, return it to your feet and wait for it to be thrown again. She particularly liked the small hard rubber balls available at the toy shop on the corner, where Peckam's delicatessen now flourishes. These tiny balls were just the right size for Biba to carry in her mouth. If no one were around to play with her she was happy to knock a ball down the two flights of stairs to the basement, galloping noisily after it as it bounced wildly downwards. Then she would pick it up in her mouth and return to the upper floor to repeat the process. She might do this twenty times and then she would come and lay the ball at my feet, entreatingly, as if to say,

"I've played by myself for long enough, please throw it for me."

I had been vaguely aware of this ball play during the night but when Yoshido was studying it was evidently more than he could stand and he confiscated Biba's night time balls. The toy shop must have benefitted, for we were always buying more little super balls and Yoshido was continually snatching them away from Biba in the night. I suppose one can hardly blame him at two o'clock in the morning. I just wish he had returned them to me.

Next there was Renato from Brazil. Although only a few years younger than I was, I always felt he treated me like a mother. Other younger students had been more equal and I had appreciated their camaraderie. When Renato had to pay a visit to the hospital for some very minor complaint, I sensed he was really unhappy. He hovered at my kitchen door for no particular reason and eventually I asked if he would like me to accompany him to the clinic and he was pathetically grateful. What a baby!

In her youth my mother had a reputation for reading teacups or telling fortunes with a pack of cards. She could spin a good dramatic story and make it sound convincing, although she had absolutely no belief in her own powers.

For her it was a party trick and the fact that sometimes her predictions had proved uncannily correct was more of an embarrassment to her than otherwise. Sometimes she vowed to tell no more fortunes but friends wheedled and once more she would gaze at the tea leaves or lay out the cards and weave a tale which, according to her own account, was a lot of nonsense. It so happened that she had been in hospital and to while away the time, had told some fortunes with spectacular success, her predictions proving correct within twenty four hours. When Renato heard of her 'gift', he was most anxious to have his cards read. Without knowing anything of his life in Sao Paulo, my Mother, with that thoughtful, indefinite quality so necessary to the successful fortune-teller, described the various positions he might apply for. She would learn later that she was uncannily close to the reality. Her reading convinced him which job to choose! Renato was delighted to have her help him to make up his mind but she was appalled that he should take her blethers seriously. We lost touch with Renato after he left. I hope he was happy in his choice.

Then Carmen returned and she was the dearest of my lodgers. She was with me for several years for she seemed in no rush to complete her degree. No doubt it requires motivation and disciplined application to achieve a PhD and perhaps you will suggest that these attributes are foreign to a Latin temperament, but I formed a different theory. She had obviously grown up in an affluent family with servants and every luxury. She described herself as a very spoiled girl who would lie on the floor and kick the door with her heels, if she could not have what she wanted at that moment. As she watched my busy life, she felt she had taken her Mother too much for granted and I received the benefit of her guilty conscience for she often washed dishes or swept my kitchen floor. When she spoke to me of the extremes of wealth and poverty in Bogota, she showed a deeper side of her character. Slowly I formed the impression that she was unwilling to return to such an unbalanced society, a society which she was helpless to change. I suspected that if she met the right man, she would be happy to marry and settle in Britain. In the meantime, she was content to be part of my family. She attended my dance classes and later, when my mother needed more care, Carmen was my companion and a wonderful support.

I have just returned from a stay in her beautiful home in Athens where she now stays with her Greek husband Piero and their three marvellously multi-lingual children.

THE LODGER'S STORY

Carmen spoke often of her life in Bogota and I listened like a child, for strange as it may seem, South America had never held great importance in my mind. How ignorant I felt when I studied my atlas and realised the extent of these vast territories which I had blithely overlooked for most of my life.

I was considerably impressed by the fact that Carmen was capable of writing her thesis in impeccable and complex English. Her spoken grammar was always perfect, though her pronunciation had many defects, which was charming and added emphasis to the exotic stories she told, though it necessitated a degree of concentration on the part of the listener. As I have not the power to represent her eccentric speech in print, I must tell you her story in my own words.

She was eighteen and in her first year at the University of Bogota when her friend Hans suggested that five of them should make an expedition to a cattle ranch, far out in the country. Hans' great grandfather had come to Colombia at the start of the century and had made a fortune in cattle. He had long wanted to take his friends to visit the distant ranch and he made it sound very exciting. He was tall, blonde and well-built. No drop of Spanish blood had entered his family for seventy years and his blue eyes sparkled as he described the project with typical Teutonic attention to every detail of organisation.

"We must leave the city early by bus and travel to Puerto Triom Triomfo on the Matelan river where we'll stay the night. Then we'll take a boat down the Rio la Miel, it's not too long a journey. There is no way to reach the farm by ordinary transport, so there will be horses waiting for us and we must ride for four or five hours in the last part of the journey. It is important that we are not too late in the day, otherwise we might have to ride in the dark and that would be a great pity, for the scenery is magnificent. Also, the path is far from easy."

Here he was interrupted by someone asking how many times he had made the journey himself.

"Never! No, I've not actually travelled this route myself, but I have studied the maps and taken advice and made all possible inquiries and necessary arrangements. So do not worry. Now, listen carefully, I will give each of you a saddlebag and you must take *no more* luggage than it will hold. We must put all our money into a common fund and please bring as much as you can, in case of unforeseen adventures! Let's do it!"

The enthusiastic group would consist of Hans and his fifteen-year old brother Reiner, Carmen, Bernardo and his girlfriend Patricia.

Carmen described Patricia as small, with very large teeth and wearing a lot of make-up. She brought a small suitcase as well as the saddlebag but Hans insisted the case must be left at the bus station in Bogota.

"What was Bernardo like?" I asked,

"Dark, a typical South American I suppose."

And Reiner?

"Just like his brother, only smaller and quieter and squarer."

Carmen assured me that she and Hans were just friends.

From the maturity of her twenty five years, Carmen looked back at those naïve and spoiled teenagers and smiled. Each one had lived a cossetted life in a city apartment with a plentiful supply of food and Coca Cola in the fridge and servants to deal with the small every-day chores.

"We were not ready for such an adventure." And she shook her head.

Anxious parents had obviously provided enough cash to deal with possible problems and when they arrived in Puerto Triom Triomfo they had a great deal of money in the kitty. They booked themselves into a luxury hotel for the night. All afternoon they lounged around the swimming pool, enjoying the hot humid climate and exotic vegetation, so unlike the cool mountainous environment of Bogota. After a splendid evening meal, they visited some of the nightspots in the town and had a very good time.

In the morning, although there were several ferryboats, they decided it would be more pleasant to hire a boat all to themselves. Quite a large boat was the only one available and a surprisingly large sum was spent on this hiring.

They immediately changed into swimsuits and sunbathed on the deck in spite of the disapproving glances of the captain. When Patricia, in her glamorous bikini, applied more make-up, he muttered audibly,

"I don't like *shiny* women, I like them to look *healthy*."

As they sailed down the Matelan, tributaries joined it, some only streams while others were small but forceful rivers. After half an hour, the boys got bored with sunbathing. Hans suddenly stood and dived over the side and in spite of the captain's warning shout, Bernardo was close behind him. They had no idea of the dangerous currents of the unpredictable river.

The captain slowed the boat and fumed loudly about these 'idiots', but they were both strong swimmers and were enjoying the challenge, though almost immediately Bernardo lost his trunks. The Captain grabbed Reiner by the arm to stop him following the others and shouted directions and imprecations at the two in the water. Realising caution was the better part of valour and not without some difficulty, they returned to the boat and grabbed the ropes which the sailor had slung overboard. Patricia quickly produced a pair of underpants from Bernardo's satchel that he might return on deck with some modesty. The young men stood smiling sheepishly while the Captain ranted at their stupidity, demanding that they do no such ridiculous and dangerous thing again on his ship. No one noticed that Carmen, feeling too hot and also cross at the telling off which the captain delivered, stepped to the side and leaped over. She too was a strong swimmer but unfortunately she had entered the water close to the point at which a turbulent stream joined the broad river. It was the worst moment she could have chosen and she was washed helplessly downstream, struggling to keep her head above water, as the boat dwindled impossibly quickly into the distance. A large bend in the river accelerated her pace alarmingly but once around it, the river broadened and the current became less overpowering. She could see a tiny fishing dugout up ahead. Death, which had seemed inevitable, was no longer imminent and for a brief moment she was exhilarated as she

was carried swiftly past the luxurious growth of the riverbank
The fishermen hauled her from the water with some astonishment and immediately started to reproach her bitterly for
such foolishness. She did not like the insults these peasants
heaped on her in their rough accents, but sat listening
sullenly until the rented boat appeared and her friends
shouted their delighted relief to see her still alive. She must
bear more and even sterner admonishments from the captain
before they disembarked a few miles further down the river. It
was a small landing place with few houses and a tiny grubby
café but they were glad to be on dry land, rid of the throb-
bing engines of the boat and the bad-tempered reprimands of
the captain.

A middle-aged cowboy stood smoking a cigarette beside
the uninviting café. He was waiting for them with their
horses and would guide them to the hacienda where they
would stay. He was anxious to start as soon as possible.
Discarded stubs around his feet showed he had been there
some time, but the young people were determined to take it
easy. They had travelled for five hours since their splendid
hotel breakfast and insisted on a snack and a Coke in the café
before setting off.

Here I interrupted Carmen with surprise that they could
find Coca Cola in such an remote place. She shrugged,

"Oh, you can buy it anywhere you like in South America."

The scenery on their ride was spectacular. Though it was
cattle country, they were never far from mountains. They
rode steadily, occasionally galloping, although Juan, their
guide, was not happy about that and warned them that they
must think of the horses, for they had five hours' riding
ahead and the last miles were the most difficult.

Hans had heard of La Laguna Azul and wanted to see it
though Juan frowned and shook his head. However, after two
and a half hours' riding, the guide sullenly changed direction
and they started to climb, at first gently then much more
steeply. When they reached the highest point of the trail, they
dismounted and followed Juan to where he stood pointing
downwards. Forty feet below them, at the bottom of a small
extinct volcanic crater, lay the lake. It was quite exquisitely

blue, a blue that glowed as though lit from within. It hardly seemed real. For a moment they stood silent and awestruck until Hans shouted,

"We *must* swim in it! Come on guys."

Juan was violently shaking his head and the girls looked doubtful, for the steep walls of the crater were clothed with impenetrable foliage where small trees, shrubs and ground cover had grown undisturbed for unknown decades. Undaunted, the three boys threw themselves down the slopes enthusiastically, Hans taking great bounds and reaching the water first. It seemed possible and the girls soon followed, though taking greater care. Juan sat down beside the horses and lit a phlegmatic cigarette.

The young people splashed and swam with delight.

How delicious and cool the water was. How calm and friendly after the terrifying river. How magical to bathe in what seemed like liquid lapis lazuli in a gigantic bowl with green shaggy sides, the cloudless sky like a lid above them.

Though it was getting late, they found it too difficult to tear themselves away. At last, when Juan had shouted impatiently several times and dusk had started to fall on their deep pool, they reluctantly left the water and dressed. The steep climb to the rim of the crater was much more taxing than the descent. Grabbing at bushes, tripping over roots and vines, cursing the rampant vegetation with groans and exclamations, they struggled up the punishing slope. They had spent a long day of unusual activity and were experiencing exhausted muscles, perhaps for the first time in their pampered young lives.

The boys were nearly at the top and the girls half way when Carmen suddenly screamed. She had slipped and landed in a three foot high anthill. Immediately she felt ants scrambling all over her, biting madly. Even her hair seemed filled with them. Momentarily she became hysterical with the agony and horror. Hans and Bernardo shouted to her to go back and jump in the lake, but she knew she had not the energy for that and continued to climb upwards, slightly calmer with the forced exertion. When she reached the top, she ripped off her clothes, it was no time for modesty, and Patricia helped her rid her body of the maddening creatures, while the boys twisted and stamped on her jeans to crush the ants which were hidden in every fold. Darkness was now falling quickly and Juan sat smoking beside the horses. His face was expressionless but who knows what dark Spanish oaths he silently swore, for he was responsible for the safety of these imbecile youths and they must ride for another two hours on an unknown and dangerous path in pitch black night.

Before they mounted, Juan spoke to them seriously about the journey ahead. For the next forty minutes the path was only a foot wide and to the right of them a cliff fell steeply away for hundreds of feet. He advised them to keep the reins loose and trust their horses completely. Each rider would light a cigarette and hold it so that the glowing tip would be seen by the following rider, but the cowboy warned that this was *only to comfort them*, for they must *never* try to guide the horse. The horses knew best and did not themselves want to go over the cliff. Perhaps it was his solemn tone or perhaps the adventures of that day had chastened them, but the group listened and for once did exactly as they were told.

After half an hour the sky cleared and the bright stars were magnificent although their light also made plain how narrow their path and how steep the precipice. It was blood curdling.

After they left that hair-raising part of their journey behind, they entered a long valley where an electrical storm blinded them with magnificent flashes of lightning. The periods of brilliance showed that they travelled through a petrified forest and the eerie shapes around them seemed like monsters and skeletons. It was a long time since they had eaten and hunger added to their depression. It seemed that they might never reach their destination.

At last they came to the hacienda, a large elegant building. Unfortunately it was in darkness and closed, for the party of young people were to bunk with the cowboys. The hacienda had an outside lavatory of which they made use, and noted that it had very nice showers, but Juan vetoed any more delays and they wearily climbed back into the saddle to ride the last mile to the wooden huts where the cowboys lived. This would be their home for the next five days and it looked terribly primitive to Carmen and Patricia. They would sleep in hammocks in a room with a few wooden chairs, a table and an oil lamp, while all around outside was the continuous lowing of countless cows as they surged restlessly back and forth over the vast grassland.

Carmen was sure she would never sleep in such surroundings, but after a simple meal cooked by Juan's wife, the five young people quickly fell into unconsciousness in their hammocks.

Next morning, after a race on horseback to the hacienda for a shower, they shared the cowboys' substantial breakfast of large steak, two fried eggs and tomato sauce, with a cup of hot chocolate, before setting off to ride the range and check the stock. Unlike the cowboys, they returned at lunchtime for a siesta in their hammocks. Patricia preferred to lie outside under a large romantic tree. That night, after a second large meal, they played cards in the hot humid evening. When Patricia felt some discomfort in her back and buttocks, Carmen investigated and found several ticks had lodged themselves in the poor girl. Sandro, the youngest cowboy, was the expert on ticks and with no embarrassment, he applied gentian violet to Patricia's unwelcome parasites.

Each day followed the same pattern of immense breakfasts, gentle riding in the morning, sleeping in the afternoon, more food and cards at night. It was a wonderful holiday and no one worried about the return home.

On the third night, Carmen spied a large creature moving across the floor of the girls' bedroom. It was an enormous and hairy tarantula and Juan came immediately with his machete and destroyed it with a blow. He warned them that tarantulas were always to be found in pairs and the place was thoroughly searched until the second one was discovered and dealt with. The girls were shaken and did not fall asleep quite so quickly that night.

It was on the fifth night that Carmen awakened with terrible earache. It was something she had never experienced before and the severity of the pain frightened her. She arose and found Juan still awake, smoking outside under the stars. Perhaps he was enjoying the thought that his young guests would be gone in twenty-four hours.

He was sympathetic but could offer no help. There was no aspirin left in the first aid box. It was a five hour ride to buy more and somehow it had never seemed too important. Cowboys seldom suffered headaches. He suggested she put a wet cloth to her cheek and rather than disturb Patricia, she could lie down in a small room that had a wooden bed. Carmen followed his advice, noticing that in the corner, a mother cat lay in a box with her sleeping family. The wet cloth seemed to help at first but, soon spasms of unbearable pain travelled up and down her cheek and her ear felt as though pierced by a red hot poker. Then one of the kittens awoke and disturbed its neighbour. Soon three kittens were wrestling and fell out of the basket. It seemed to Carmen, who might have taken pleasure in their antics at any other time, that they were little demons sent to taunt her. She turned from side to side on the hard bed and her agony seemed unbearable. Was she in mortal danger she wondered? How terrible to be so distant from civilisation. Tears welled and she sobbed miserably as the five kittens chased each other across the floor, mewing and squeaking loudly when their play became too rough. It seemed as though she might go mad.

And she knew she was too ill to contemplate that long journey home tomorrow.

Their main problem was that they had no money left. Hans explained to Juan that they must have some cash to travel back to Bogota. They were taking a different route home and might be in transit for nearly three days. He assured the cowboy that if he would advance a reasonable sum, he would certainly be handsomely recompensed by Hans' father. Juan looked unsure, but as it was the boss's son, Juan brought a fat roll of bills from his pocket and slowly peeled some off, though not enough as far as Hans could judge.

"Could you not be more generous?" Hans enquired rather loftily.

Juan shook his head and replaced the roll in his pocket, mumbling 'wages'.

First they must ride for an hour to a farm where they would leave the horses and though Carmen felt impossibly weak and ill, the fresh air and movement helped her a little. She said hardly a word, but the others, thinking she had recovered, chatted merrily, looking forward with pleasure to the various aspects of their journey. At the farm, a tractor would be hired to take them ten miles to a tiny nameless village, where, hopefully the train from the coast to La Dorado would stop for them. La Dorado was a fair sized town where Carmen could see a doctor and buy painkillers before they started on the last leg of their journey, a four hour bus ride to Bogota. They were unsure of quite how many hours they must spend on the train but everyone, apart from Carmen who remained silent, agreed that travelling with the peasants would be a very interesting experience.

Before they reached the farm where they must leave their horses, it started to rain, which quenched their mood. The tractor was incredibly old and rusty and caked in mud. Carmen, surrounded by the five saddlebags, sat with the driver, but the others must cling precariously to whichever part of the vehicle they deemed trustworthy. The track was rough, the rain did not stop and it was a very long ten miles. The five fastidious youths were filthy as they stood there in the deserted space between the few houses and the railway station. Suddenly Patricia noticed two large shallow tanks of water. With a shout of delight she stepped into one and started to sluice the dirt off her face and limbs. Carmen, smiling for the first time that day, followed her example in the other tank. Immediately, five furious women appeared from the houses, screaming that this was drinking water which they were using as a bath. The two girls were roughly dragged out. Everyone was shouting at once, the girls apologising for their mistake and the women reproaching them bitterly. Hans, afraid of real violence, produced money and was able to appease the angry villagers.

It was late afternoon before the train arrived and they sat in the humid heat, uncomfortably aware that furious eyes watched them from every window. They were all hungry but there was no café and obviously no hope of hospitality from the insulted villagers. Each of them drank two cans from the Coca Cola machine on the platform and thought Hans mean when he refused them a third but Hans was realising the

bitter truth. With at least thirty hours of a long unknown
journey ahead of them, his wallet was inadequately filled.

The hot train was crowded with country people from the
coast, some had travelled since early morning. All were laden
with produce to sell in the town, bulky sacks of fruit and
vegetables were stowed in every space and the air was rich
with the aroma of nature and noisy with unhappy babies,
whimpering children and the squawking of chickens im-
prisoned in baskets, Hans and his friends, used to several
daily showers throughout their young lives, had never
encountered such an environment.

There was no chance of their sitting together and they
squashed in just where they could. Bernardo was unhappily
squeezed between an aged man who smoked a stinking pipe
and a large breasted woman who regularly gave her baby
sustenance.

In spite of their surroundings, they were all terribly
hungry. As food was produced regularly by one group or
another, the smell of cheese, ham and onions constantly
overpowered the other perfumes of the carriage and tortured
the friends. Unsuccessfully, they tried not to gaze at their
neighbours as they ate.

Fortunately the kindly travellers, used to noting the
misfortunes of others, realised that the young tourists had
brought no food with them and generously shared their
picnics. Young appetites are happy to discard standards of
hygiene and the rough peasant food was handed around and
eaten with gusto. Only Carmen did not eat, but leaned her
head against the shoulder of a fat old lady and slept fitfully
until they reached La Dorado in the very early hours of the
following day.

Though they were again hungry, Hans was forced to be
miserly. There was the doctor, medication and the bus journey
yet to be paid for.

"These are absolute necessities!" he said sternly.

"But food is the greatest necessity of all!" Bernardo
protested and Reiner and Patricia vociferously agreed with
him.

Hans held up his hand and shook his head and indicated
Carmen who was white and looked as though she could

hardly stand. Bernardo looked ashamed and relieved Carmen of her heavy saddlebag.

The young doctor on duty at the clinic looked serious after examining Carmen and spoke to Hans.

"This is very bad, very serious and there should be a doctor standing by ready to deal with the case as soon as you arrive in Bogota. You must get in touch with her people to arrange this. When will you get there?"

"The first bus leaves at midday, we should reach the city before five."

"I will prescribe Darvon, a very strong painkiller, to help her get through the day."

After payment was made for the phone call, the medicine and the bus tickets were paid for, there was only enough money to buy one can of Coca Cola each. It was a starving and dejected crew which climbed aboard the old bus.

Reiner, who felt somewhat ashamed of his brother's financial mismanagement, tried to cheer them up.

"Only four more hours to go, then we will be in civilisation again and eating our heads off. I shall have soup and a hamburger and French fries and..."

But they all shouted at him and threatened to punch his head if he did not shut up.

Bogota lies high in the mountains and straightaway the road started to climb steeply. After half an hour, the ancient engine overheated, the bus filled with smoke and the passengers quickly left their seats and stood waiting patiently at the side of the road for another bus to come and return them to La Dorado. Evidently this was not an unusual occurrence.

There was nothing to do except sit on their saddlebags and wait.

After an hour a bus returned them to town where they found that the next bus would leave La Dorado at seven.

The bus station waiting room was crowded with people. Food sellers constantly pushed amongst them proclaiming their wares, tasty sausages, crisp rolls and succulent fruits. It was a sort of torture for the starving, penniless young people.

Eventually hunger proved too much for Patricia.

"It's all your fault!" she shrieked at poor Carmen who was in a drugged daze of misery. "We are *suffering* and have not eaten for *hours* because you must have that expensive medicine. It's not *fair.*"

"I'll go back to the pharmacist and try and sell it back to him." Carmen offered, but the boys would not let her do that.

Once again they were aided by the generosity of others for a motherly woman nearby had heard Patricia's outburst and offered them a loaf, while someone else gave them bananas. These snacks only served to whet their appetite. In desperation, Hans offered to exchange his fine leather jacket and a splendid knife for some food. After much bargaining and shouting, this was arranged, with the food vendor making sure that his side of the transaction was obscenely profitable.

Hans was past caring and they ravenously devoured roast chicken, sausages and mangoes in the middle of the surging, smelly waiting room.

The next bus to Bogota was in better condition than the first and the exhausted, but no longer starved, group of young people returned to their cossetted and luxurious lives in Bogota at eleven that night.

Carmen was taken immediately to the best hospital and quickly recovered.

FOLK UPSTAIRS

Tenement living has many benefits and a few problems. Neighbours can fall into both categories. Mostly I have been lucky but there have been a few problems. The worst one happened a few years ago when the hose became detached from the washing machine belonging to the students in the flat above me. I was not even in Glasgow at the time but *very good* friends left their warm bed at midnight to help deal with the incredible mess and give aid to the tenants in my basement flat who discovered the disaster and, who were also inundated. It seemed to be like Niagara in my kitchen with water pouring through the ceiling, sheeting down the walls and six inches deep on the floor. There was no response from eleven 24-hour ads in the Yellow Pages and it seemed impossible to find a plumber. Eventually, one of the students upstairs, who had remained deeply asleep and unaware of the calamity, was roused and the hose replaced.

Another flood happened in a different flat when I was a child. It was one of the cruel winters of the war and my mother and I were living on the east coast. My father had gone to check that all was right in the empty flat. He walked into the kitchen and immediately fell flat on his back for the floor was like an ice rink. Mrs Williams upstairs, a plummy-voiced aristocrat who perhaps enjoyed a slightly extravagant alcoholic intake, had let her sink overflow, not for the first time, and the temperature had dropped. Many years later a friend of hers, also plummy-voiced, rang our doorbell.

"Good *morning*! Now my friend, Mrs Williams who lives upstairs, is apparently not at home at the moment. *Could I trouble you* to keep this *pheasant* for her... so kind. Thank you *very much* indeed."

We kept it for five days without hearing any footsteps overhead. Next day in the kitchen, my mother said,

"Hand me that bird, I'm going to pluck it. No use it going to waste. She might not be back for a month."

We stuffed it with sage and onion and the delicious smell of roasting was filling the air when the sound, or rather the vibration of feet above us stopped us in our tracks. We looked at each other in dismay, then my mother smiled grimly.

"Well, I've plucked it and stuffed it and I'm not giving it up now! We can always buy her another one."

Next day, when Mrs Williams came to our door to collect her pheasant, I 'chickened out' and insisted my mother deal with the problem. My mother was apologetic and made the offer to buy another pheasant, but the heart of a gentlewoman beat beneath that battered, baggy suit.

"Not at all, my dear. My pantry is full at the moment and I do hope you enjoyed it."

When Mrs Williams moved out, we were less lucky with the new neighbours, probably the only really unpleasant ones I have come across. They were a pushy couple who owned a pub, a large car and a heavy-footed boxer dog that whined and barked and wailed whenever they were out.

When we moved to my present flat, the folk upstairs were elderly and apart from the hurried sprint to the bathroom each morning, we heard not a sound from them. It was a different matter when their nephew came to visit with his three children and a large energetic dog. The worst of the nephew was his habit of throwing his boots to the floor when going to bed. He was a late bedder and those boots were perfectly timed to waken me from my first sleep. One night about 2am he obviously noticed a piece of floor maintenance required and took his hammer to it there and then, immediately above my head.

When the old couple left, a young newly married couple moved in. They each followed demanding careers and were hardly ever at home. All that I heard of them was the regularly used vacuum cleaner, which nudged my guilty conscience, for it is not my favourite domestic appliance.

It would be some years after they had left that I learned from my daughters that the nightly amorous enthusiasm upstairs had been a noise nuisance.

Lastly there is the problem of music practice for which I must plead guilty for I attempt to play the piano regularly, though badly. I try to play quietly and always stop by 10pm, nevertheless, it must be an intrusion. I hope my neighbours forgive me and are sufficiently grateful that I did not choose to study percussion, trumpet or bagpipes.

A MATTER OF TASTE

Tom came to Glasgow from Wales. He was a clever young man with three degrees and many more ambitions. With some help from his mother he bought a small top flat in Novar Drive and proceeded to drive towards the aforesaid ambitions, which were admittedly vague but included London, New York, Paris and an important place amongst the higher proponents of Literature or perhaps Modern Art. You will notice I have used capitals. The eclectic research on which he was engaged at Glasgow University was fascinating and meant that he travelled and came in contact with many interesting people and this experience did not at all detract from his natural self-confidence.

After three months Tom was surprised and somewhat disconcerted to be joined by Gwyneth, who was of course no stranger to him. She came to the Novar Drive flat without asking permission and arrived with her cookbooks and her cat, which added a look of permanence to her proposed stay.

Tom and Gwyneth had known each other from schooldays in Aberystwyth and had shared a flat for three years while studying at Liverpool University, their relationship apparently very happy and close. Their student friends predicted a Darby and Joan future for them.

Gwyneth was an exceptionally pretty girl with clouds of soft brown curling hair, large green eyes and the sort of smile that cheers folk up. Few young men would have failed to greet her arrival with pleasure.

And Gwyneth was clever. She had two degrees and could have had three if she had wanted. She was ambitious too, but her ambitions were different from Tom's. She wanted a family, Tom's family to be precise. She was happy to use her excellent brain to make money for a while, but her true goal in life was to be Tom's wife and the mother of his three children. Call her old-fashioned if you like. When she had properly realised her own wishes, she set herself to earn enough to help support Tom in that last crazy expensive year of study for his PhD, and had helped him with hard cash for the books and travelling that were so necessary for his complex research. Also, with little fuss, she maintained a cosy organised house, clean clothes in the drawer, food on the table and that constant undemanding silence so necessary to the thinking man.

At Tom's *viva voce* there were delighted questions, admiration, awe even from the visiting examiners. It was a wonderful and successful thesis, an academic marvel, it was aesthetic, philosophic, esoteric and any more words ending in *ic* that you can think of, but no, wait a moment, that is not true, for the word *domestic* was not included. Domestic was a word absent from Tom's vocabulary.

Of course he was grateful to Gwyneth for her unfailing support. He had said so to his mother once and he said so to Gwyneth at least three times. He said he could never have achieved it all without her, though he probably did not quite believe that.

When Tom moved to Glasgow, he continued to write to Gwyneth now and again, in a friendly brotherly sort of way for he knew that he had *moved on* and she was *in the past*. Unfortunately, in spite of his academic prowess, his letters did not make that situation clear to Gwyneth.

When Tom opened his front door and found Gwyneth there with her suitcase, haversack (full of cookbooks) and cat basket (full of Arnold the tabby), he naturally invited her in. He was not so crude as to show his dismay and made quite a good show of pleasure at her arrival in fact. As I said she was a very attractive young woman. Also, the house had reached that stage of chaos and degradation which only an intellectual can achieve, (*hygienic* was another word absent from Tom's vocabulary).

Within a few days, Gwyneth had the little flat scrubbed and under control.

Also she had a job and had regained her ability to sit quietly. She felt it imperative that she should not interrupt him, for her own studies had been handicapped by a mother who considered conversation a natural and continuous human activity. After Gwyneth had made and cleared up after the evening meal, she would sit silently sewing or reading on the couch with Arnold's warm furry body for company. Tom tapped at his laptop or hunted and shuffled through myriad sheets of papers. Sometimes he had long phone conversations with academics on the other side of the world and often he gazed for extended periods at the calendar on the wall in front of him, no doubt wrestling with some knotty intellectual problem. It was a lonely life for Gwyneth and she longed to share her day with him, but she said nothing. She knew his need to concentrate was paramount for their future happiness. Perhaps he found her presence relaxing. He was certainly unaware of any difficulties attached to her determined silence. He took her silence as his right.

Weeks passed and there was very little conversation, certainly no outings. Her suggestion of a stroll one sunny evening made Tom very irritable. Did she not realise how busy he was? She was welcome to go herself if she wanted, but he was up to his eyes in it.

Though Arnold was a particularly affectionate cat, it was a lonely life for Gwyneth. She found nourishment in dreams of a future when Tom was established and need not work so hard and when those babies arrived, she was sure he would almost certainly become a tender and devoted father.

Did I mention that Gwyneth was an excellent cook? Taking great interest in the health-providing properties of food as well as the various delicate and exciting flavours, she took pride in presenting meals that were balanced, energy-giving, appetising and attractive. Sadly, she need not have bothered. Her knowledge and skills were wasted, for the light of her life demanded chips at every meal, grimaced at any suggestion of salad, eschewed all vegetables and insisted on preferring a hamburger in a bun. He joked about garlic, chilli, herbs and spices as something to hide the taste of bad meat and he condemned, not very originally, broccoli, lettuce, cabbage as rabbit food. Had he always been like that? Perhaps in the early days of wooing, he had forced down the mushroom soup, the roast pepper, the chicken ragout and the lemon soufflé with some show of enthusiasm. Perhaps he had even enjoyed those delicious dishes. Now, after these months on his own, he was determined to eat as he liked. *He had found himself.* He was a simple soul and liked quick simple food. Food was only fuel to keep the body ticking over and not a subject on which to waste mental or physical energy. In the three months that he had lived alone, he had simplified his meals and shopping drastically, depending almost totally on a freezer full of frozen burgers and oven chips (for Tom did not believe that frying was unhealthy) with Sugar Puffs for breakfast or a late night snack. He stuck to this narrow menu even after Gwyneth arrived, though it was surprising how often his brilliant mind considered this regime, justifying its adequate balance, assuring himself of how much he enjoyed it, how much time was saved. His next line of thought would almost certainly, feature Gwyneth and her seldom expressed but obvious disapproval of his diet. but then no one had asked her to join him and cook fancy stuff to fatten him up.

Tom certainly was a simple soul, for his inner mutterings hardly recognised the fact that refusing to eat her food was the strongest psychological tool he possessed in his struggle for masculine freedom.

✧◆✧

One evening Tom was more communicative than usual. It was a long and bitter complaint but Gwyneth was happy to listen and commiserate.

"Shit, I don't believe it, just when I'm so busy!" he grumbled, "Some damned American woman is visiting the department next week and the professor wants me to *look after her*. Take her round the city, he says. Make sure her stay is enjoyable and memorable. Help her with her research. What does he think I am? Some sort of nanny? Or maybe a gigolo. She's supposed to have written several books, he says, *important books* he calls them, but I've never heard of her. I have my own work and that's important to me. What am I supposed to do with her? I bet she's an old hag with short blonde hair and too much make-up and I bet she never uses words of less than four syllables. What the hell am I going to do with her?"

"How long will she be staying here?"

"God knows! Too long."

"It might only be a week or two..."

"Two weeks wasted! I can't afford two weeks."

Gwyneth agreed that it was a shame and expressed her sympathy several times throughout the evening but there seemed little she could do about it.

She offered to prepare a meal for the lady. That was swiftly rejected.

"No, no she's not coming here, thank you very much. Don't want her hanging round here all day, far too much to do. Besides she's a Yank and probably wouldn't care for that fancy food you make."

Next day the news was worse. Although Gertrude Birtle was American, she lived in London at present and would be travelling back and forth over the next six months.

"Well, believe me, I don't intend to run after her or pander to her every whim for six months. I know how demanding these bloody American women can be."

Gwyneth tut-tutted sympathetically and hid her amusement at his fury. Nor did she ask how much experience Tom had of demanding American women.

"I expect she won't be as bad as all that, Tom."

"*Oh yes she will.*"

Many a girl might have pouted and questioned what she was supposed to do while her boyfriend was squiring a strange American around town. But Gwyneth loved him and trusted him and saw this as part of that great preparation for their joint future, nor did it strike her that she had any rights in the matter.

Next day Tom came home carrying a large bunch of flowers and presented it to Gwyneth rather awkwardly. He had never given her flowers before for they had always agreed that flowers were a completely unnecessary luxury.

Gwyneth smiled but also raised her eyebrows questioningly.

"Yes, yes, I know it's a bit strange. I hope you like them."

"I love them, they smell delicious, thank you, darling, but what...?"

"It was Gertrude that suggested them."

"Gertrude? The horrid demanding American? You've met her?"

"Yes, and already she's asked me to do something and it involves you, I'm afraid. She doesn't live in the States, she has a place in London and she has a cat, but because she's moving around Britain so much, just now, she wondered, I wondered if we could have the cat here for the next six months. You can understand why she couldn't haul it from hotel to hotel."

Gwyneth was rather taken aback but said,

"You would need to ask Arnold how he feels about that. He's a hospitable relaxed cat and I expect he could take it in his stride. As long as it's not a nervous demanding pedigree cat."

"Well it's a Siamese cat, I believe. And interestingly, Gertrude herself is part Chinese, with some Russian blood too I believe."

"They sound an exotic pair. Well unless Arnold objects horribly, I suppose the cat can join us. Is it a she? I hope it's not too particular about food."

"Oh no, but it does need a litter box."

Gwyneth looked dismayed. Arnold was an independent cat who liked his daily outdoor exercise.

"But I'll see to all that sort of thing," Tom added hurriedly.

"And is Gertrude the old hag that you feared? Does she use long words and expect to be obeyed?"

"No, she's quite interesting really, I suppose. Small and thin, fragile almost and talks in a terribly quiet voice. I have the feeling she's not very strong and she doesn't order me about. Well, she hasn't started yet."

Tom smiled his charming little boy smile, a smile that melted Gwyneth's heart and reminded her how very much she loved him.

"Bring the pedigree moggy here if that will help and why not bring Gertrude too sometime. I'd be happy to cook her a nice meal."

"No, I wouldn't bring her here but I'll let her know about the cat. She'll be grateful, I know."

Princess Woo moved in and proved unfriendly, neurotic, fussy about food and erratic about her litterbox. Needless to say, Tom had forgotten his offer of responsibility as far as that was concerned.

Arnold, instead of lying companionably on the sofa beside Gwyneth in the evenings, secreted himself in a cupboard, where he need neither see nor hear the unwelcome guest. He also began to stay outside for longer periods. Tom, too, was often out in the evening and Gwyneth started to feel forsaken, though she said no word of reproach. Princess Woo was not a friendly cat and often exited through the door which Gwyneth had just entered. If the cat remained, she perched uncomfortably on the opposite side of the room staring at Gwyneth with what seemed like suspicion.

Certainly Tom had plenty to say when he came home, complaining about the crazy length of time the meeting had lasted, and how he had been forced, yet again, to take Gertrude somewhere to eat.

"It's bloody ridiculous how much time I'm supposed to give up to that woman, when I have all this work to get through. There's hardly any of the evening left. How do they expect me to do it? I'm just a work horse. And it's costing me a fortune."

He looked so stressed and miserable when he came home, it was impossible to mention the litter tray. Gwyneth would make tea for him and say not a word to interrupt him as he worshipped at his computer screen, occasionally cursing under his breath when it failed to produce the required result.

It was the eleventh time this happened that Gwyneth ventured to speak in what she hoped was a teasing tone.

"Just as well Gertrude's an American."

"What? What are you on about?"

"I expect you took her to a MacDonald's?"

He grunted in reply.

"But I suppose even Americans must get tired of hamburgers, *sometimes*?"

He peered purposefully at his screen and made no response.

"Which one did you go to?"

"Which what did I go to?"

"Which MacDonald's did you go to? Were you over on the south side?"

"Oh no, Gertrude never eats that sort of food. It was a Thai restaurant tonight."

"A Thai restaurant!" Gwyneth's voice was faint and her face wore an expression that was new to it.

"Yes, Gertrude always likes Asian of some kind, Chinese or Indian. Sometimes Japanese. Thai food's quite good. Better than Chinese, though curry is quite tasty I suppose."

Tom's eyes did not leave the screen. He would never realise the destructive power of this statement. Nor would he see the expression on Gwyneth's face with its mixture of misery, disbelief and even a little bitter amusement.

Without a word, Gwyneth rose and went to the freezer where she regarded the packets of hamburgers, the bag of oven chips. She stood there gazing into the cold cavern, perhaps searching for some sort of reality.

She was a clever girl as I told you and suddenly that well-known madness, that ancient craziness, that terrible magic spell of love just disappeared! Like a puff of smoke! She felt empty and alone, but very clear-sighted.

As usual, Princess Woo was wailing and begging for treats, tuna, salmon, cheese, eggs, anything. Gwyneth threw a couple of frozen hamburgers across the kitchen, narrowly missing the surprised cat. Then she hauled Arnold from his cupboard and fastened him firmly into his travelling basket. Next she packed her clothes, then phoned for a taxi. The cookery books could stay. There would be no time for elaborate cuisine while she worked for that PhD

Morning Cinema

Let us not discuss how many years it is since I attended the morning film matinee for children at the Ascot cinema in Anniesland. What a splendid art deco palace it was, now converted to equally splendid luxury flats. There is even a roof garden where one can sip a long cool drink and view (or ignore) the relentless traffic of Great Western Road as it dashes east and west far below you.

Though I enjoyed watching films in the morning, I did not go very often. I was a quiet, only child and did not care for the ear-splitting noise of the unaccompanied children around me. There was usually a large part of the programme that did not appeal to me. Cowboys and other masculine heroes were just to be tholed until the 'big picture' started. That was what I was there for. The films were not very new and would feature a child star. Shirley Temple or Jane Withers were my favourites.

This week, when my friend Jean suggested we might go to the *Silver Screen*, the 10.30am film showing at the Grosvenor cinema in Byres Road, it seemed a charming idea. A gesture towards that distant past of childhood and a snook cocked at all those adult duties we should be performing.

It was a film we had missed when it was on general release.

"And you get a cup of tea or coffee thrown in!"

"Oh well, certainly. Sounds a good idea. Let's go."

"And," she added enticingly," for an extra couple of quid, you get a fish supper!"

"What! *A fish supper!*"

It was not to be missed.

We entered from Ashton Lane, where the old cinema exit was in days gone by. This little street, only a hundred yards from Byres Road, is an unlikely looking corner of G12, a quaint mews with white-washed walls and shining black woodwork. Balconies and outside staircases give the several restaurants and pubs almost a Mediterranean atmosphere and it has become a very trendy place indeed, mobbed on a Saturday night, I believe. It is almost like a stage set and you might be tempted to think it had recently been created to meet the modern demand for dining out, but it was there in my youth. Though much shabbier then, there was always a foreign glamour about the place. Fifty odd years ago, when an art student, I depicted a horse and cart delivering milk in the picturesque lane.

How changed the Grosvenor is since my youth. The large cinema has been chopped into unrecognisable portions to create a shop, bar and restaurant, toilets and two minute cinemas connected by a labyrinth of winding carpeted corridors. By the time I was seated I had no idea which direction I was facing, but there was no denying the luxury of the leather armchairs in which we sat. Classical music was playing discreetly. Compared to the large space of my youth, the auditorium seemed hardly worthy of the name, being not much larger than a very big sitting room. Only a few other seats were taken but perhaps more folk would arrive? Jean collected her coffee to enjoy with the film, but I saved mine for after my fish supper.

Can it be called a supper when served at 1pm?

The film was well made, though perhaps a little self-indulgent. It was set in the sixties and it was nice to be reminded of how well-dressed people were in those days. Even the students looked groomed and colourful, with not a pair of jeans in sight. Colin Firth's performance was marvellous.

And the fish supper, which we ate in the bar, was superb! A large piece of haddock in a perfect crisp batter. I did enjoy it. Most of the rather sparse audience also indulged in the treat. A lady on her own, Marie, who has attended the *Silver Screen* regularly since her retiral, joined us at our table. Her husband comes along when he likes the sound of the film and in future, I might follow his example.

AIRLIE STREET GAMBLER

It had been his usual, and his favourite, supper of ham and eggs and baked beans, with plenty of HP sauce and he did not take long to demolish it. Then Stephen cleared the dishes from the kitchen table and wiped the yellow patterned formica thoroughly with a damp dishcloth. While the surface dried, he went to the sideboard in the bed recess and took from the drawer a small box, two plastic cups, and a roll of bright green cotton fabric, also a notebook and pen and placed everything, except the cotton, on top of the sideboard. His movements were slow and calm and there was an element of ritual in the deliberate way he handled each object though his face showed a contained excitement, his eyes darting quickly back and forth and the corner of his mouth twitching, as though he must smile.

Stephen was a small slight man in his early sixties, with carefully brushed thinning grey hair.

Completely unremarkable.

He would have told you that himself. He had lived a quiet life in this top flat since his boyhood in the late fifties. Because of a modest inheritance, his widowed mother had been able to buy the flat for £500 and they had lived in it together until her death ten years ago.

The flat had only one bedroom which had always been Stephen's. His mother had insisted that he needed a room of his own in which to study. She was quite content to sleep on the sofa bed in the sitting room. It meant folding bedclothes, shifting and rearranging furniture each morning to return the sitting room to its proper elegance but she did not mind. Though not a large room, it really was elegant, with well polished furniture, attractive ornaments and the bay of three windows overlooking the trees on the other side of the street.. She did not mind the extra work entailed, for Stephen's studies must come first.

Unfortunately, Stephen was not ardent in his studies and did not fulfil his mother's high hopes. He became nervous at

examinations and failed in most subjects, forgetting even the
small amount that he had learned.

However at fifteen he found a job as an office boy, for his
writing was neat and, if not rushed, he was reasonably good
with figures. When he became proficient with a duplicator
and a comptometer, he was promoted to an office clerk and
there he stayed until he retired. Unfortunately for Stephen his
career was contemporary with the explosive advances in
technology. And as the years passed, the skills which he could
offer were required less and less and he had not the self-
confidence nor the ambition to enter the age of computers.
When still in his fifties, he was referred to as 'old Steve' and
gradually his duties returned once more to the simple ones of
an office boy.

It was just a year after his mother died, a very old lady, that
it became impossible for management to justify Stephen's
modest salary. He was given a dinner, and a presentation clock,
for he had been with the firm for over forty years. Although
there were some kind speeches, no doubt many believed the
business might have prospered just as well without him.

Stephen was sorry that his mother had not lived to see the
clock, which was very handsome, though never a reliable time-
keeper.

✧◆✧

Stephen methodically unrolled the green cloth, then folded
it exactly in half and spread it carefully on the table. It was
part of a summer skirt that his mother had worn when he was a
teenager and he had always liked the colour. He remembered
her wearing it on several pleasant excursions to Largs and
Rothesay. It was a generous piece of fabric, for the skirt had
been voluminous and, as she herself was first to admit, she was
'pretty broad in the beam'.

He laid the colourful box and the notebook and pen beside
the cloth, then taking a jam jar of coppers down from the
shelf, he counted out fifty pence and placed it in one of the
plastic cups. After putting the same amount in the second cup,
he put the kettle on.

✧◆✧

It was on one of those long ago visits to Largs that his
mother had told him some surprising news. He was twelve that

day they sat on the beach. They had just finished their tomato sandwiches.

"Stephen, I have something I must tell you and I know you'll find it difficult to believe, dear, but," she paused and tears came into her eyes. Stephen was terribly astonished and worried. He had never seen her cry before. She turned her head away, as though she spoke to the small waves that lapped relentlessly a few feet from them.

"I have to tell you that I am not a widow, Stephen. Your father is not dead. Ssh! Just listen to the whole story before you say anything. Your father, Jim, was a very weak man. Not exactly a wicked man but the result of his weakness was wicked. He had a terrible, terrible vice. He was a gambler! I worked for years before you were born and every penny that we earned was thrown away on his gambling! Just as soon as we got it, he would gamble it away! It was as if those hard-earned pound notes were thrown immediately into the heart of the fire. It's a fiendish curse, gambling. Of course I had no inkling of what he was like when we first married. My parents and his parents were good to us and we both had steady jobs and rented a comfortable little house in Bishopbriggs and furnished it smartly, too, but soon it all went on his dreadful... habit. Every weekend was the same... oh I can't bear to think of the waste..."

Then she broke down completely and Stephen was really glad that it was a windy day and the beach deserted. He put his arm awkwardly round her shoulders. He wanted to ask lots of questions but felt it was the wrong time. She was terribly upset. He did not know that adults could be so upset and it scared him.

Through her sobs she explained how Jim had left when he found she was expecting a baby. They had been married for nine years and had moved to a one-roomed flat in Partick. They were in debt and her fine furniture and wedding presents were all pawned or sold.

"I was exhausted and dispirited, I had struggled and strug-gled all those years. I really loved him at the start, but I was worn down by it all and when he disappeared I felt rejected and angry and miserable but deep down, I knew it was for the best. I would manage somehow and surely a baby would be less of a responsibility than Jim had been. Aunt Jeanie came to the rescue with a loan of a hundred pounds, then the old soul died the next year and left me everything. You should be eternally grateful to her for her little savings lifted us out of absolute poverty. And we've been able to live in a nice area where you can go to a good school and I hope you're working very hard, Stephen. I have such high hopes for you."

Stephen wanted to ask where his father was now, but his mother continued speaking.

"I don't know what happened to Jim or where he went and I don't want to know. He only meant trouble to me and I have put him out of my thoughts long ago, but I wanted you to know the truth. It was only right that you should know he is still alive. I suppose he is anyway. Now Stephen, your father was a worthless man and he deserted us and I hope that you will put him out of your mind and forget all about him."

Stephen said nothing but thought that might be very difficult.

His mother again turned towards him and gazed into his eyes,

"There's an important reason that I've told you this. I want you to make a solemn promise to me that you will never, never gamble. Promise me, please promise me that you will never, *at any time*, gamble in any shape or form. Bad blood! I've heard it's a vice that runs in the blood and I'm terrified, for Jim had an uncle who gambled. Perhaps my own son has inherited this destructive flaw. You are still so young, my darling, but please, please *never* gamble, *never* be tempted. Will you promise me, please?"

How dramatic she seemed. Stephen had never heard her speak like this before. She had never called him darling that he could remember and her voice sounded different. It was as though they were acting in a play and he must now say his part.

"Of course, I'll promise, Mum. I've never gambled, ever and I've never wanted to and I'm positive I don't have that 'bad blood' so don't worry about it." Then in a deep slow voice quite unlike his own he added, "*I do solemnly vow that I never will gamble in my life.*"

As he said these words, he felt very adult and serious, almost holy, like a knight of old. They were reading about King

Arthur at school just now.

After he had made his vow he suddenly wondered if winning and losing at marbles, which was a constant pastime in the school playground, counted as gambling. He decided not to ask about that.

"That's a very good boy, such a wonderful, good boy! You've made me so happy and we'll never talk about your father again."

And they never did.

The kettle boiled and Stephen made a pot of tea in the dented aluminium teapot. Then, covering it with the blue and yellow striped tea cosy that his mother had once knitted, he felt the usual pang of guilt that it was so grubby, but wool could shrink and he was afraid to add it to his weekly wash at the laundrette.

When he had filled his favourite striped mug he sat down at the table with a happy little groan and opening the box, which held two packs of cards, he chose the pack with roses on the back rather than the one with lilies and bluebells. Then he laid out his patience. The first card face up, then six cards face down, then one card face up and five face down until there were seven neat, evenly-spaced piles, ranging from one card to seven.

The first moments after the 'laying out' might be exciting, with a lot of shifting to do, or possibly disappointing, but Stephen was always optimistic and you never could tell how it might turn out. Aces were put above the layout and black threes were put on red fours, red queens on black kings, etc. It was disappointing if there were no aces to put up and nothing much to shift. He went through the remaining cards one at a time and only once. He disapproved of those folk who searched through the pack several times.

This was the game that he and his mother, until her last illness, had often played together as double patience, sitting on either side of the table with the green cloth spread right across and each with a pack of cards. His mother always chose the lilies. As she got older and slower she started to miss opportunities and make mistakes and Stephen had to keep a sharp eye open and play her side of the game as well as his own. But it was always an enjoyable triumph for them when it came out and they would smile happily to each other as they separated the lilies from the roses and shuffled them ready to lay out another game.

After his mother's death he had continued to play patience each night, but though he and his mother had often succeeded with the double pack, that game seldom 'comes out' when played singly. After a few weeks it seemed pointless.

One day in the cut price bookshop in Byres Road, he found a book called *Fifty Different Types of Patience*. It cost a pound and he bought it. The illustrations and instructions looked complex and he hardly knew where to start. The first game he tried to work out had no skill attached and depended only on the luck of the cards. It was boring. Then he noticed a familiar row of seven cards going from one to seven, but in this game they were face up and spread out so that every card was in sight. There was no search through the pack, but seven cards were laid out, one on each column, between the normal shifting of aces and building on them until there were no more cards left. The unusual fact that red card was placed on red and black on black made Stephen smile. The book said this was an old Japanese game and that exotic idea appealed to him.

He decided to search for one more game and chose Demon, which started with thirteen cards counted out, then four laid out to build on. Spaces were filled from the pile of thirteen and the remaining pack was searched through three cards at a time and as many times as necessary. As with the other two games, the aces were placed above the cards and built up in sequence.

For a month, Stephen played these three games in strict rotation. They provided a pleasant variety of method that kept him alert and on his toes. He played many games each night and the two new games were more likely to be successful. When a game 'came out', it gave him a surprising glow of satisfaction and well-being. With a curiosity which had never previously manifested itself, Stephen started to wonder which of the three games gave the most successful results. At first he jotted down which game had come out that night on a scrap of paper, but his years in the office had instilled in him the need to be neat and accurate and he soon invested in a small note-book. In it he marked the date, naming the three games,

Japanese, Scottish and Demon and marking a perfect circle in the appropriate column when he had a success. Occasionally there was a game where not one ace showed itself. That was dispiriting, though fortunately it happened more rarely than winning and it seemed worthwhile to note it down as well. Stephen used a large asterisk, one cross on top of another, for this disappointing result.

These were both unusual results so the marks in his notebook were sparse. After a week, he decided to grade every game he played. Stephen reckoned it a poor game if the build up on the aces was less than five cards. More than five was the most common result and he awarded that a plain little cross in the notebook. Whether there were ten or forty cards up, it was all the same and received a cross, but if only one or two aces and a couple of twos had been disclosed, that game was a failure and he marked it with a cross enclosed in a square.

He found great satisfaction in devising this method. It added to the enjoyment of playing cards and somehow gave the occupation some point.

"It makes it more worthwhile," he said to himself several times.

Perhaps it was the first time since his boyhood that Stephen had used his ingenuity to create something.

As he played, Stephen quietly advised and pleaded with the cards,

"Now how about a red ten or a black four. You can do it. No I said a *red* ten, not a black one. Oh no! not again... *Ah, Hah!* that's the stuff. And there's the ace... and a two... very well done. Now a six, any old colour will do, I've got the two sevens... YES, that's what I wanted.'

Sometimes the requested card popped up immediately and it really seemed as though the cards listened to him. It had more than a touch of the supernatural which delighted him. The neatly marked pages of the notebook definitely gave a sense of purpose to the evening's steady application.

Though his days were rather empty, Stephen would only play after eating his supper, looking forward to his evening as a treat and a reward for the small slow tasks which filled his mornings and the afternoon walks to Botanic Gardens or Partick Library.

The notebook was quarter full when the idea occurred to him.

Who will say where it came from? Was it the curse that his mother had feared, the bad blood of his father? Or was it simply the logical and creative enrichment of the pleasure he had found in cards?

Stephen decided he would add cash to the evening's entertainment. He would have a bank and play against it. As it was all his own money, it could scarcely be called gambling for he remembered his mother had been very much against that sort of thing. His memory of the solemn vow on the beach had faded away, but he could never forget the fuss she had made when he was twenty and had told her of the office sweepstake. Her shouts and tears had seemed out of all proportion to the half crown that her son had ventured on the Grand National. And he had won nothing.

As he walked along Highburgh Road, he planned exactly how it would all work. Then, sitting in the pleasant warmth of Kibble Palace, he made notes as he decided how much he would win or lose on each different symbol in his little book, awarding himself tenpence for a circle (a win) and losing tenpence for an asterisk (no aces up at all), winning three pennies for an ordinary cross, which most games were, and losing three when the cross was enclosed in a square. He had complete power over this decision, but he would not be greedy. He wanted to be fair.

When he returned home, he again remembered his mother's strong feelings, for her presence was never far from his mind in the flat. For more than an hour he piled up justifications for his plan. Surely his proposition could not be called gambling. It was completely harmless, for no one else was involved. And it was impossible that he should lose, for it was all his own money. He was in his sixties and he should be able to spend an evening just as he wished. Surely she could not want him to be unhappy.

Anyway, it was not gambling!

After he had eaten his sausages and beans, he felt better, practically free of guilt and certainly ready to enjoy his new game.

He felt so positive that he decided to add another winning

symbol. Seven was a lucky number and if seven cards had built up on the aces, he would give himself a little bonus of seven pence for that. He chortled to himself as he took a new page and marked the five symbols and their minus or plus allocations.

He found two plastic cups, and using a felt pen to mark one with a B for bank and the other S for Stephen, he placed fifty pennies in each.

A tune was beating at the back of his mind but he could not quite catch the melody and it disappeared as he laid out the cards.

He played each type of patience ten times and it was a splendid night. He added another fifty pence to B, and finished with one pound forty-two pence in his own cup.

As he tidied the cards and rolled the cloth he whistled the tune that had escaped him earlier. He was sure there were words to it, but his memory was not as good as it used to be. Perhaps all this counting would improve the old brain box.

Stephen slept very well that night.

In the library next day, the tune hammered in his head until suddenly, so suddenly that he nearly shouted into the silence of the high ceiling above him, he remembered the words,

...with an independent ai-ya,
You can hear the girls decla-ya,
He must be a millionai-ya..

He left the building immediately and climbing up North Gardner Street, whistled "*The Man that Broke the Bank at Monte Carlo*" until the punishing hill deprived him of sufficient breath to whistle, but he smiled as he continued to walk purposefully.

His euphoria faded as he cooked the bacon that night.

It was all too easy. Fancy trebling his money last night. Some might say it was beginner's luck, but he had decided himself how much the bank should pay and he could make the rewards even greater if he wanted, but that would be ridiculous, for it was his own money he was winning so what was the point? Tonight he must adjust the amounts before playing and make his winnings more realistic. He knew nothing of the law of averages, but he felt he had an instinct for this business, which he still refused to call gambling, and he was sure he *should* lose sometimes, perhaps quite often.

"*Lose every time, if you're like your father,*" echoed in his brain, but he whistled his tune loudly, and drowned out his mother's voice as he broke two eggs into the pan beside the bacon.

He amended his notes, modifying each sum considerably and that night after playing eighteen games, six of each type, he had won fourteen pence. It was less exciting, but probably more normal.

On the third night he won eighteen pence.

Luck was against him on the fourth night and he lost fifty pence. By the end of the week, he had only three pennies left in his cup.

He bought another notebook and as he sat by the boating pond in Whiteinch park he made calculations in it for another change in the amount allotted to each symbol. Swans and ducks swam past, watching him hopefully. He made sure the new numbers were in his own favour, for it was no use depressing himself, but he tried not to be greedy. He gave a generous twelve for the lucky seven that happened so seldom and surely that seemed quite 'fair'. For an instant he wondered just who might suffer from his unfairness but quickly dismissed that thought.

After six months, a change had taken place in Stephen. Even his neighbours noticed it. He was fatter for one thing, but though his spare figure had thickened, he held his shoulders straighter and marched to the shops with a smarter step. And though his shopping bag was fuller and heavier than previously, he climbed the stairs to the top flat quickly, like a much younger man.

He was more sociable, too, and would chat to neighbours in a way that he had never done before, helping young Betty Graham carry her pram up the twenty four steep front steps to the close and sometimes even knocking at old Mrs Peter's door to ask if she needed anything from the shops. But he was never to be seen in the evening and everyone thought he probably went to bed early as he was so active during the day. They were wrong. Stephen played patience each night until two and three in the morning. It was a task to which he devoted himself assiduously. He worked as conscientiously as he had in his office job and with more energy. And he applied himself with a great deal more enjoyment. His evenings were a delight to him. At the end of his last game, if he had won, he would have a small whisky. If he had lost, which was very seldom, due to his own cleverness, he would shrug philosophically and also have a small whisky. Alcohol was another thing of which his mother had disapproved, but nowadays her voice seldom commented and when it did, it seemed fainter than before.

For nearly a year, Stephen never tired of his evening occupation. Then one rainy morning, in an unusual fit of domesticity, he decided to clear out the hall cupboard. Perhaps he was looking for something in particular. He certainly found many things which he had not seen for years and most of them reminded him sharply of his mother. A coat with a velvet collar and a pair of red sandals were particularly evocative. It was not the delicate, elderly lady of her latter years that appeared before Stephen's eyes, but the energetic woman of his youth, dogmatic and dominant.

Shaken by strong memories, he felt he must get out of the house and shoving everything back into the cupboard except for an old schoolbook, he set off for the Botanic Gardens.

The rain had stopped and the sun shone and choosing a bench, Stephen opened that long ago schoolbook. It was the story of King Arthur and the Round Table. Cold and unmoving, as if turned to stone, Stephen sat gazing at the first illustration. It had always been his favourite, he remembered, with the knight humbly kneeling in front of the King, as he promised loyalty and devotion. The black and white picture faded and changed to a vision of a beach with tomato sandwiches and ginger beer and his mother's sad eyes gazing at him. He remembered the sound of the small waves lapping and the strange way his mother was speaking just before he made his promise. His Vow! That picture had been his inspiration on the beach, when he made that solemn vow to his mother never to gamble. Now, it all came flooding back to him with terrifying clarity. How wrong he had been to forget that declaration. His guilt was almost unbearable. Jumping to his feet, he hurried home, leaving the book lying on the ground. Gambling! Of course it was gambling.

He had been gambling for months!

Stephen climbed the eight flights of stairs two at a time. In the kitchen he yanked the sideboard drawer open so violently that it came right out and everything in it scattered on the floor. The green cotton had unrolled, pennies from the plastic cups were everywhere and various other long forgotten articles, table mats, serving spoons, sugar tongs, postcards, butter knives, nutcrackers, buttons were strewn across the linoleum. The bright box of playing cards lay in the midst of it all, like a terrible reproach.

He gazed at the floor for a few moments, then turned away and opening the kitchen window wide, leaned out. With his hands gripping the red sandstone sill, he gasped at the fresh air as if he could not get enough. Far beneath him lay the small back green with its few shrubs and neat bin shelter. How far away it was. He had never looked down from this height before. So much air and space between him and the ground. There was a fascination in that immense drop. He smiled slightly. It provided a distraction from his mental agony.

Withdrawing his head, he stood for a moment as a wave of dizziness swept over him. He shook his head, then stepping carefully over the scattered articles on the floor, he picked up the box of cards and returned to the window.

He chose the rose pack and tossed the top three cards out into space, then leaned out and watched as they fluttered down and finally reached the grass far below. Two showed their rosy backs and one was a black face card, though at this distance he could not be sure what it was, king or jack, spades or clubs. What did it matter? He dropped a single card, then another and another. His movements were careful and unhurried and the cards were handled with the same respect and deftness as in the evening games. It was only the fling from the window which suggested violence. When a bunch of ten or twelve cards sailed from the window, some were clinging together and descended quickly, while others floated down, as if unsure of their target. A gust of wind caught the next batch of cards and distributed them over a wider area, some landing in the service lane, others drifting into the next door garden. Soon the rose pack was finished and after contemplating the random scatter on the grass far below him, Stephen ducked inside again and took the lily pack from the box and thoughtfully shuffled it several times before violently casting all fifty two cards out into space at once. He did not watch their descent but stood gazing at the disorder on the floor for a few dazed minutes.

Now that the house no longer held any playing cards, Stephen felt some of his guilt assuaged, but also there was a terrible emptiness. For months he had seemed to live life with a purpose. Each day had held the promise of an evening's busy enjoyment with the possible delight of a game that came 'right out' and the certain pleasure of totalling his winnings. Even a 'seven' could give him a glow of happy satisfaction.

Now it was finished.

Nothing.

Once more he looked from the window at the scattering of cards so far beneath him.

How easy it would be to follow them, to put one foot on the sill, a hand on the stonework on either side, then duck under the window and push off into that void. His descent would be very different from the graceful flight of the cards. Almost certainly he would die though it would be even worse if he did not. But of course he would die and that would show how sorry he was to have broken his vow.

It was tempting, with all future problems of loneliness and boredom solved.

With a bit of difficulty Stephen put one foot up on the sill and for ten minutes, he stood at the open window, seriously considering this simple conclusion. It seemed the only thing to do. The right thing to do. A leap into space would be dramatic and almost noble. He remembered the flying leaps that he took as a boy from some high rocks at the beach, soaring through the air with his arms spread like wings and laughing as he landed in the soft sand.

But it would not be like that, for he was no longer an agile boy and it would not be easy to squeeze through the open window, then find his balance on the sill. He would probably just topple out sideways.

Stephen brought his foot back to the floor and once again leaned from the window. Suddenly he realised the implications of what he had contemplated. He pictured his broken body added to the scattered pieces of pasteboard so far beneath him.

Betty! How terrible it would be for Betty on the ground floor, happy with her nice little baby, to discover such a horror lying there just outside her kitchen window. She might never get over it. How would she ever take her rubbish out to the bin without reliving the tragedy? No, he could not do such a thing to a nice young woman. In fact he should not leave the back green in such an untidy state. He must go down right away and pick up all those cards. And his kitchen was such a mess too! He shuddered at the thought of what his mother would have said had he chosen to die and leave the house in such disarray.

Stephen counted as he gathered the hundred and four cards into a poly bag, retrieving them from the next door garden, the lane, shrubs, pot plants and long grass. It seemed important to make sure that every one was collected and deposited in the bin.

His mind relaxed wonderfully as he worked and he started to think of a visit to Byres Road tomorrow. He would buy doughnuts at Gregg's, perhaps treat himself to a cheese and onion pastry.

Last week, Stephen had noticed that Bargain Books had very nice and inexpensive playing cards in their window. They were decorated with a picture of a pretty Geisha girl. Those roses and lilies had been getting pretty grubby and it would be a pleasure to play with new cards and truly it could hardly be called gambling when it was his own money.

BRIEF ENCOUNTER

In my long lifetime I have enjoyed the incredible benefits of advances in technology. As a mother of four, washing machines and dishwashers have saved me immense drudgery. Nowadays the computer has made the writer's life simple, safe and independent. Just imagine entrusting your only existing manuscript to a careless typist or a busy publisher. Even a friend might not be trusted with those precious scribblings, for consider the perfidy of Hedda Gabler. However, in the last few years, technology has advanced so speedily that I cannot keep up with it and have decided to opt out. Technology is only a tool of which I have sufficient and I can lead a comfortable life without any more of it. I do have a mobile phone but cannot think it a good thing to be always available to the demands or boredoms of others. I keep mine on silent and use texting as a quick and convenient method of communication. I do not use the internet. It would not suit my purposes and, as well as the expense, I hear of too many problems and drawbacks attached to it. I prefer the more immediate phone call or the old fashioned letter and I resent the fact that the Government and the world of business are forcing us to depend more and more on a facility which is unlikely to be available to the elderly or less affluent members of society. We are urged and herded towards dealing with income tax, banking, telephone and fuel payments on the internet. My insurance company no longer accepts payment by cheque and previously I have paid by phone and Mastercard, but this time I was greeted by a machine, rather than a person. It was very slow and had repeated difficulty in 'reading' my voice. What would it have done with a strong regional accent? Eventually I gave up. It seemed insane and frustrating that it was so difficult to pay them money. Alternately, one can pay by logging on to the internet and save £10 to boot, but when my daughter attempted this in the evening, that too proved impossible. My insurance remains unpaid and I shall transfer my business to a different company. A few weeks ago I renewed my car insurance by phone. A business-like and cheerful young man dealt with it in about three minutes and we exchanged a couple of pleasantries. I put down the phone with a charming feeling of being a valued customer and an interesting person. I hope he felt similarly satisfied with the way he had conducted the transaction. I think this sort of human contact is vital and I am prepared to pay a few more pounds to retain it. I think it disgraceful that people should lose their jobs to a machine that wastes the customer's time and patience. And if I should ever wish to make an insurance claim, I shall certainly want to speak to *a real human being.*

I think it worrying that small everyday transactions are being whittled away. Perhaps time is saved, though I would question that fact in many instances, but I treasure those daily encounters with a wide variety of people, shop assistants, bus conductors, bank clerks etc. They provide the opportunity to use agreement or disagreement, kindness, wit, (especially in Glasgow) flirtation and often sympathy, those human interactions which hold a community together and make for a wealth of experience. A brief meeting with an acquaintance can often be as enriching as a chat with a friend. When I lived in Canada, I realised how people, especially the older generation, were isolated by the terrible climate. A taxi to the supermarket once a month might be their only outing during the winter, and with an impatient queue waiting, it was unlikely they would get more than a nod from the check-out clerk. When I returned to Scotland, how pleasant to see the senior citizens standing chatting in the street every day. We have such a wonderful climate and we are always complaining about it. Rain cannot change your life in the way that extreme cold, with snow and ice underfoot does. Perhaps that lesson has been learned in the unusually severe and extended cold spell of this last winter of 2009-10.

Normally I never shop on a Saturday but recently I was in town on that day. I was meeting a friend for lunch and as I was recovering from a bout of flu, I left early to give myself enough time to wander. Leaving the bus at the top of Renfield Street, I strolled slowly downhill towards the Merchant City where Jan and I would meet in the Citation restaurant. The last time that I had entered that splendid pile in Wilson Street was in the mid-seventies when it was the Sheriff Court and I was on jury duty. I could hardly imagine it as a restaurant. As I walked I passed many coffee shops and some sad vacant stores and closed restaurants, victims of the credit crunch. I was particularly impressed by the smooth pavement underfoot. Walking was pleasant and easy, which is not always the case with city streets. In the last few years, Glasgow has worked hard to improve the pavement surface in the city centre and is to be congratulated on using fine materials and splendid workers.

I was heading for the late lamented Borders Books in Buchanan Street in order to take a quick, inexcusably vain, peep at their shelves, where my books had recently found a niche, though sadly that success would be short-lived.

After Jan and I had enjoyed a delicious lunch and a long chat about our summer, I returned to the west end via Great Western Road. As I walked along Byres Road and collected various items of shopping. I had several of those brief but pleasant encounters, described above, in Hillhead Library, Oxfam bookshop, Clarks shoes, Gregg's bakery, fruit shop and Corrigan's wonderful fish shop. And as is usual in Byres road, I met a friend and stopped for a quick word.

I just missed a 44 bus and stood waiting, alternately accusing myself of laziness for not walking the short distance to Clarence Drive, and justifying myself, for I was laden with shopping, had left home more than six hours ago and had my bus pass.

I was alone in the bus shelter in Highburgh Road and leaning my elbow on a convenient ledge with my chin on my fist, I gazed disconsolately in the direction from which the next bus would arrive. After a moment I turned my head, perhaps I felt myself watched, and was immediately hailed by a cheery voice from a city-bound taxi on the other side of the road, which was waiting for the lights to change.

"Aye, ye're lookin' awfy fed up there," the driver shouted.

"I'm just thinking of a cup of coffee in my own house!" I replied at the top of my voice, for he was twenty yards away from me across the noisy road, with occasional traffic passing between us.

"Aye that'll be whit ye're needin'. Been in town?"

"Yes, all day!"

"No' great weather for it, wizzit."

"It could have been worse. I was lucky and I had my brolly with me."

I waved it in demonstration and paused while a red Honda passed between us, then yelled. "Had a very nice time."

"That wiz good." And he nodded as though he was really pleased about that.

The lights changed and he put his car into gear,

"Keep good health, now!" was his parting roar, accompanied by another encouraging nod and I wished him the same.

Although the conversation had been short and shouted and interrupted by various vehicles, I had enjoyed it very much and no longer felt at all jaded. Perhaps his kind attention was jogged by pity for an old lady at a bus stop, but his manner made me feel like an interesting and attractive woman.

I wonder if taxi drivers in other cities strike up this spontaneous sort of conversation? But I consider Glasgow has a very special quality of friendliness and surely my fear that technology will change that is groundless.

MISS GERTRUDE THEOBALD

It was in 1952 that Miss Theobald's parents died. Mrs Theobald had a heart attack. Then, as with so many devoted couples, swans for instance, the relict found life impossible without his long familiar partner and succumbed within a few weeks. Though this romantic fact did not help their daughter's financial position, it supported her in her grief.

For more than forty years Gertrude had lived in the comfortable Theobald home in Cleveden Crescent, a house which was perhaps not quite a mansion but certainly spacious and impressive. Before the war, a staff of three had inhabited the tiny spartan top flat and worked continuously to maintain the eight luxuriously furnished rooms to the high standard considered acceptable by Mrs Theobald.

Gertrude had grown up without any thought of independence. There was no need for her to earn money. Her father would have been offended if she had suggested it. He had been a successful businessman, now retired, and was happy to see his wife and daughter such good companions, for he could leave all the feminine occupations to them and need never go shopping for hats or make decisions about wallpaper or any such fripperies.

The war had been a great nuisance in his lifetime what with food and fuel shortages, staff problems at home and in business. Fortunately it was now all in the past and strangely it had improved his finances rather than otherwise. He now intended to enjoy his retirement and was more than happy to support his undemanding and demure daughter. She had at no time caused him trouble and had happily allowed money to be spent on her in the way he wanted to spend it. He considered her a model daughter.

Gertrude's teachers at Laurelbank School for Girls would have described her as a 'very sweet girl' rather than a 'clever girl' or a 'hard worker'. Her fellow pupils would have labelled her as a 'kind girl' or some, more cruelly, 'rather wishy-washy'. Gertrude lacked that sparkle, that inexplicable allure for which

Laurelbank girls were renowned.

Of course, if the right young man had come along, no doubt Gertrude would have accepted his proposal and become a model wife rather than daughter. But that did not happen. Many young men of her generation had not returned to Glasgow after their experiences in the war and the wider world. Many had not returned to anywhere at all.

In her twenties, she met a few fellows at the tennis club dances, After a visit from a nervous young man, her mother was wont to make remarks such as,

"Quite a nice-looking boy, that, but, oh dear, his conversation is terribly dull, don't you think?"

Or with another potential suitor,

"What a nice suit he was wearing but somehow I wasn't very impressed with the *calibre* of that young chap."

And her father would nod his head portentously and admit that he was forced to agree with his wife.

Then the scales would fall from Gertrude's eyes and she would see the many defects in his character and quite soon her lack of enthusiasm would lead to a cessation of phone calls from yet another young man.

Later when her mother might comment that Charles or Richard or whoever did not seem to have called for a few weeks, Gertrude was quite offhand and dismissive and Mrs Theobald, without quite knowing why, could relax and breathe a sigh of relief. She was so very anxious that her daughter should choose the right man to marry.

When the war started, Gertrude at twenty-nine expected to be called up and awaited the unknown experience without much excitement or fear. However her father knew many of the *right people* and with a little exaggeration of his wife's health problems, he was able have Gertrude exempted from active duty. If she felt disappointment she did not admit it, even to herself. As it was almost impossible to get domestic help, Gertrude became more involved in keeping the beautiful house as spotless and elegant as it had always been. They had one faithful daily cleaner, Mrs McGill, who was in her late sixties but still able and willing to deal with the rough work, scrubbing floors and washing windows with apparent verve and enjoyment. Gertrude, who was a kind-hearted girl, often carried the heavy step ladder and the pail of water to where Mrs McGill needed it. Then she would leave the room hurriedly for she could not bear to watch the old soul get creakily down on her knees or shakily mount the steps. Twice Gertrude offered to wash the windows herself,

"It would be safer, Mother."

But Mrs Theobald was very much against that, for Gertrude's domestic input would then have been obvious to the outside world.

"It would be unsuitable," she snapped and the matter was closed.

Nevertheless, Gertrude worked hard and continuously. To reach those Theobald standards, the carpet sweeper, the O-cedar mop, the Mansion polish, Brasso, various brushes and a complicated hierarchy of rags and dusters must be wielded daily with religious fervour. Gertrude found herself devoting more and more time to the care of the shining mahogany, the glittering and plentiful ornaments and the richly hued Persian rugs. She accepted it. What else was there to do? She no longer played tennis and thought a woman in her thirties rather old for tennis dances. She did not resent the demands made on her. She loved and respected her parents and her home. In the evenings she was happy to read a little or bring out her embroidery. Really, *what else was there for her to do?*

If you have read this far and have any natural perspicacity, you will have guessed that Gertrude was born to be a confirmed old maid.

Not that I think for one moment that her life should be categorised as a failure on this score. If her parents had lived the long lives that they no doubt expected to live, Gertrude would have shared her life contentedly with them and I think that shows a courage and a philosophical bent to which few of us can aspire. To these praiseworthy traits, Gertrude Theobald added commonsense and determination at the time of her parents' death. What is more, she would display ingenuity and a taste for adventure in her long future life.

The lawyer looked across his large untidy desk at the very neatly dressed woman. Neat but dowdy, he judged and hardly over forty. Every article she wore was of the best quality, yet her

appearance was uninteresting. Could it be the colours she had chosen? Or was it her self-deprecatory air? Her French suede gloves must have cost nearly four pounds. He knew the outrageous price because his wife had bought a similar pair and his anger at such extravagance had disrupted their matrimonial calm for some days. Yet he had finally admitted that those gloves added undoubted chic to her entire outfit. But this woman across the desk gained no such benefit from her gloves. Why was that, he wondered. And how was she to continue buying expensive gloves after hearing the bad news that he must impart?

For the first time in her life Gertrude would be forced to consider money and how she might work out a budget.

It was obvious that she could not afford to continue living in her vast home, even if she had wished to. She had no income herself and her father's comfortable pension had died with him. Like so many wealthy men, he had been unwilling to consider that time when he would not be around to lavish money on his dependants and had made no provision for them. He had bequeathed some securities but Gertrude decided to cling to them as a nest egg in case of future ill health. The lawyer commended this idea. But of course there was the beautiful well-maintained home filled with fine furniture.

"What about the house and furniture? Won't that be quite...?

"Miss Theobald, I'm afraid your large house may not fetch a large price. Property is at an all-time low just now, especially at the top end of the market. No one can afford to heat or maintain those enormous mansions. And of course the rates are astronomical. No doubt it is a beautiful home in a splendid area but... a bit of a white elephant if you will excuse the expression. Now if you were speaking of a two-room and kitchen flat in Hyndland, hardly the size of your drawing room, I could sell it for you tomorrow, no bother at all. Five or six hundred pounds, right away. But your house... just too cumbersome."

He shook his head sadly.

"But there's the furniture?" her face expressed confidence in its excellence as well as those hours of labour expended on its worship.

"Ye-es, but again it's big, much too big for what folk need

nowadays. Houses are smaller. Sadly, some of the best stuff hardly covers its carriage to the saleroom. I'm sorry, Miss Theobald to give you such bad news."

Gertrude took a deep breath,

"Roughly how much *would* the house fetch, d'you think, Mr Haroldson?"

"The question is whether it would sell at all, Miss Theobald. There is a story, perhaps apocryphal, I couldn't say, but an old lady on the South side of the city, is reputed to have begged a young couple to *take* her large home in Nithsdale Road, *take it for nothing* and relieve her of the terrible burden of its upkeep!"

She smiled for she did not believe him. The lawyer admired her calm determination.

"I certainly don't think I'd be quite as stupid as to *give* it away. Rather than that, I would stay on and take in lodgers, although I must say I don't care for the idea of being a landlady."

"I'm sure you'd make an excellent job of it, but we'll hope it doesn't come to that. Let's advertise and see if we get a bite. The west end is always popular and I believe that quite a few of the larger houses are being *developed* these days, you know, divided up into two or even three smaller flats. Not in the same way as the pre-war service flats but with more reconstruction to make each flat completely self-contained. I believe it is a very profitable venture. It is said that some developers 'make a killing' but one needs capital of course. The ad will be in the Glasgow Herald next week, Miss Theobald, and we'll keep our fingers crossed."

Gertrude walked away from the office with new ideas in her head. Could she be a landlady? Probably not, with the present staff shortages. She knew only too well how much effort it took to keep that house maintained and there would be cooking and accounts to do. No, that was impossible to imagine.

It was a Spring day as she walked along Great Western Road. The trees on either side were just opening and the green veiling of fresh little leaves added optimism and poetry to the vast elegant terraces. Gertrude felt strangely full of energy in spite of her sadness.

She considered her small capital. She had never heard the expression 'a developer'. Could she be a developer and 'make a killing'? She considered how the house might be divided into two very spacious flats. Then, realising the possibilities, she tried to re-allocate space and imagine it as four much more modest apartments. The little top flat could be separated successfully but the size of the main rooms was a problem. She decided she must wait until she was at home and had paper and pencil to work out her ideas.

Then the idea of a small flat in Hyndland that could be purchased for £500 was interesting! That would be all she would need for herself and surely her own house would fetch at least three thousand. She would have a roof over her head and there would be much less housework to do. But how would she fill her time? Perhaps she might find a little job, but what could she do except housework? She was certainly well-trained in that art. She stopped in her tracks for a moment, shocked at how horrified her dear mother would have been at the very idea of her daughter going out to clean! But then she walked on, smiling to herself, and unusually for Gertrude it was an ironical smile. There would be a wage if she went out as a cleaner. That would be a change! Those years of devoted menial work in the family home had been *unpaid* labour. What had it all been for? The Theobalds were not particularly hospitable and there had been few visitors to appreciate the high shine and spotlessness of it all. And now to learn that it was worth very little!

As Gertrude turned the corner, she considered the terrace of four storey town-houses climbing the hill on one side of Cleveden Road. Across from them were austere mansions with-drawn behind shrubs and trees in their own grounds. They were even larger than her own home. How many people had continuously scrubbed, cleaned and polished behind those soaring walls since they were built. And for what reason?

She walked slowly along Cleveden Drive and climbed the steep driveway to her house. The same thoughts kept whirling in her brain. All those years of wasted toil and her house was *worthless,* unless she undertook the even greater task of land-lady.

Perhaps for the first time in her life, Gertrude felt real anger, undirected as yet. There is no emotion like anger, especially if it is mixed with financial necessity, to produce the adrenalin and energy required for immediate decision-making. Gertrude stood in the beautiful oak-panelled drawing room and tried to imagine it with the grand piano replaced by a large table at which she, with a kindly, false smile, would preside over a motley crew of lodgers. Some would be sure to smoke and those golden panels would soon become darkened with nicotine. She thought of all the food she must cook each day to feed them and how she must satisfy their appetites and yet make a profit for herself. She turned quickly and left the room. She knew she could never be a landlady.

Neither could she make changes to this house that she had loved and cared for with such vigilance She could not carve it up into small ugly apartments, even if she could afford to do so. She stood in her father's study, so perfectly and lovingly fitted out in the finest of wood by some long dead cabinet maker. The soft patina of dedicated polishing shone from the mahogany desk, the filing cabinets, cupboards, safe and book shelves and paid tribute to her years of energy and many tins of Mansion polish. If this must be demolished she knew she could not be the one to do so. Some hard-hearted developer with enough money and absolutely no investment of toil or sentiment to handicap him might destroy the beautiful, demanding house but she could not. She pulled open a cupboard, the one that was fitted inside with six little drawers each with a beautifully finished brass handle. One drawer was deeper than the others and was divided and marked for index cards. She had loved these drawers as a child and although forbidden to do so, had sometimes explored them. It was almost the only naughty act of her childhood. Tears came into her eyes but they were quickly followed by another ironic smile. Had there ever been such a well-behaved and obedient child as little Gertrude? Resolutely, she closed the drawers and the cupboard, walked into the large kitchen and made a decision as she drank a glass of water. The little flat in Hyndland would be her future. The fact that she could neither visualise the flat nor the life she might lead in it had a spice of the unknown which Gertrude found frightening but also intriguing. Her surge of anger had faded and she felt apprehensive, but pleasantly excited, which was a state she had not experienced since she was a young child.

✧◆✧

The house and contents realised a little more than might have been hoped and Miss Theobald of Cleveden Drive became Gertrude Theobald of Polwarth Street. The flat was large enough for a few of the smaller pieces of furniture and also for a lodger, which brought in a small and welcome income. Gertrude found that being a landlady to Lucy, an interesting single woman of her own age, was not at all demanding. Very pleasant in fact. They shared the kitchen and quite soon the cooking and washing up. Gertrude would learn a lot from Lucy about dressing, make-up and enjoying oneself generally. It was Lucy who suggested Gertrude should apply for the job of receptionist at the Highburgh Road surgery. This not only augmented her income but she found great satisfaction in dealing with the variety of people of all age groups and backgrounds. She had never quite realised the humour and brisk intelligence of the Glasgow population.

Lucy suggested they attend yoga classes, which was something very new and physical for Trudy as Lucy now called her. They went to the cinema each week and sometimes the theatre or a concert, for Lucy liked to go out in the evening and Trudy found that she did too. Sometimes they bought themselves a nougat wafer in the Clarence Drive ice cream shop, Sometimes they walked to Byres Road for a coffee in the Cosy Neuk. It was a very pleasant life and there seemed little time left for dusting or polishing. Lucy had no time for that sort of thing anyway.

"Oh just leave it, Trudy, and come over to the fire and read your book, no one will notice a little dust. I know I don't."

When the summer evenings started, they walked round to the bowling club in Queensborough Gardens and drank ginger beer as they watched the players. One evening, a tall interesting man, a doctor and a widower, joined them on their bench and spoke to them. Within six months, Lucy was renting the Polwarth Street flat and advertising for a lodger, while Trudy was married to her doctor and off to Africa.

I did say she had a taste for adventure.

✧◆✧

STRANGE ECONOMY

In my younger days, many ladies of the west end took it as a matter of course that Saturday morning meant a visit 'into town'. Wearing a smart outfit and certainly a hat, they would look around the shops, perhaps make some small purchase, then probably meet a friend for coffee in Fuller's, which had delicious cakes, or perhaps Coplands where a black silk-clad trio of females played light popular music. Perhaps they would prefer Daly's where in the tearoom, remnants might still be seen of the outré décor of Rennie Mackintosh, whose genius was at that time still rather unappreciated in his own city. I was never of that genteel group, for my visits to town were always hurried and with a special purpose in view (probably buying material for some new outfit) and I never stopped for coffee. Time was always precious for me and there was never enough of it. I liked to shop alone, make decisions quickly and waste no time dallying or dithering. While a student and a teacher, I galloped around the stores during my lunch hour. When I became a mother, I would visit town, buy what was needed and be home in time for children returning from school for lunch. Of course, with a growing family, there was more shopping required in those days, but I always saw it as a job of work, to be accomplished as quickly as possible and with the least outlay of cash. I cannot say I did not enjoy it, but I did not consider it a leisure pursuit. The weekend stores were too busy. Those in Sauchiehall Street closed at 1pm on Saturday and all city stores closed on Sunday. Besides, there were other things to be enjoyed then, swimming, going to the park or out into the country, perhaps cutting out and sewing that pretty fabric I had bought during the week. Nowadays with the much extended opening hours, shopping has become an almost overpowering hobby. It has become the fashion to say that shopping is one's *favourite pastime* and as a certain amount is necessary, I suppose it should be as enjoyable, as possible though personally, I have no desire to shop when there is no need. Do people really find satisfaction in spending money for goods which they do not require and will shortly discard? It seems a great waste of circulatory effort. Surely there are more interesting, constructive and entertaining ways of wasting time, energy and money.

Even my contemporaries, mature ladies who, like myself, must be burdened with a plethora of goods and with no need for any more, admit to enjoying the experience of shopping. One friend pleads that she only handles the goods momentarily but many do more than that of course and purchase articles that either take their fancy, or seem an irresistible bargain. I can only suppose they must be much more successful than I am at ridding themselves of the redundant, otherwise they would hardly find room to live in their houses.

This fashion of unnecessary buying and throwing out what is hardly worn, (pristine goods still wrapped in plastic are not unusual) is what has made the charity shops so successful. But then those same friends who supply Oxfam and Cancer Research, also like to purchase there! In what a strange economy we exist, where, as I have heard, one charity shop in a small but affluent market town can make £3000 in a week. Perhaps the goods sold represent an original nine or ten thousand pounds spent, articles bought and then discarded to allow the buyers to go in search of yet more on which to spend their money. That charity shop is only one of seven in the town and that town is only one of thousands throughout the country. You can do the arithmetic yourself.

There has always been a market for used clothing and furnishings but with the advent of the charity shop, the wealthy are customers as well as donors. Formerly, second-hand clothes came more directly from the wealthy classes to the needy through direct gift or from the 'old clothes woman'. The latter was an important channel who travelled the country, trading cheap china for discarded clothing in affluent districts and re-selling the garments in poorer areas, probably not making a large profit but providing a service. There was a touch of romance about her profession and I have written of her elsewhere. Possibly things are better nowadays, for the charity shop offers dignity and independence in choosing and paying for cast-offs and there is no longer a stigma attached to the wearing of them. Of course it is not only clothes which are donated, a very wide range of articles, practically anything you like to mention, will find their way to the charity shop.

While these second-hand stores provide an income for the different charities which they represent, and may, for some people, fulfil some deep psychological need, I cannot approve of them. They encourage the materialistic 'shopaholic' tendencies which seem to have overcome the population. This relish for shopping blights many conversations with tales of latest purchases and boasts of 'great bargains'. Sadly homes and land-fill are stuffed with unwanted goods. It is a kind of madness.

Do I hear you say 'Think of the economy'?

I suspect that if I were a small local merchant, struggling to buy stock, pay full local taxes and wages, I should feel rather ill done to and might even put a brick through the window of my local charity shop.

AT AN OPEN WINDOW

It was June 1949 and a Saturday morning. At that time, we lived half way down the long slope of Clarence Drive, at number 46, opposite Hyndland Secondary School. The windows of the flat were higher than the pavement by ten feet or so and a large tree grew in the small weedy front garden, which was about five feet above pavement level. In those days there was a tram stop just outside the window.

As it was a beautiful summer's day my mother, who was confined to a wheelchair, sat at the open window, almost hidden by the thick fresh growth of leaves on the lime tree.

In good weather she often sat there, practically unobserved, enjoying the fresh air and watching the residents of Hyndland as they shopped, gossiped or waited for a tram to take them into town. If the weather were good she would say,

"If you'll open the window, I might as well sit in my bower today and get a spot of fresh air. And I might see something exciting. You never know."

Once or twice she did see something. An elderly man fell down one day and I was able to rush out with a chair for him, then bring a glass of water, while others tended him until he felt better. Another time two cars collided. They were both moving slowly and no one was hurt as they slewed awkwardly across both sets of tramlines. As they waited for the police, a tram came from each direction but could not pass the cars. A real traffic jam, almost unheard of in those days, developed, for next a horse drawn coal lorry came to a standstill to watch the drama. And when the number five bus trundled up the hill, it could not pass. Soon several motorcars were sitting behind the bus. Some blew their horns once or twice but motorists were rather polite in those days. (I was taught to use my horn only in a dire emergency and *never* at a pedestrian). Another bus, another cart, another tram arrived.

"This is a peliperty and a half!" my mother chortled.

Eventually the well-known figure of our local policeman strolled down the hill. Though perhaps not always instantly available at a crime scene, he was a comfortable and reliable presence, never hard to find. There was a blue police box on Hyndland Road where he often roosted and if not there, he was probably having a cup of tea and a blether in the garage in Lauderdale Gardens. Failing that, one or other of the local shops would certainly know his whereabouts.

Three more trams and two more buses arrived before the tangle was unwound.

"We'll never have such an exciting scene again, I'm afraid."

My mother shook her head and her voice was full of regret.

Usually the happenings outside the window were less sensational and more along the lines of noting the different stages of a baby's progress; the first time a young mother proudly pushed her pram up the hill, the day the baby could sit upright and later when it metamorphosed into a toddler who would soon graduate to the next adventurous stage of 'walking on the wall'. The railings which had once surrounded the front 'garden', if I can use that word to describe such a neglected plot of land, had been confiscated at the start of the war and the red sandstone coping stone was studded with their small metal roots. These low walls were a perfect height for young children to walk along, balancing precariously, while clutching an adult hand. There must have been a fascination in this walkway nine inches above the pavement for all pre-school children insisted on attempting it and older independent children tramped and sometimes ran along it. Even the odd teenager strolled negligently along it or perhaps made use of its height while chatting to friends standing on the inferior pavement. Already the rudimentary remains of the railings were worn to smooth and shining buttons.

There were occasional moments of excitement amongst these domestic scenes, perhaps enough to make my mother lay down her knitting and pay attention.

Heated arguments between couples as they stood at the tram stop were not unknown. One morning she heard a fiercely whispered lover's quarrel. They carried tennis racquets and as they both seemed so furious, she wondered if they might start to wield them. But of course Hyndland was too well-behaved for any such real violence to take place, although another time she did think she heard a slapped cheek, followed by a gasp and a muffled curse. Immediately after, a tall young man swiftly walked off up the hill. But she admitted it could have been her imagination. Sometimes she was forced to use a little imagination to add interest. She had various nicknames for the regular faces that she saw and, while not exactly unkind, these names used personal characteristics which might not have pleased the recipients.

She was also tempted to create scenarios involving the passers-by and her inconsequential stories made me giggle.

"I think there's the possibility of a romance there."

She had indicated two people who appeared to my seventeen year-old eyes as much too aged for anything like that. He had thinning grey hair and walked slowly with a stick, while she was taller than him and had fat ankles.

"You can look disbelieving if you like, but he is carrying her basket and she's fluttering her eyelashes in quite a girlish way."

I shook my head.

"Look, there, he's transferred the basket and stick to one hand and he's helping her across the road. Just a gentle guiding hand under her elbow. What a true gentleman. Just you wait! I think we'll see developments there."

While her tone was always a joking one, my mother's prophecies were sometimes fulfilled and I was never ready to disbelieve her completely.

One Saturday morning I was discussing what food I should buy for the weekend when she interrupted me,

"Here's the butcher's boy again. I think he's going upstairs to Mrs Laurie. Yes, he is too. It's only half an hour since he was here before. I bet he brought the wrong order and she's been on the phone at once. Furious. I expect he brought her sausages when she ordered black pudding. Hmmm. There'll be no tip for him today! Although I suppose she would give it to him the first time he came, before she discovered... I wonder if she'll ask for her tip back?"

Mrs Laurie, our upstairs neighbour, was well known for her complaints and her careful use of money.

Another Saturday I was called to the window to join her.

"Look at those two fellows hanging about at the close next door. What do you think they're up to?"

I thought they looked quite respectable and said so.

"Yes, but they keep looking up and down the street in a shifty sort of way and they've been there for nearly quarter of an hour."

We watched them and quite soon another young man joined them. He carried a large camera, the kind that flashed.

"Aha! That's what they are. Journalists. They're waiting for someone important. Someone worth photographing. I wonder who's coming to 38 Clarence Drive that's so important."

We watched them for another five minutes as they tramped back and forth, looking at their watches, looking down the hill and up the hill.

"I know what you should do. Away and put on that nice new yellow dress and the green sandals and walk slowly up to the shops. Perhaps they'll take a photo of you. You might be in the papers tomorrow."

I greeted this suggestion with the derision it deserved, for if they were waiting for someone important, they were unlikely to notice me, certainly not waste one of their bulbs on me. However my mother was insistent, having greater confidence in my appearance than I had.

"Och, go on. You can get some small message when you're out, then saunter back down again. And don't look too grim as you pass them. You don't need to smile, but don't glower."

Sometimes it is easier to fulfil a request than to fight it. A loving mother in a wheelchair, who makes sure she is not too demanding, has a lot of power over a daughter. Besides, I rather fancied being photographed in my yellow dress. It did suit me and her admiration bolstered my confidence and fanned my vanity. I changed, tidied my hair and strolled up the street past the journalists to the little wooden fruit shop on the hill where I bought half a pound of tomatoes before strolling back again. I did not look at the men as I passed but with that sixth sense that every female possesses, was well aware that they looked at me. However there were no flashing bulbs. I had not been photographed and would not hit the headlines tomorrow.

I was neither surprised nor disappointed. I had done my best. I was glad to have pleased my mother and also to have met the challenge she had set me. I have always found it difficult to resist a challenge.

She was philosophic.

"You looked lovely anyway. They missed themselves, silly asses. *I wonder who it is they're waiting for?*"

Just then the three men turned to gaze down the street, then quickly leapt to the various positions which they had no doubt already arranged.

An enormous black car drew up and stopped.

"That's a Daimler. I wonder if it's Winston Churchill?"

A slender female emerged from the elegant vehicle. She was wearing dark glasses and, despite the blazing sunshine, a long and voluminous fur coat. After an exchange of only a few words and not more than three flashes of the camera, she hurried up the front steps of 38, leaving the three fellows standing looking at the limousine.

"Well, they didn't get much after all that waiting around, did they! They look like knotless threads now, poor souls. Who could that woman be, I wonder? Someone important obviously. I bet that's a mink coat and I expect she's sorry she wore it on a day like this. Look at those poor blokes. They don't know whether to go home or wait for her coming out again."

After five minutes the three journalists walked slowly, perhaps reluctantly up the hill, with only a few backward glances.

And who was the unknown lady?

In the Glasgow Herald next day, under a very blurred picture, a short paragraph informed us that,

Deborah Kerr, the well-known film actress, was in Glasgow yesterday. Miss Kerr was born in Helensburgh but moved to London to further her career. This week she has flown North to pay a visit to her cousins, who live in Hyndland. Miss Kerr recently starred in the film Black Narcissus and will shortly be travelling to Hollywood, where she and several other British actors will appear in a three million dollar epic of ancient

Rome. A very bright future is predicted for this attractive Scottish actress.

Unaware and uncaring of the brilliant future that certainly lay ahead for Deborah Kerr, I was fascinated by her dark glasses. No one then wore sunglasses as a fashion statement and I was very impressed. I yearned for a pair and the fact that normally only blind people wore them did not deter me.

There would be five years of study before I earned my first monthly pay packet of twenty-eight pounds and acquired this desirable luxury for the enormously extravagant sum of two pounds and five shillings.

About Money and Writers

L ots of ideas leap into every head throughout each day. Some, probably most, are immediately forgotten again and this is perhaps fortunate. Often some brilliant thought cannot be followed through because other tasks and duties must take precedence. Or so it seems to the thinker. Then, some hours later, when you no longer have the energy to carry it out, or the plan that struck at 8am no longer seems viable, the application, ingenuity and problem-solving which you applied so assiduously as you lay in bed or munched your muesli, fades and disappears, seldom to return. The whole elaborate structure is discarded. What's more it is forgotten. It is quite sad to think of so much mental energy being wasted. Waste is certainly one of my favourite hates, but more of that later.

If your creativity leans towards the practical, your planning will consider the materials that you require to carry it through, tools, nails and wood perhaps or cotton fabric and thread or even the raw ingredients to make a tasty dish. These are possibly to hand or easy to buy in a local shop. Perhaps your inspiration is more ambitious and abstract, perhaps an idea for a business that would make a fortune. If your ambitions are political or philanthropic they require some steady consideration, probably help from other brains which might not agree with your point of view. An excellent supply of cash would also be advisable.

To those of us who are addicted (I use the word advisedly) to writing, the ideas come thick and fast. Nothing can fly more swiftly through your brain than words and ideas and how you will use them to describe, astonish, amuse, mesmerise the lucky reader with a series of brilliantly depicted characters, plots and scenes. However, once I sit down at the keyboard, I hardly ever follow the scenario which I have rehearsed in my mind. I might use some aspects of it and I think the process was useful in that it shoe-horned me into the mode of thinking about whatever subject I wanted to write about, but the actual piece of prose is never a reproduction of my earlier thoughts. Perhaps technology will one day advance to the point that those first thoughts, which seem so lucid and compelling as you lie comfortably in bed, can be transferred and recorded immediately. Perhaps they will horrify us by their poverty and scrappiness, for I am sure that mental composing must be a type of shorthand and would need a deal of working over. Some writers have continuously and obsessively worked over their prose, honing and polishing. I believe PG Wodehouse, Henry James and Flannery O'Connor, three very different writers, all did. But what about Anthony Trollope who streamed out two thousand words of impeccable English every day before breakfast? And he was writing in longhand! How did he have time to polish it? He published more than eighty novels, all of them long complicated and most of them enthralling as well as several travel books and many short stories. This immense literary work was achieved at the same time as he held a responsible job with the Post Office which required him to travel all over the world. How much more might he have written with a laptop, not to mention the thought technology I have suggested above.

I have read that each night Mrs Tolstoy carefully copied the output of her genius husband's pen for that day. Did she perhaps correct spelling mistakes? Grammar? Did she put in a metaphor here and moderate a long description there? Perhaps she tweaked conversations to make them more natural? And if she did, was he aware of her input? Did he accept her alterations? Sofia Tolstoy was certainly an exceptional and intelligent woman but we will never know how much we are indebted to her. Perhaps she copied his illegibly scribbled prose in a mechanical, unimaginative way and we are indebted to her only for her dedicated toil.

If you are going to write, you should probably jot down those fleeting thoughts as soon as they strike. Lots of them will be daft and useless, but if there is even just one little good one that escapes your grasp and disappears irretrievably into those unknown folds and crevices of your brain, you may retain a sense of loss for years.

Recently I read 'The Assassin's Cloak'. This strangely named book is not a historical mystery, but a fascinating collection of diary extracts, reaching from Pepys in the seventeenth century to my own contemporaries at the end of the twentieth century. Some of the diarists are famous, some are completely unknown. Some extracts deal with important historical events, some describe the trivial exploits of every day life and I probably prefer the latter. One entry which particularly impressed me and has been retained at the front of my mind, was by a wealthy fellow, Chips Cannon. I had never heard of him before. He was Canadian, but lived a luxurious life in London in the twenties and thirties, working for the Foreign Office and eventually becoming an ambassador in many of the European countries. I was intrigued to learn from his extract that '...when you go shopping in the morning, it is *so difficult* to spend less than two hundred pounds."

That was in 1934 when my father, a professional engineer, was earning around four pounds a week. Though we were always rather 'hard up' we were certainly not poor, for my father ran a little car and was a member of a distinguished golf club, while both parents and I belonged to a private swimming club. There was no large mortgage payment, for our spacious three-roomed Hyndland flat was rented for a moderate sum.

My parents were married in 1929 and as both families were fairly comfortable, they 'got off to a good start' with wedding presents of furniture and household necessities. My father did no domestic chores whatever, for my mother did not work outside the home. Though she did not have a washing machine, towels and linen went to the laundry, returning ironed and pristine. Occasionally she had a woman to help with heavy cleaning. In spite of the high ceilings she papered and painted the house, made most of her clothes, hooked rugs and knitted. She also painted in oils occasionally but domestic chores took precedence. We went to the cinema regularly and often and occasionally to the theatre. She and I often spent a day in town lunching in Coplands, an elegant department store where a trio of ladies played genteel background music. In fact it seems that we lived a more comfortable and much less demanding life than the young families that I know nowadays.

I seem to remember that my mother mentioned that the very nice lunch (brown soup, braised sweetbreads with carrots, ice cream and fruit) cost something like one shilling and threepence. For those whose youth limits their knowledge to decimal money, one shilling was one twentieth of a pound. Thus the meal cost one sixteenth of a pound or one sixty-fourth of my Father's weekly income. Because of inflation, it is difficult to compare those costs of long ago, but you might like to do a comparative sum on your calculator the next time you have a three course lunch in elegant surroundings with uniformed waitress service, sparkling linen, fresh flowers and live music.

Of course so much depends on your income.

Obviously Chips Cannon was not eating sweetbreads at one and thruppence a shot after his morning's shopping. My parent's expenditure was very modest compared to Mr Cannon's, yet we lived in moderate comfort. *How did he manage to spend so much in a morning?* I do wish he had itemised his purchases! And his lunch afterwards. What did he eat and what did it cost?

We talk about the Great Divide nowadays but surely it must have been even greater then. At four pounds a week we felt far above the poverty which surrounded us. My father talked of the unimaginable closes and dens of the Gallowgate where his employees lived in miserably unfit conditions with no hope of improving themselves. Perhaps Chips regretted his two hundred pound-a-day shopping spree but it did not seriously damage his financial position. What was his weekly income? I expect his friends were not much less well off than he was, although no doubt there were plenty of hangers-on and scroungers in his life.

It was Chips' diary entry that partly inspired this piece of writing, for I do think that money and the spending of it and the inequality of its distribution is a fascinating subject. Is it really true that 'the rich get rich and the poor get poorer'?

Incidentally the law forbade any increases to the modest rent my parents paid for the Hyndland flat between 1920 and 1954. Inflation meant that by the 50s this rent was ridiculously low, making it impossible for landlords to maintain the buildings adequately and tenement flats came on the market at very modest prices. My father was able to buy our three-roomed flat in 1959 for £800 which at the time might equal one year's salary of a young professional man in his thirties. Within six years it was sold for £3000, possibly three times what that same professional man might hope to earn annually. For a lot of my life the subject of money was never discussed, which seems strange when it is such a vital part of existence. Wages were often a secret which husbands kept from their wives. They may still do so for all I know. I hope not. I was given a weekly threepence from an early age but when I became a parent, I did not give my first two children any financial independence when they were young. I did not care to hear five and six year-olds drooling over how much cash they had and this happened quite a lot in Hyndland in the sixties. But with my third and fourth child, I changed my philosophy, realising that in order to deal with money, you must have it in the first place. Each of my four daughters had a weekly allowance from which fines would be deducted for untidiness or chores missed. They also had a modest dress allowance from the age of twelve though I still bought the basics. If they wanted something special but unaffordable they could withdraw a future allowance but the books had to balance eventually. My banking system meant extra work and I admit it was not perfect but I think it helped the girls' awareness of money matters. Many families in Hyndland at that time had two generous salaries entering the home and some children were spoiled. I was a single parent who could not afford to have my children make expensive mistakes. One only learns how ephemeral cash is by making mistakes. Once you see how easily it disappears, you should, if you have any sense, learn how to hang on to it for necessities, or for what you deem necessities.

Anthony Trollope is one of the few nineteenth century writers who talks about money. He tells us what people earn and what things cost and it makes his story much more real. I thought I would like in my writing to note down some of the daily costs, which have changed so much in my long lifetime.

Long lifetime! That was the other spur to write this piece. Last week I had my seventy-fifth birthday. Nobody really believes that they will ever be seventy-five. It seems an incredible age. I know of people that are eighty, ninety, one hundred and two but for me, Nanzie, to be seventy-five is hard to accept.

I consider myself lucky to be still physically fit and without aches, very loose jointed and able to swim a kilometre. Long may this last.

UNFINISHED BUSINESS

Jill sat at the end of the back pew in the Memorial Chapel with her soft wide-brimmed hat pulled well over her face, as if to achieve as much anonymity as possible. She had no experience of crematoriums and she had arrived early, partly to find her way around, more especially to avoid encounters with the other mourners. Jill considered that Memorial Chapel was a rather pretentious name for the small bland room with its overpowering amount of shiny brown wood and the awkwardly curved end wall, presumably meant to simulate an apse. A monumental yellow vase full of lilies and other stiff flowers mixed their perfume with the strong smell of polish. Beside the modest reading desk was a low platform set at right angles to the wall. Where it touched the wall hung a small crimson curtain. Jill thought it looked just about the right size for a puppet theatre. She regarded the curtain for several minutes in the complete silence of the chapel. The platform was where the coffin would rest and presumably the curtain concealed the exit? The exit to the... *furnace*? If that was what it was called. The furnace. *The fiery furnace*. What evocations her mind was conjuring up. She remembered the myriad of lurid details in a painting by Hieronymous Bosch which had disturbed her sleep when a schoolgirl. She had never quite considered the implications of cremation before. As a member of a long-lived family, death of a loved one had never touched her. And what was the alternative to cremation? Worms and decay. No she did not care for those thoughts much either.

Now, she really must stop thinking like that. Why had she come here today? That was a much more demanding topic to consider. Just *exactly why* was she here? She knew that later her daughters would certainly be interrogative and they might be cross. She could imagine their questions and her own unsatisfactory answers. Their genuine, if diluted, grief at their father's death would not abate their curiosity in the least.

What *were* her motives at this late date? For it was twenty years since her marriage to Jack had crumbled.

Jack and Jill. Everyone had thought them such a wonderfully happy couple, though never failing to make the obvious remarks about hills, pails of water and broken crowns. And it had been an uphill struggle, with Jack suffering damage to his crown on several occasions, figuratively speaking, and Jill always ready to apply the psychological vinegar and brown paper. Jill kept hoping that they might find a modest 'hill' on which to settle and enjoy their youth and family, but Jack would so often be allured by yet another misty mountain. There was a boyish charm about his obsessive enthusiasm for the new and unknown. It was one of the things that had first attracted her to him. He was so completely joyful and fulfilled when researching and planning ahead. Jack was at his very best when 'Starting Afresh'. Unfortunately this was at complete variance to Jill's character. A sense of establishment was important to her and she had little need for adventure. Their marriage had been tough going and yet, at one time, they had loved each other. Jill was sure of that. And they had such lovely children. Really an ideal family. No one could believe it when Jack, after fifteen years, walked away to start a New Life in Canada. Least of all Jill. But Jack wanted to find himself and indeed it was a very popular thing to do in the seventies, that decade of the 'Me Generation'.

Jill suffered some years of sadness and feelings of rejection but the task of parenting the children and earning enough to create a comfortable life kept her too busy for self-pity. A handsome young lover helped her self esteem enormously. After three years, however, she decided that her girls and her career did not leave enough energy for romance and her life was sufficiently fulfilled without the young Adonis, who soon found another mature intelligent divorcee with children.

As Jill grew older, she felt relieved that she did not have to deal with the strange quirks and illogicalities of the male animal. Those eccentricities, exaggerated by age, were becoming only too apparent in the husbands of her social group and she sometimes caught a glimpse of envy in the eye of a married friend. The solitary state had many benefits.

So why was she here today? Unfinished business?

Just then two uniformed men entered, talking quite loudly until they noticed Jill sitting in the corner. Even then, they scarcely moderated their voices. Surely officials should show a little more sensitivity. It was all in the day's work to them she supposed but she might have been in the throes of great sorrow and distress.

The men were showing signs of distress themselves as they seemed to have lost something. They were searching through all their pockets. Then they left the chapel by a different door which Jill had not noticed before.

"A little more reverence and peace would be desirable," thought Jill.

Soon the men returned.

"Have ye no' goat ony?" the tall thin one shouted across the pews to his colleague.

"Naw, Ah cannae find ony." returned the small plump one with a note of desperation in his voice.

Again they went out and almost immediately returned. They whispered together and seemed very agitated. The tall one approached Jill.

"Excuse me, m'm," he spoke quickly, "D'ye have sich a thing as a match?"

"No, I'm sorry I don't."

"Oh it duzny matter, never mind."

He looked at his friend and shrugged helplessly. Then both left the hall again hurriedly. Jill sat there stunned. What did they need a match for? Did they want a quick cigarette before the service began? Or was it something much more vital to the morning's work? Could it be possible that they needed a match to light the furnace? Would they approach a *mourner* for the means of incinerating the corpse of their nearest and dearest? Surely not... that would be beyond belief. In another few minutes, Jill became aware of a distant hum. The furnace was alight. Jill remembered that Shakespeare had introduced clowns to his tragedies and she felt pleased to place these two characters in the scheme of things.

But why was she here? Perhaps she knew now. Yes, she was meeting a deadline. The last deadline in this instance.

Jill's married life, with an ambitious and changeable

husband and an ever-growing family, had consisted of meeting a succession of almost impossible deadlines, usually just at the last minute. She prided herself that she had, almost always, met them. Jack had accused her of manufacturing deadlines and perhaps in some small domestic ways she had. A kinder husband might have complimented her on her self-discipline.

Yes, that was it. She shivered with the realisation. She was here today because it was a last chance for her to be a part of Jack's life.

Or death.

While having no religious beliefs about the sanctity of marriage, Jill knew that Jack, as the father of her children, was the man in the world with whom she had most in common. Twelve years ago, he had deprived her of the power to share in his life. Now she would assert her right to share in his death.

She felt a faint flush of satisfaction, and was immediately ashamed.

Jill consciously relaxed her shoulders as though to slip off her feelings of guilt. Pulling her hat down firmly over her eyes, she looked around at the sad walls.

A group of five men filed into the chapel and moving carefully as if to make as little noise as possible, arranged themselves in the third row from the front. When an umbrella dropped with a clatter some of them jumped visibly. One smiled slightly. They spoke to each other seldom and in hushed voices.

Who were these men? Jill recognised none of them. They were certainly behaving with sad decorum.

Perhaps she herself should have felt more reverential or solemn at such a time, but after acting so impulsively in coming here today, she was glad to have clarified her own motives. She had followed her instincts and she was pleased that she had done so.

Jack had always said that she was instinctive but she never knew if he meant it as a compliment or otherwise.

Another three people came in and chose seats in the fourth row. Then, after a short discussion, they moved back two rows. Jill did not know them either, some very distant relatives perhaps. They talked and were more restless than the first group.

Then Jack's mother Eunice, arrived, escorted by his much younger brother Grant and Mona, his droopy wife. Eunice noticed Jill immediately and gave a nod and then a shake of the head with a twist of her lips which was almost a smile. Well into her eighties, she looked sad and disbelieving but dry-eyed. Suddenly, Jill felt the first real pangs of sadness that day.

How terrible to see your first born child die before your own life came to an end. Jill's eyes filled with tears of sympathy for Eunice. In some ways Jill and her mother-in-law had grown closer since the marriage had broken up. Jill had seen no reason to deprive her children of a grandparent, nor why Eunice should miss out on the delights of her charming grandchildren. The two women skirted the subject of Jack as much as possible and got on well together.

Jack had been paying one of his rare visits to Scotland when he had suffered the fatal heart attack. He had brought Dinah, his third wife, over to meet his daughters and mother. It was typical of Jack to expect the meeting to bring pleasure to everyone.

"Perhaps I am quite cold and hard," thought Jill, "I have not thought about how much sadness my daughters may be suffering and I haven't considered Dinah at all."

But she could not take Dinah's sorrow too seriously. Dinah had twitched Jack away from his second wife in a fairly bare-faced way and Jack was her fourth husband.

Just then Dinah arrived, sobbing noisily under a large black veil, such as members of the Royal family wear at funerals. She was supported on either side by Lorna and Helen, Jill's two daughters, who had met Dinah for the first time the previous week. The two girls looked remote and embarrassed.

"I know they are hating this situation but how very smart they both look in black." thought Jill, then immediately castigated herself. "What a hard unfeeling person I must be. I am so completely objective. I feel like an invisible spectator. But I am not invisible and I dread the moment when the girls notice me. Why did I come here? *What will I say to them?*"

The three women seated themselves in the front pew and Jill's momentary panic subsided.

The minister took his place in the pulpit and the coffin was carried in and deposited on the platform by several men, also strangers to Jill. Were these new friends of Jack's or were they hired coffin carriers? Jill suspected the latter and again accused herself of lack of charity.

During the non-denominational service the minister spoke kind words of the man about whom he obviously knew nothing. Inevitably he made a few blunders. In referring to Dinah's deep sorrow he suggested that the support of her beautiful daughters would be invaluable at this time of trouble. Dinah was hardly five years older than Lorna and the stiffening of her back and the stretching of her neck showed her insulted feelings. Lorna and Helen showed a similar offence. This was all that Jill could see from the back row, but she expected the minister had a battery of indignant eyes fixed on him. Probably those behind the black veil would be fiercest.

After a tape was played of two sentimental Scottish songs, the congregation sang "Abide with Me" in the usual hesitant manner. Then the curtains swished aside with a little rattle and the coffin disappeared soundlessly and electronically through the aperture, which was immediately covered again by the crimson velvet. A silence ensued and Jill had to stifle her strong visual imagination.

"How distastefully theatrical," she thought, "Must remember to say that I do not want my coffin to disappear at my funeral. All those evocations of taking a last curtain call, or heading for the fiery furnace."

Then she remembered the men and the matches and smiled inwardly.

Outside in the bright icy day, Jill kissed Eunice, nodded to her daughters, avoided Grant and Mona and left as quickly as possible.

Strangely, her daughters never did mention the funeral or her presence at it.

✧◆✧

It was some months later that Jill bumped into Grant in Sauchiehall street. After asking how Eunice was and Mona and the children, Jill broached the subject of the funeral.

"Where did you - ah - scatter the... ?"

"The ashes? Oh I didn't," replied Grant "Life has been just too hectic with us, as per usual. You know how things go!"

He gave an apologetic smile that was reminiscent of his brother. Jill suffered a slight pang at the resemblance.

"I don't know if you heard but Mona is pregnant again... and... eh... "

"Oh... yes... good." although Jill was not sure if a sixth child warranted congratulations.

"Yes, well, it's rather awkward really, as we feel that our marriage, just like yours, has started to disintegrate... and... "

"It was only Jack that felt the disintegration, but never mind. I'm really sorry. Mind you, I've never thought that Mona could be very joyful to live with and all the problems of a big family too..." her voice trailed away and a silence developed.

"I expect Dinah would really like to have them sent out to Canada."

"What?" Grant was completely bewildered, still contemplating his children's future.

"The ashes I mean, Jack's ashes."

"Oh yes! well no, not really. She was so distraught, you know and keen to get back home and see her lawyer."

"Yes, I bet, I mean I expect so. It must have been such a shock."

"Yes, poor girl. So she left it up to me, just to do what I thought was best."

Another silence.

"What about Eunice?"

"Oh no, the ashes would just upset her, I think. She seems wonderful but I can't manage to get up north to visit her just now, of course, when everything is so unsettled and... well you know how it is."

Another awkward pause,

"Where are the ashes?" asked Jill.

"Still with the funeral directors, just round the corner there."

He indicated the marble-front of the long-established Glasgow firm which had carried rich and not so rich to the cemetery in black Daimlers for nearly a century.

Grant grinned boyishly, reminding her again vividly of Jack when life became difficult.

"They said they would keep them for me until I wanted them."

"Oh well, I'll be in touch. I hope things work out for you."

She hurried off with an uncomfortable feeling of deceit. She had no intention of keeping in touch.

◇◆◇

Five years passed by. Each time Jill drove along Sauchiehall Street, it was in her mind that there in that imposing office, lay all that remained of Jack, unwanted and uncared for.

The thought would nag for a mile or two and then she would forget until the next time she drove past. Jack had once said accusingly,

"You and your bloody conscience!"

But her conscience could not be too demanding, for she thought less and less of him as the years passed.

The girls were maturing now and seemed to have conquered the emotional scars resulting from their parents' breakup. Lorna was thirty-five with her own little boy and a large devoted teddy bear of a husband. Helen had a hard-working husband, three little girls and a thriving interior design practice. In fact they seemed to have made very happy and successful lives for themselves. Jack was seldom mentioned in her presence.

But each time Jill drove past the Funeral Director, she felt a tiny stab of guilt.

It was nearly fifteen years since Jack's death and Jill was in town without her car. She found herself walking past the familiar shiny marble frontage and impulsively walked into the hushed and sympathetic foyer. She gave Jack's name, her own name and the date of the funeral all those years ago to a dark-suited, lugubrious young man and was asked to wait for a few minutes.

Perhaps Grant had eventually collected the remains for Eunice. Poor Eunice herself was now dust. Possibly Dinah had sent for the ashes and scattered them on the shores of Lake Ontario, but that was unlikely. No communication had ever come from Dinah, only a regretful letter from her lawyer,

explaining in obscure legal language why there was no settle-
ment from Jack's estate for his daughters.

Through the tangible silence of the thickly carpeted foyer
Jill was aware of the distant traffic. She felt a shiver of
apprehension. What would she say if the ashes had already
been collected. How awkward it would be and what sort of
explanation could she give?

A swing door brushed open and the deferential young
man presented her with a parcel about the size of a shoebox,
neatly wrapped in white paper.

Jill walked out into the noisy city and wondered what on
earth she was going to do now. It seemed irreverent to drag
Jack's earthly remains around Marks and Spencers. She
decided to forgo her shopping expedition and go straight
home.

She put the box, still wrapped, into the bottom drawer of
the small chest of drawers beside her bed. This drawer held a
conglomeration of souvenirs: Lorna's first doll, a Christmas
musical box, a small sketch book from a Greek holiday, a
magazine which had run a feature on Helen's unusual home,
odds and ends of out-dated make up and several little hand
made gifts from her grandchildren.

For the next three years the white-wrapped box sat neatly
in a corner of that drawer of memories.

Jill was, as yet, unwilling to admit to more than late
middle age. She was still working, still social, still very
active but various small annoying signs of age were making
themselves felt. Though her hair was still thick and brown,
her feet, which had tramped so continuously and so willingly
for over sixty years with little or no heed, were starting to
complain and need a little attention. On holiday in the
Highlands, she found herself quite lame after three days'
walking. Obviously a half hearted rub with a pumice stone
twice a week was no longer enough. Lorna, a mine of practical information on all subjects, suggested regular creaming
and also the use of an implement of thin wood with heavy
emery board on each side and immediately supplied her
mother with these necessities.

"It's called a foot-file and use it *before* the bath," Lorna
advised in her omniscient way, "Use it when your feet are dry,

it works much better. Then be generous with the cream, *after the bath.*"

Lorna was, as usual, right. The file was a little miracle worker and with hardly any effort, Jill was able to remove the unsightly and painful bumps on her toes and heels. As she worked, with quite a feeling of enjoyment, she noticed an almost invisible dusting of particles of dry skin accumulating on the green vinyl of the bathroom floor. Being a saving sort of person, Jill bent down and pushed the pale grey substance into a little pile with the edge of her hand. She had grown up in the lean years after the war, when it was a crime to waste anything and though it was only a very small amount, she considered momentarily whether it might make good nourishment for a potted plant.

Then, in a flash, Jill knew exactly what was the right thing to do. Fetching a sheet of notepaper, she carefully collected the fine powder and carried it into her bedroom.

In moments, torn white paper littered the floor and the open box lay beside her on the bed where she sat. Solemnly and with a sense of completion, Jill added the minute quantity of whitish dust to the very similar powder in the small plastic bag which the box had contained.

As she did so, she whispered triumphantly,

"And in Death they were not Divided".

KENSPECKLE FIGURES

When a friend recently applied the adjective kenspeckle to me, I felt vaguely insulted. I had always known the word but never used it. Mistakenly I would have defined it as describing a degree of eccentricity, even absurdity. On looking it up I found I had misunderstood it for all these years. My friend had been complimenting me.

> Kenspeckle; adjective <u>Scottish</u> easily recognisable; conspicuous. – ORIGIN mid 16th century: of Scandinavian origin, probably based on old Norse <u>kenna</u> 'know, perceive' and <u>spak-</u>, <u>spek-</u> 'wise or wisdom'.

I could live with that. I liked it.

G12 has always had its full complement of kenspeckle figures.

They were there in my youth and are still there, though nowadays, those with a real claim to fame, have learned to preserve their incognito by assuming the ubiquitous fashion of worn and wasted jeans and thus disappear into the crowd of middle class pseudo labourers. How different was that film star of the 50s that I describe in another story with her Daimler, dark glasses and ankle-length mink!

What constitutes a kenspeckle figure? Possibly their way of dressing or the indefinable air with which they carry themselves makes them instantly recognisable at a distance. One should know something of their standing or repute (*perceive and wisdom*). They should be an ikon which declares their place in the world as soon as you spot them. Though film and television have created a plethora of easily recognisable celebrities, I do not believe fame is an absolute necessity.

My music teacher, Elizabeth Main, was a perfect example of a kenspeckle figure in G12. It was partly due to her unforgettable features, for she was no beauty. Let me paint her for

you. Her large face had small close-set eyes and an extra long
upper lip. Her black hair was dragged unforgivingly back
from a middle parting, smooth and shining and might have
been painted on. Not tall, she favoured dramatic dressing.
Rich colours, flowing capes and enormous silver brooches
camouflaged but could not hide her impressive bust. She
walked purposefully and sternly through Hyndland for many
years and no doubt through Lambhill where she taught. (I
believe the school children called her 'Geronimo'). As well as
her large and splendid service flat in Sydenham Road, she
had a cottage in Ardnamurchan, though I find it difficult to
picture her in that bucolic environment. She gave me my first
and only piano lessons, choosing simple but delightful music
for me to study. Despite her intimidating expression, she was
probably too kind a teacher, though as a late starter, I was
very keen and worked hard.

As secretary of the Glasgow Chamber Music Society, Miss
Main was instrumental in introducing some world class
performers to Glasgow in the fifties. I listened to the Amadeus
String Quartet give a marvellous concert in the McLellan
Galleries and was honoured to be introduced to them later that
evening in Sydenham Road.

Though she was the kindest and sweetest of friends, there
was an aura of power about Elizabeth Main which enhanced
her unusual appearance. I suspect she would have been just as
at home in the musical world of Paris or New York. She will
always be my *beau ideal* of a kenspeckle figure.

Until recently, the BBC had its headquarters in G12 so it was
a convenient area for its employees to live. Our witty local radio
host Fred Macaulay started his married life in Hyndland and
newsreaders, presenters, musicians, actors well known and not
so well known might be glimpsed, shopping or leading their
humdrum everyday lives in Great Western Road, Hyndland or
Highburgh Road. The Curlers pub and the Ubiquitous Chip
restaurant in Byres Road were favourite haunts. That busy street
now has a plethora of eating places and coffee shops which
must be sadly missed by those TV and radio exiles now based
on the south of the Clyde. Perhaps their splendidly palatial new
building and the excellent fish suppers at Harry Ramsden make
some recompense for the loss of Byres Road.

In the sixties and seventies, my mother-in-law, an avid TV fan, would be disappointed if she had not encountered at least one well-known personality while out for an afternoon walk with her grandchildren. She was thrilled that I had actually met a TV celebrity socially one evening, but I did not tell her how boring he had seemed. Even his wife did not smile at his jokes. But that was long ago.

Cliff Hanley was another face that my mother-in-law often triumphantly spotted in the sixties, for literary folk have also been drawn to G12. Nowadays the poetic playwright Liz Lochhead lives across the road, and at least two folk dwelling in my own tenement write. Frank McKee describes the esoteric advance of modern art and Roddy Woomble, as well as composing the poetic words for his songs, has a charming quirky literary style which I trust he will develop and enlarge. I have suggested we call our corner the Writers' Block.

I am sure there are many more scribblers living in G12 and I apologise for not mentioning them.

Ann Laird has produced a comprehensive factual account of Hyndland, full of fascinating details and charming old photographs. The idea of this area being countryside rather than tall red sandstone building is difficult to comprehend. Although Ann describes it as an Edwardian suburb, I was intrigued to learn from her book that my tenement was one of the first to be built and that it was given planning permission in the 1890s, so was actually Victorian. How strange it must have been to live in this great pile with a wide view of lonely countryside. I try to imagine it but fail.

Yes, kenspeckle figures should be immediately apparent. Unfortunately the species has almost disappeared. As I have already said, everybody seems to strive, and succeed, in looking similarly dull and unimportant.

Yes, I have seen Ewan McGregor standing beside me in a patisserie and I nearly bumped into Robert Carlyle outside my grocers but it was only at second glance that I recognised either. Neither fell into the category of a kenspeckle figure but perhaps one cannot blame the famous for maintaining a low profile in everyday life.

As I walked up Clarence Drive the other day, I spotted a truly kenspeckle figure in the distance. Could it be the person

I thought it was, as he strode towards me with his abundant flying white hair and beard? Was it really that important person? Or was I mistaken? Could it be? Surely not. As we drew near, I decided not to look at him but at the last minute my curiosity proved too strong. I glanced towards him and he was looking steadily at me! As soon as we made eye contact, he shouted a cheerful,

"Hullo there!"

Was it really Billy Connolly? He looked like him at close range and the voice was right. But what was he speaking to me for?

Did he, too, recognise a kenspeckle figure when he saw one?

CREATIVE WRITING

Bridget was nearly forty and worked as a clerk in the City of Glasgow council offices. She dealt with council tax problems and it was not a difficult job but it was repetitive and it required her to turn down a lot of requests, which she found dispiriting. It would have been more pleasant to help people, rather than tell them they still owed money. Not that it was all bad news, but she hated to see a client walk slowly away from the counter, gazing sadly at a bill as though there might still be an overlooked detail. Sometimes she dreamed of more positive employment, perhaps in a glamorous dress shop where satisfied customers, wearing pleased excited smiles, waved to her as they carried off large parcels. That was just a fantasy. Bridget had always had a great imagination, for her own life left a lot to be desired. Born with one leg a little shorter than the other, she walked with a limp. She also spoke with a slight stammer. Perhaps the limp had caused the stammer. Perhaps her mother's early death had contributed. Her father died when she was twenty and Marie, her sister, twenty-two. His death left the two girls in a very shaky financial state but they were both hard workers and were settled in respectable if unexciting jobs. By the time Bridget was thirty, they lived a secure if mundane life. Bridget was content for she had learned to search for the best in all situations and if there was no best, she escaped to an alternative imaginary world.

The two girls had lived all their lives in the flat in Dudley Drive and had both attended the large school which was further up the hill. Marie hated the noise the children made when they came out of school and constantly complained about their rudeness and untidiness, but Marie tended to complain about most things. Bridget liked to see the young people for it reminded her of her own schooldays. She had been a bright, intelligent pupil, well appreciated by her teachers. When she saw the children laughing and pushing each other around as they trailed slowly to school each morning, she was reminded of her own youth. Not that there was so much horseplay in her day, but it looked friendly. She had read voraciously throughout her childhood and specially enjoyed English classes with Mrs Macdonald, who commended her vivid essays and did not insist on her reading aloud too often. The school was disappointed that Bridget did not continue with tertiary education, but at the time her father and Marie had decided it would be too difficult financially.

Bridget loved their Dudley Drive flat and often gloated.

"Isn't it *lucky* Mum and Dad bought this flat when they did. We could never afford it nowadays."

Marie would grunt, then after a moment grumble,

"I'd move tomorrow if I could. I'm fed up with constant plumbing bills and noisy kids and as for those damned parked cars outside, they'll drive me crazy, you can hardly get across the road."

Like the other side roads in the area, Dudley Drive was overpowered by parked cars. Sixteen trees planted in the railed grassy centre plat of the short street aggravated the problem. Marie also complained about the trees, finding them too shady in the summer and the fallen leaves a nuisance in the autumn. Bridget thought the trees pretty at all times and believed they added great charm to the street.

Apart from Bridget's personal memories, she knew that their flat was *very special*. During the second world war, a landmine had completely demolished several tenements in the street and one of those had been on the very spot where they now lived. On the night of the terrible Clydebank Blitz, by mistake or bad judgement, four landmines were dropped on this residential area which had nothing of industrial importance. There was considerable loss of life in the west end that night with thirty six killed and many injured in Dudley Drive and over fifty killed less than a mile away.

Eventually the tenements were replaced by new, red sandstone buildings, which, because of shortages, were less decorative than the original, though now, sixty years later only an observant passer-by might notice the variation.

Bridget had always been fascinated by the idea that she lived exactly where such destruction and death had happened all those years ago. Few buildings could boast of such a history. Sometimes she imagined the terror, noise and screams, dust and smoke of that fearful night as clearly as if she had lived through it herself. Then she pictured the rebuilding of their block amidst the rubble and broken bits of furniture. As she grew older she realised that was nonsense, but found it hard to discard the image. She often wondered what had happened to those people who had experienced such a night of horror. Had it changed them forever? Or were they just glad to survive? Perhaps only desperate to find a new home and try to live their lives again as normally as possible. Most of them would be dead now, she supposed, though there was a story of a teenage boy who was buried in the debris for more than forty-eight hours. He might still be alive. How she would love to meet him and hear his story.

As Bridget's fortieth birthday approached, she decided, as so many people do at forty, to branch out and try something new. She decided to enrol in a creative writing course at Glasgow University and asked Sandra at work if she would like to join her but Sandra shook her head decisively. When she made the same suggestion to Marie, she sniffed and said nothing so Bridget went by herself.

For twenty years Bridget's daily bus journey had taken her past the various impressive buildings in University Avenue and it was a disappointment to find that the classes would be held in a ramshackle terrace house in Southpark Avenue. She had hoped to sit in a real lecture theatre. However, the old house was interesting and as there were only twelve students, the room was quite large enough. The lecturer was a tall self-confident lady called Pam who smiled at the group in front of her,

"Good evening, ladies and *gentleman*. As usual, I see the weaker sex is predominant but that makes *your* presence all the more welcome."

She beamed at the bearded young fellow who huddled unhappily in his seat at the back of the room.

"I shall look to *you* for an interesting masculine approach."

The rest of the group, mostly well-dressed ladies in their sixties, turned to smile and nod to the young man who gazed steadily at the notebook in front of him without responding, though his ears turned bright red.

The woman beside Bridget, who was more her own age, nudged her gently, made a 'cringe making' face and whispered.

"Poor git."

Rather confusingly Pam started talking about the Impressionist painters of the nineteenth century and Bridget wondered if she had come to the wrong room.

"With the invention of the camera, the traditional way of painting pictures *died*. The artist with his ever creative mind must find a *new way* of expressing himself. Why should painters continue to work so painstakingly when the camera could capture every detail in a moment? Photographs often showed a *cropped* picture. Perhaps only *part* of a figure was caught in the frame, perhaps *only* a head and shoulders. Painters found this *releasing* and *inspiring* and started to edit and chop their compositions in the same way. And it worked *marvellously*! Renoir, Cezanne, Manet..."

Pam talked on for quite a long time about painters and their philosophy, about which Bridget knew very little. She wondered if the camera could really take the blame for everything that had happened in the art world. It seemed too simple an explanation. Besides, the way that Pam spoke sounded affected and dogmatic and Bridget had noticed that people tended to be most dogmatic when they were least sure of their position. However she was here to learn, whether it was about painting or writing and she must keep an open mind.

"And now, dear class, we must look at how the Arts *influence* and give *sustenance* to each other. Quite soon, this idea of editing and chopping spread to other areas of artistic endeavour, literature in particular. Editing and chopping became *the rage*!"

"She likes big words, and lots of them, doesn't she." whispered Bridget's neighbour. "Shame I forgot to bring a notebook."

Though Bridget had one with her, it remained blank as long as painting was the subject, though the rest of the class scribbled assiduously.

It seemed that Pam spoke for a long time and many names of authors of short stories were added to the list of painters. Conrad, de Maupassant, Kafka and Turgenev were all mentioned. The names were foreign and unfamiliar and Bridget started to feel confused. Nothing was said about some of Bridget's favourite writers. Not a word about Anthony Trollope, Somerset Maugham or Jack London.

"Of course there was the old fashioned idea that there should be a *twist* at the end of a tale, as in O Henry, but..." Pam paused and shrugged as though there was nothing good to say about that.

They learned that their first assignment would be a short story of two thousand words, to be completed in four weeks.

"Perhaps you have tried to write a story before?" she raised her eyebrows and looked around the class. One or two simpered and nodded, "*However* as this is your first attempt for my eyes, I shall give you *very exact instructions* concerning your *method* of writing... and indeed *preparing* to write it."

Bridget's neighbour nudged her,

"Don't like the sound of that much!"

Pam noted the whispered interruption and paused with her eyes downcast before continuing. She emphasised that she considered Chekhov very important. Influenced by the Impressionists, he often chopped off the first and last sentence or even paragraph of a story. He shared this strange habit with someone called Katherine Mansfield. Bridget had not heard of either but Pam advised them to read all they could of these two.

"They provide a literary watershed which you must learn to appreciate thoroughly. Eventually we will study more modern authors, Angela Carter with her wicked magic and Nick Carver with his splendid sparcity of prose though we have recently learned some *sadly unsettling* facts about that..." her face expressed grief as her voice trailed away "... but never mind, I suggest you choose one author of short stories, the choice is yours, and read as much as you can of that author in the *first week*. Do not even *think* about what you are going to write until the second week. In the *second week* start considering but *do not discuss your thoughts* and *write nothing down.* Just keep reading the works of your chosen author and *mull* over any ideas for your story in your head. I suggest you *mull* while lying in a hot bath! Very inspiring! Only in the third week should you stop reading and start writing. *Do not copy the style of your chosen author,* though possibly your story will have inadvertent echoes. Don't worry. Eventually you will find your *own voice!* Yes?"

A lady in a good tweed suit had raised a hand to ask if two weeks was enough for a two thousand word story.

"I'm sure it is. But do not worry if it is not quite so long. Next?"

"Does spelling matter?" there was a ripple of laughter.

"I expect your spell-check will help you there."

"I'm afraid I always write in longhand."

"Oh! Well, never mind. Yes?"

"I'm sorry, I've forgotten what I..."

"Next... is that everything? Just one more word of advice. It's a good idea to make the first sentence of your story have *great impact.* It should grab the reader's attention. Hit him between the eyes! It's *never too soon to start thinking* about that all-important first sentence!"

As they left the shabby room, Bridget's neighbour spoke to her.

"Bit of a drama queen, isn't she! My name's Hilda and I'm a nurse and I don't see how the hell you can think up a first sentence before you know what the story is about, do you? D'ye fancy going for a coffee?"

"Love a coffee. Yes, and then when you've written your story, what if you decide to chop that sentence off, like old whatisname?"

They walked down to the Left Bank coffee shop and laughed a lot as they criticised Pam's tone and advice, both agreeing that the necessity of writing a story was the best part of the course.

"I've always meant to write, but never quite got round to it."

"Me too."

✧✦✧

That first week, Bridget selected a book of Chekhov short stories from the library and read until 2am each night.

Though some words seemed wrongly used, that could have been the translator's fault. If Chekhov had ever tried the hit-you-between-the-eyes first sentence, he had certainly later cut it in one story which started,

"All Olga's friends and acquaintances were at her wedding."

Bridget would have chopped that without a moment's hesitation.

Another was called 'A Boring Story'. And it certainly was and sixty pages long. One was about a married woman who almost, but not quite, had a love affair. Bridget was unsure of what had actually happened in the story and found it very unsatisfactory. Most of the stories were unsatisfactory in one way or another. She could not really believe in the characters and there was a lot of sadness which was depressing. Surely the translator was to blame.

Eventually she brought out her well-thumbed Somerset Maugham and comforted herself by reading 'The Letter' and 'The Three Fat Women of Antibes'.

She reached the end of the first week with no ideas for that introductory sentence.

✧◆✧

"Now my dear literary pupils, this week you must start *thinking,* not writing, only thinking, musing, considering and *planning* your story. Forget what you have read! Put it out of your mind. And *not a word down on paper!"*

She gazed for a few moments at the bearded man who continued to scribble, then sighed and continued.

"I am sure you have heard the old advice to write always about things *in your own experience.* To write only of what you know!" Pam shook her head vigorously, she would certainly have none of that.

"No!" She often started a sentence with the word 'no'.

"No! Never write a catalogue of your own boring, minimal life. Do not let your story be something like a letter home to Mummy. Let your imagination *soar.* This week I want you to let your mind experience the Joy of Creation. You have the power to go *anywhere,* to be *anyone,* to do *anything.* Make full use of the morbid, the gruesome, the sexual. Rip away that genteel curtain! Gaze into the abyss. Do not be afraid to shock your reader! The reader *loves* to be shocked! But remember, not a scratch of the pen or one touch on your laptop. It must *all be in the mind.*"

The nicely dressed elderly ladies sat in front of her and apart from a momentary tightening of the lips or a brief subliminal raising of the eyebrows, hardly one face showed any expression. The young man was bowed over his desk, writing steadily. Hilda nudged Bridget.

Undismayed by the lack of reaction, Pam, with a flourish of her impressive arms, continued,

"You must seek out and examine those dark corners that you have perhaps been afraid to peer into... heretofore."

Pam was very careful never to split an infinitive or finish a sentence with a preposition for there was bound to be a retired English teacher or two at the back of the class ready to pounce on any grammatic error. They probably attended the course for the sole purpose of superior nit-picking. Or perhaps they were spies? Pam knew her qualifications were minimal. Two plays and a self-published selection of short stories that Gilbert, her husband, had somewhat ungraciously bank-rolled. He had made it clear at the time that unless they recovered their investment, this was a one-off project. Not quite five hundred of the great rampart of books in the garage had now gone, some as presents admittedly. But with help from some of Gilbert's many contacts, she had been awarded this teaching job. Anyway, who could define the qualification for teaching creativity?

"No classes next week, but I will see you in a fortnight and I can hardly wait to read your work. Good luck to everyone!"

As they waited for their coffee Hilda asked,

"What d'ye think of all that morbid, sexual, gruesome stuff? Will you give it a try?"

"*I don't think so,*" Bridget laughed, "Wouldn't know where to start and I don't even like reading that sort of thing. Not interested. I suppose I want to write the sort of story that I would like to read myself. Though I don't exactly know what that is. I suppose I look for believability. I need to iden-tify. But then I love all sorts of adventure stories, situations where I would *never* find myself. What about you?"

"I suppose those lurid sexual ones are more likely to get published these days and I did try once, but... I suppose because I'm a nurse, it turned out more like a clinical report!"

They both laughed so much that people turned to look at them.

Bridget admitted.

"I have absolutely no idea what I'm going to write about. Have you?"

"Not really. And I think I have fewer story ideas than I had before I listened to Pam and read Katherine M. I enjoyed her stuff and I think you'd find it very real, but just not always... *enough* somehow. Sort of unfinished and leaving you wanting to know more."

"Too much chopping, I expect! Those Impressionists have a lot to answer for." Again they laughed.

By the fourth week, Bridget had written nothing at all. Her mind was a blank. She had read too much about spoiled aristocrats and miserable peasants in Russia and Pam's advice had only confused her.

"You'll be punished," Hilda warned," I expect you'll get lines or even the belt. Anyway, mine is rubbish and far too short. I wrote it last night. And no sign of our only man. Chickened out, the coward."

Pam looked displeased when she noticed his absence but made no comment as she shuffled through the pile of stories.

"No, ladies, do not worry. I shan't read them aloud nor shall I make any comment tonight on your work. I'll return them to you next week with some of my thoughts noted and then talk generally of the successes and errors. I don't expect to discover any Flannery O'Connors!"

Hilda and Bridget raised questioning eyebrows at each other at this unknown name.

"So I shan't be disappointed and one *never knows.*" Pam smiled encouragingly at the class and continued,

"This evening I want to talk to you about the *subconscious*. Remember, no matter how well you may plan your story beforehand, once you start writing, at some point, the subconscious will take over and then *beware of your careful construction*. I expect some of you may have already experienced this and it can be *unsettling* when, like a runaway horse, your story rushes off in its own direction. My advice is to *listen* to your subconscious, never fight it. Go with the flow. If it tells you to change a character or even the whole plot, pay attention. It probably knows more than you do!"

She spoke for an hour on this theme and Bridget felt more and more dazed. This was another problem to face, assuming she ever started to write at all.

Pam also advised them to start reading different authors now and explore more modern experimental writing.

"For the tenth and final week of the course, I want you to write another story, three thousand words and no more than that, please. Think carefully about this one, using all the ideas which we have discussed. In the meantime, I want you to try a very short piece for next week, one hundred and fifty words, more or less. Do not think it's easy to write an abbreviated piece," she bit her lip as she looked down at the pile of stories in front of her, most of them longer than the two thousand demanded, "So much easier to write one thousand than one hundred. Best of luck and *never be afraid!*"

They did not have coffee that night. Bridget went home and started to write. She headed her page,

Wicked Magic

"With one stroke of the very sharp knife, Susan cut off the pig's left ear. The pig shrieked loudly, then stood gazing at her in a sad offended way, moaning and breathing deeply. Susan noticed that the heavy rain had washed the top surface of the pig's vast mud-spattered body and her many teats showed clean and pink on her filthy belly. Each teat trembled slightly.

Susan stood deep in inches of stinking mud and her feet were freezing in the green wellies that had looked so shining and attractive in the shop window. The smell was abominable and the rain continued to pour down. Her wet hair streaked across her face as she contemplated the morsel of gristle and hairiness that she held in her hand. How was she to turn it into

*a tiny exquisite purse for the ball tonight? A perfect
purse, with beads, embroidered flowers and a purple
lining. A purse just large enough to hold a wisp of
lace handkerchief and the little programme with the
tiny tasselled pencil. How quickly the tall Hussars and
dashing princes would rush to initial her programme.
Every dance would be a triumph... but the problem
remained. Her delicate eyebrows frowned and her
small white teeth chewed her soft pink lip. How could
she make a silk..."*

Bridget had written quickly and used too many words but
where on earth had such strange nonsense come from? Had
she tapped into her subconscious? Yes, Bridget thought, she
was rather good at that 'hit you in the eye' start with lots of
description to follow, but it was only the beginning of a story.
Would Pam accept that? She had no idea how to finish it.
Any continuation of the plot eluded her.

At least she had *written something down* at last and she
slept well.

The following night she told Marie she was going to bed
early and her heading was *Morbid and Sexual*. She found
writing less easy this time and after several false starts,
considered changing those daunting words, but that seemed
like cheating. Eventually she again wrote quite quickly,

*"The blind prostitute, cold and soaking wet, sobbed as
she limped along the dark alleyway. All day the rain
had dropped down in large fat globules. Fumbling her
way along, her hand brushed against the rough, stone
wall until she reached the heavy iron door. Taking her
last coin from her pocket, she tapped out the code on
the metal panel...*
   tippy-tippy-tippy-TAP
TAP TAP TAP TAP.
*"A thin, bedraggled cat sat at the kerb and seemed
to watch her with mournful sympathy. The animal,
obsessed by its own hunger, hardly noticed that its rat-
like tail dipped in the filthy rushing waters of the
gutter.*

With a loud shrieking of hinges, the metal door
was thrown open, a large hand covered with thick red
hair emerged, grabbed the woman's emaciated arm
and hauled her roughly inside.
The cat slunk away, its empty belly dragging on
the wet, shining cobbles."

That was the required amount of words but again it was
only a start. Bridget was at a loss. How did one proceed? She
knew very little about prostitutes and the lives they lived
behind iron doors in alleyways. Pam had advised them to
explore and research the unknown.
"Research! Research! A few basic facts can *authenticate*
your story wonderfully! Be brave and work hard."
But where did one start researching the lives of those
miserable women? Police records or the Social Work
Department perhaps? She had no enthusiasm for such delving
and not at all sure that such research was possible, nor could
it ever give a true emotional picture. Had those two pieces of
writing been a complete waste of time? No, they had served a
purpose, for Bridget now realised what she wanted to write.
Rather than wildly sensational experiences of unfortunates
that she had never met, she wanted to give a true picture of
ordinary people who, found themselves unexpectedly in a
dramatic situation.
Suddenly she knew what her story would be. The possibilities of this story had hovered in her imagination all her
life. There was some research which she must do, but it
should be comparatively easy. No doubt Google would give
her enough information.
She started her story that night.

Jack was eleven. He sat underneath the massive
mahogany table and was completely happy. The heavy
chenille table cover which almost reached the floor on
all sides made it a perfect den. Beside him was the
large paper bag of little red apples that Uncle Bob had
brought. It was an annual custom that Jack receive his
share of the old tree's harvest and with the fruit
shortage this year, they were specially welcome. There

were thirty-five apples. Jack had laid them out in five rows of seven, then carefully replaced them in the carrier. They were hard, though very sweet and he was trusted not to eat too many at once. Jack hoped to make them last for two weeks for he was interested in rationing. Grown-ups spoke of little else. Tonight he would have a feast, for old Mrs Pierce upstairs had given him a bar of Duncan's Hazelnut chocolate for running a message and his father had brought in ginger beer. This evening would be perfect. His Meccano set was laid out in front of him and he had a brilliant idea for constructing a vehicle that no one else had ever thought of.

It was quiet in the room now and Jack could hear the extra fast clicking of his mother's knitting pins. They always went at top speed after the deafening shriek of the siren died away.

Mary was trembling as she knitted. The siren was sited on top of the nearby school and its inhuman wailing was loud, long and terrifying. She worried terribly about her husband Robin, out on ARP duty, ushering people off the streets, reproaching residents who showed a chink of light at their windows and encouraging others to seek safety in the damp smelly shelters. And few trusted them. It was so hard to know what was the best thing to do. Who had any idea what it would be like? Nothing had happened yet and it might never happen. She knew the people in the top flats came down to the back close for safety during an air raid, but that was cold and uncomfortable. Bombs were unlikely in this vicinity but there were terrible tales of the blast damage from quite distant explosions. Mary shivered and gazed at her grandmother's table. What a big ugly brute it was, she had never liked it, but Jack was protected from falling plaster or flying glass underneath it and he seemed so happy in his den. It did not occur to her to join her son.

Robin paused for a moment outside his own flat, tempted to pop in for a cup of tea. Although Dudley Drive seemed like a calm little backwater, there was a strange turbulence in the air. The branches of the trees moved restlessly, though there was no wind. Robin was aware of irregular, almost inaudible sounds in the distance, a faint pounding roar interrupted at intervals by dull thuds. He almost wondered if it was his imagination, but no, something was happening somewhere. He looked up at the clear sky. Not for the first time he considered what a hopeless task it was to attempt to camouflage this great city. Even the most complete blackout was useless on such a moonlit night, when the glitter of tramlines defined the streets and the Clyde was a shining, bright ribbon. The plan of the city must be instantly recognisable to enemy planes.

Just as Robin caught the sound of a lone aircraft high overhead, there were distant fire engine bells, probably racing along Dumbarton Road. Next, several heavy lorries thundered down Clarence Drive. He relinquished any hope of a cup of tea and returned to his duties.

The street returned to its uneasy silence. In the sky, a rough circle of four grey mushroom-shaped objects drifted gently and silently downwards. The large metal canister suspended from each parachute made it sway slightly in its descent. Each canister was eight feet in height and tightly packed with high explosives. One of them would completely wipe out of existence a large villa with its residents and contents. Another would drift south before bringing death to fifty people. The third would not explode on impact.

The fourth was slowly and fatefully heading for Dudley Drive.

FIRE

It was a normal autumnal Wednesday in 1977 that my daughters arrived home from school hungry for lunch. Hyndland was quiet, for in those days only the fish and chip shop furnished fast food and fewer schoolchildren thronged the streets at midday.

We ate in the quiet kitchen at the rear of the flat but, before our bowls of soup were half finished, I was aware of noisy excitement in the street. When we ran to the front door, police were cutting off access to Clarence Drive for normal traffic and folk were shouting as they ran down the hill. Within minutes two fire engines screeched round the corner from Hyndland Road and hurtled in the same direction. Another soon followed. A neighbour breathlessly informed us that the school was on fire.

The girls were astonished as it was hardly fifteen minutes since they had left the building. Regardless of maternal duties, I grabbed my cine camera and followed the crowd down the hill.

Hyndland Secondary School is built on a hill and consists of two buildings divided by a large playground. The fire had started in the lower building which was originally built as a primary school. I had started my schooling there in the thirties, with my two older daughters following in my footsteps in the sixties. Some smoke issued from the roof but there was nothing very dramatic to see at first. I felt quite emotional for I had spent most of my life in a flat just across the road, at 46 Clarence Drive.

As I made my way through the crowds of people who were gathering, I remembered the infant mistress, the well-named Miss Noble, telling me how upset my imaginative oldest daughter, Kate, had been when they had a practice firedrill one day. When the classes mustered in the playground, Kate was inconsolable, weeping hopelessly at the thought of never seeing her Mummy again. The fact that not a flame or wisp of smoke was in evidence and her home was in sight only a few hundred yards across the road, could not comfort her.

Just as I thought of that poignant memory, a sudden enormous burst of flame, together with vast billows of black smoke shot into the air from the roof of the school. It was a conflagration. I started to film.

A high extending ladder was in place and the crowd became quiet as the fireman climbed to the top and directed his hose. Sadly the water dribbled from the nozzle with less force than a kitchen tap, arching uselessly away from the firemen, quickly succumbing to gravity and returning to the ground only yards from the foot of the ladder. It was frightening to realise that the powerless stream of water would never come near the roof and hard to understand this inadequacy so near the foot of a long hill. What hope would there be for those of us at the top of the hill if we should need the services of the Fire Brigade?

How alone, frustrated and possibly embarrassed the fireman must have felt, perched high in the air, his bravery and expertise nullified by the lack of pressure. It seemed almost cruel to film the futile attempt.

Cine film was expensive and one learned to be miserly with its use, editing as one filmed in a way that the camcorder does not demand. I needed a different viewpoint and looking up I saw old neighbours of mine watching from the second floor window of 46. At their beckoned invitation, I rushed upstairs to join them and was able to film a bird's eye view of the death throes of my first alma mater.

I later heard that the fire had started through a workman's carelessness with a blowtorch, though whether this is accurate or not I have never found out.

The damage was extensive and it was decided to demolish and rebuild the sixty-five year-old school, replacing it with a modern building, better suited to secondary education. Strange how often good comes out of bad.

When I returned home, I was greeted with,

"Well, did it burn to the ground, I hope?"

"Were there any casualties?"

"They surely won't expect us back this afternoon, will they?"

"Did you get some astounding historical footage?"

"Did people stare at you filming?"

"Our mother, the *roving reporter*!"

A prophet hath no honour in his own land.

❖◆❖

TALL BEAUTY

Back in the seventies, Beatrice was known as the department beauty. She was very nearly six feet tall and not particularly slender. I do not mean she was fat but her bones were big and well fleshed. Her hands and feet were masculine in size. Both in person and personality, she seemed overpowering to me, but then I am a fairly short fellow.

As was appropriate, her face and its features were large too, with a well-shaped nose and an exuberant mouth and she made the most of her eyes with clever make-up. She dressed in a spectacular and dramatic style with many richly-coloured layers of drapery, which swished around the desks and typewriters and must have picked up a lot of dust in a day's work.

A gift shop called Aquarius had opened in Byres Road a few years previously. Gift shops were a new concept then, though all too familiar nowadays. Aquarius offered all sorts of small, charming articles at modest prices; little bibelots, knick-knacks, silk scarves, jewellery and useless adornments of all kinds. Things that you had not realised you needed until you saw them temptingly displayed. I guessed that Beatrice was a regular Aquarius customer, though it seemed to me that she must have been permanently too warm in all those velvets and silks, for the office was over-heated for my comfort. She also wore what seemed an impractical amount of rings on her large hands. Perhaps women do not mind suffering discomfort for the sake of style.

Beatrice's most outstanding feature was her abundant brown waving hair, which she wore in a loose, flowing mane, cascading over her shoulders and down her back, finishing well below her waist. Free-flowing hair was not an unusual style in those extravagant years of the seventies but Beatrice had taken it to an extreme that few others could match. Few could boast of quite so much hair as Beatrice had, or owned such a large back on which to display it.

I thought it a over the top myself, almost intimidating in fact and unsuitable for an office, but then I suppose I am a conventional guy.

Beatrice used a gracious, affectionate manner towards everyone with just a trace of coyness. In spite of her size, she would often employ a little feminine helplessness when problems arose. She was certainly generous with compliments and most of her comments could be described as sweet, but somehow I could never quite trust her and always remembered the saying of my clever old Aunt Ada,

"Aye, that yin's ower sweet to be wholesome".

There is no doubt that Beatrice successfully presented herself as a beauty and a charmer. Everyone described her in those terms. Perhaps her confidence tended to influence others, but I could never see her fascination.

We both worked in the biology department of Glasgow University. I was doing some final research for my PhD and Beatrice was in administration, though I am not quite sure what she did exactly or whether she did it well or not. I remember she bustled around a lot from one office to another, exchanging little snatches of smiling conversation. She seemed to know everyone by their first name.

At that time I was hardly part of the academic set-up. I had been assigned a small office for the next ten months and would work on my own. As I was not lecturing or tutoring, I was not so much in touch with staff, students or scandal as I might have been, though it would have been impossible to avoid completely the vapours of gossip which seem always to drift about a University.

Folk in the department were nice enough to me, chatting and asking me out for a drink now and again, but there was a distance in their manner. I had no intention of spending the rest of my life in the groves of academe and I suppose I made that pretty clear.

What I did learn in my first fortnight, was that Beatrice had the reputation of being a 'man-eater'. I paid little attention to this tittle-tattle. At five foot six, I felt pretty safe from her predations. Besides I was engaged to a wonderful and perfect girl of five foot two.

I was right not to worry, for Beatrice hardly noticed me

and never quite got my name right when she did speak. Several of the men in our building were very tall, some of them were married and some not. I suspected Beatrice preferred the tall ones for she was often to be seen with one or another of them in the corridors, speaking vivaciously as she smoothed her hair or adjusted a silken scarf.

I noticed on more than one occasion that Beatrice had a habit, as she stood chatting, of pushing her heavy curls back from her forehead with two hands, her back arched and her elbows stretching higher than her head. The position was provocative and accentuated her size and I would always hurry past, avoiding her billowing hair as best I could and glad that it was not me that stood there beside her.

Of course those married men who spoke to Beatrice were the subject of conjecture, but I have no reason to believe any of the stories.

It was around Christmas that I heard that Beatrice was engaged and I felt strangely disappointed.

It surprised me that she should have been so conventional.

Her dramatic character seemed to demand that she should have unexpectedly eloped with someone and preferably a married someone.

However we soon learned that Morton, her fiancé, was an ordinary fellow, although "just wonderful". He worked in the City Chambers, although in what capacity we never learned. They *adored* each other and would marry very soon.

On the first day that he came to the office to collect her, I was even more astonished. He was slightly made and not an inch over five foot eight! His out-dated clothes were also a surprise. Most younger men dressed very casually at that time, in polo necks or open-necked shirts, often brightly coloured or patterned. George was dressed much as my fifty year-old father dressed, in a nondescript tweed jacket and grey flannels, with a checked woollen tie!

Without actually discussing it, we all felt that this was a strangely boring mate for the exotic Beatrice to have chosen.

Yet I must admit she showed the greatest pride in him and treated him with an obvious tenderness. He showed no embarrassment, nor did he seem quite pleased. He accepted her ministrations and fussings with a small amused smile and hurried her from the building as quickly as he could. They were married shortly after.

No one from the department was invited to the wedding, but the professor and his wife and a few other bigwigs, were asked to dinner a few weeks later. The following week, the rest of us, five to be exact, were asked along 'just for drinks and nibbles'

I must admit that I was curious about the home of this outrageous girl.

Rather than buy a new place, Morton had joined Beatrice in her west end flat. It was a part of one of the mansions that sprouted in the days of Glasgow's fabulous wealth and must have been very splendid in its heyday around 1900 when there would be many servants to run it. Now sadly, the rambling house was chopped up into several small flats. Some had been more successfully converted than others. I was told that each consisted of one large impressive room, an awkward bedroom, a poky kitchen and various unexplained corners.

We crowded into the tiny hall and Morton took our jackets and scarves and hid them in some unseen closet. I was immediately overpowered by the heat of the place. And the air seemed heavy with perfume but I soon realised that, of course, Beatrice was just the sort to burn incense. Aquarius was very big on incense and scented candles.

How long would she expect us to hang about for our drinks and nibbles? How quickly could I leave this stifling and over-scented house?

Always dramatic, she waved us into the sitting room, which was spacious and would have been airy if it were not so full of furniture and flickering candles. How could seven people fit themselves into this already crammed and crowded room? Two couches, many chairs, footstools, little tables, book-cases, magazine racks, several chests of drawers with every possible surface covered with gewgaws and bibelots. That room was more stuffed with knick-knacks than Aquarius. It seemed impossible that nothing should be over-turned or broken as we picked our way cautiously to the nearest seat. Pictures, macramé work and embroidered tapestries covered the walls, partly hiding the Art Nouveau wallpaper. A large construction of imitation birds and flowers on wires hung from the ceiling in the middle of the room. When Beatrice reached up and gave it a push, the elaborate artefact started to swing and pitch about. The birds were obviously on elastic and they bounced up and down while the large loose petals of the flowers fluttered as they flew round and round. One or two dropped to the carpet.

"How do you like my mobile?" she laughed, "Isn't it just too *exquisite*! Morton made it, you know. Isn't he such a clever boy!"

We all mumbled appreciation and she rushed at her new husband and kissed him as he stood quietly there. I will say for him that he took it all quite happily and smiled his little amused smile. And I was impressed that such a staid and apparently dull man could have constructed such a fantastic frippery.

I do not know whether it was the incense or perhaps my general feeling of unease, but shortly after the drinks were served, I suddenly stood up. I had some idea of leaving the room for I knew I was going to sneeze. There was no way I could make a quick exit and a fit of sneezing overcame me before I could manoeuvre past the first little table. I sneezed loudly and continuously, perhaps producing twenty five or thirty deafening sneezes. I have had this problem since I was a child and I am helpless to stop once I start. Possibly the fit is triggered by an allergy or perhaps an emotional response, no one has discovered. Whatever it is, fortunately it only happens occasionally and I have learned to live with it. Many of my friends have never witnessed one of these attacks but I believe they are impressive and terrifying. I am certainly always exhausted afterwards.

There is nothing more commanding than continuous sneezing and there I was, completely out of control and stranded in a labyrinth of furniture, every surface covered with articles of fragile glass and china, with even the airspace full of vulnerable and precious birds and flowers. I dominated the scene with twenty seven outstanding explosive sneeze-shouts.

I have been told that the noise I make is incredible.

Six pairs of eyes gazed at me in horror.

Worst of all, when I fumbled in my pocket, I had no handkerchief.

Once the paroxysm ended, Beatrice kindly led me away to her bathroom to wash my face and recover.

It was necessary to go through her bedroom to reach the bathroom but I was so weak and disorientated that I noticed nothing of the room.

As might be expected, the bathroom was full of perfumed soaps, powders, lotions and a large bowl of potpourri, all of which brought on another attack. I had never experienced such a violent episode before. Eventually the sneezing did stop, by then my nose had started to bleed profusely and there were spots of blood on the basin, the bath and the floor, even on some of the glass and china ornaments which decorated shelves and ledges. I used up an entire box of pink tissues cleaning and wiping before I started on the pink toilet roll. I hope I removed every sanguine spot, I know I tried.

What a disastrous evening.

When I emerged from the bathroom and saw the bedroom, I thought I was hallucinating.

It was like a scene from the *Thousand and One Nights*.

The room was long and narrow and held only the bed and a small muslin draped dressing table.

No doubt because of mundane plumbing practicalities, the bed was on a platform built about two feet above floor level, with three steps leading up to it. It was a very large bed in a small room and the fact that it was raised gave it tremendous significance. As well as the unusual height of the bed, its entire surface was piled with jewel bright cushions, round, square, heart-shaped, small and large. There must have been forty cushions scintillating on the bed. Above the bed, were many yards of diaphanous curtaining swagged, draped and falling asymmetrically to one side.

It was a vision.

I must admit that my imagination immediately added Beatrice, languishing amongst those cushions, suitably unattired.

I was paralysed with astonishment at my thoughts and blushed deeply.

It certainly put a stop to my sneezing.

Without returning to the sitting room, I made my excuses and apologies to Morton and Beatrice and left the party there and then.

She did try to persuade me to stay and she made a good hostessy show of concern for me, but her relief was obvious when I insisted on going.

The next day in the department, I spoke to Fred who, like myself, was struggling with the last stages of his thesis.

"Sorry about making such an ass of myself last night. That hasn't happened for ages. I think it was all the perfumes of Arabia that set me off."

"Yes, you were astoundingly dramatic. I've never seen the like of that before! I suppose the aroma was a bit strong but I don't have much sense of smell myself."

"You're lucky!"

"You missed the sausage rolls!"

"Home made?"

"No, Iceland's best."

"Oh well..."

"You also missed the rather embarrassing description of their Saturday night orgies."

I was speechless as I stared at him. The dusty smell of potpourri filled my nostrils and my inner eye saw the bed, the cushions, the drapery... Beatrice... .

Fred looked at me closely and laughed,

"Oh, don't worry, old man, nothing too shocking. Nothing spicy at all. Exceedingly tame in fact. They like to read children's stories to each other. Winnie the Pooh is the favourite this week, but they also like Babar the Elephant. They lie on those two couches in the sitting room, eating marshmallows and reading to each other. Seems inane to me but each to his own. What *did* you think they might be up to?"

"God knows." I smiled and hesitated, then continued lamely, "P'raps they might have been juggling with the ornaments or swinging on the mobile."

We both laughed self-consciously and returned to our damnable writing.

I left Glasgow soon after that and did not return for seven years. By that time I was married and the father of two little boys. I had an excellent job which had nothing to do with academia and in fact I never did finish that PhD. What a waste of time! Perhaps I matured in the struggle.

Sally and I bought a nice flat in Polwarth Street and settled down to the domestic scene with its mixture of joys and tribulations.

I met Fred as I was walking along Hyndland Road one day. He hadn't changed a bit and was kind enough to pay me the same compliment. We sauntered along to the Patisserie Françoise in Byres Road and over an excellent coffee, brought each other up to date with our personal news. Fred was now a lecturer in the biology department.

As we spoke, a memory of Beatrice, with her flamboyant outfits and impressive hair struck me. I swear I had not thought about her for years, but once she entered my mind, I remembered more and more about her and especially that ill-fated night in her hot, crowded, perfumed flat. I tried not to bring her into the conversation too early but eventually there was a pause.

"Whatever happened to that big woman with the long, long hair? Was Beatrice her name, I think?"

I was not being entirely honest as I knew very well what her name was.

"Oh, Beatrice!" Fred replied, "Yeah, she's back working in the office with us again."

"Is she indeed. I thought that she might be a mother and entirely domesticated now."

"Oh, no. That marriage didn't last long."

"Not even with the charming telling of kids' stories to each other? Do you remember that?"

By the way that Fred looked at me blankly, he had obviously no recollection of that detail.

"No," he continued, "It's a strange story. Morton, that was her husband y'know, was an orphan. I didn't know that at the time, did you?"

I shook my head.

"Well he was an orphan and a twin and the twins had been separated at birth and adopted by different families. The other kid, who was a girl, had gone off, or been taken off rather, to South Africa. Life's tough for some folk isn't it? Well it seems that the girl returned to Britain and decided to find her twin brother, who was Morton, and she must have been successful and they really hit it off when they met. Really liked each other and got on well. Unfortunately the sister and Beatrice *didn't* get on so well and eventually Morton made the decision to leave Beatrice. He must have liked his sister better than his wife, I suppose."

"My God, you don't mean that the brother and sister fell in... love... that it was *incestuous*, do you? Surely not!"

"No idea! Who knows?"

"That's a most tragic story. Poor Beatrice."

In my mind's eye, that proud woman was very changed, almost unrecognisable. Such an experience must have transformed her. I imagined Beatrice much thinner than before, tall and almost gaunt, dressed in a shapeless brown waterproof. Her magnificent hair would be streaked with grey and dragged back into a severe bun. Gone would be the scarves, the jewellery, the extrovert gestures and the superlative confidence of an acknowledged beauty.

I was silent and aghast as I pictured her.

"How on earth did she take it? What's she like nowadays?" I asked, half fearfully.

"Oh she's certainly different. Fashions change and she'd look a bit strange in all those falderols and gimcracks she used to wear."

"But did she fade away after an experience like that? Lots of women get depressed and really thin. And what about that hair of hers?"

Fred laughed,

"You certainly do remember her well! You weren't keen at the time, were you?"

I denied that hurriedly.

"No, she certainly didn't fade away. Heftier than ever, I would say. Her fat behind is squashed into jeans these days and very much part of the landscape. And rather inadvisedly, she sports tight T-shirts. And her hair? Well it's not so long as it was before, of course, but there seems to be more of it. It's all curly and piled up on top and falling over her shoulders. I think it's what they call 'big hair' and I mean *really big*. And of course she's a blonde now."

✧◆✧

STREET VIOLENCE

Twenty odd years ago, I was returning from a party at 1am. Friends had given me a lift home and they dropped me off on the opposite side of the street from my front door. Although I was making my farewells as I left the vehicle, I was aware that a couple who were standing nearby showed an awkward tension as I passed them. It seemed that the girl gave me an almost pleading look, but I did not know her and that stupid unwillingness to interfere made me hurry across the road and let myself in without a backward glance. I reported my safe return to my daughters who were engrossed in some infantile film on television and declined an invitation to join them. Without removing my coat, which was a particularly bulky one with a large stylish turned up collar, I ran quickly to my sitting room window where I could see the couple across the road, for I was unhappy about them. I was horrified to see that the young man had pushed the girl backwards into a small hedge which bordered the front garden and he seemed to be *raining* punches on her head. Though I consider myself rather a timid person physically, I did not hesitate nor did I stop to say anything to the girls, which was foolish, but immediately ran out of the house and across the road. The girl was now bent backwards and jammed into the hedge with the man bending over her, still attacking her. His rear end was in evidence and I drew my hand back and gave him as big a wallop on the bum as I was capable of doing. At the time, I felt it a very inadequate action, but it stopped him at once and my arm ached for three days so it must have had some strength. After hitting him, I stepped back quickly! What if he turned on me next? However, I wore very high heels that night and standing as tall as I could inside my bulky coat I gave him a dressing-down in the practised manner that only years of dealing with recalcitrant school children can teach. Fortunately he was a diminutive man and I felt I towered over him.

"What a DISGRACEFUL way to treat a woman ! Leave her ALONE and *go home at once* you nasty little man."

"Och, ye don't know what things she wis sayin' tae me..."

"I DON'T care."

"But ye see..."

"QUIET. That's a TERRIBLE way to behave. Go on! Get away home out my sight, NOW. GO. AT ONCE."

With some signs of reluctance, he slowly shambled off and I helped the girl wipe blood and tears from her face. She was gingerly feeling her front teeth as I walked the short distance with her to her home in Hyndland Road.

"I hope you'll have nothing more to do with that lout in future." I advised her, but she did not reply.

In the house the inane film was about to finish and the girls were still guffawing. When I described my adventure, the three faces were perplexed.

"But you just came in a minute ago!"

I struggled out of my heavy coat, slipped off my shoes and said modestly,

"Oh, but I went out again and it doesn't take long for me to deal with street violence."

LISTENING

James was an ambitious and hard-working lawyer. Lily was his efficient and very attractive private secretary. When they married in 1968 they bought a nice flat in Novar Drive. These desirable homes in Glasgow's west end were still financially attainable for a young professional couple, though property prices were starting to rise alarmingly.

When the twins arrived, James decided a garden was a necessity with children. After making a small but acceptable profit on their flat, they moved to a bungalow in Milngavie. Lily had been very happy in Hyndland and she was happy in Milngavie. At first the low ceilings of the bungalow were a little depressing and the carpets had to be re-fitted in the less spacious rooms and she had to chop lumps off the curtains, but Lily accepted these slight problems. She was a hard working girl and liked a challenge. The garden was certainly very nice although it, too, added to her work load. James had been more fascinated by the idea of a garden than the reality, and it would be some years before he developed into the fastidious and obssessive gardener of his later years. What Lily missed most was the gossip and friendship of her neighbours in the tenement, and Hyndland had been terribly convenient for shopping or for nipping quickly into town. Nevertheless she soon adapted and when two little girls, born separately this time, were added to the family, Lily settled into a calm and devoted domestic life with no regrets for Hyndland or her former employment. James took the blue train into Glasgow each day and Lily devoted herself to the children and the house, as well as finding time to pursue the employments open to a young mother at home, decorating, dress-making, baking and helping with the local playgroup. Lily would have described her life as "just about perfect".

✧◆✧

With no tragedies and only the usual ups and downs of family life, forty years passed and Lily and James now often spoke about his retirement and their plans for travel. They were grandparents now and, except for family visits, the bungalow seemed empty and almost large.

Suddenly, James started to complain of tiredness and a sore back. He had always taken such pride in the garden but suddenly the grass was long, the hedge untrimmed and he showed no interest in a visit to the garden centre.

He sat in his armchair at the window frowning at the neglected garden and occasionaly grunting with pain. Lily was worried.

"Darling, did you not take a pill..."

He interrupted her,

"No, I didn't take anything. They do no damn good."

"You should see the doctor about that back, James."

"Och, doctors!" His tone dismissed the entire medical profession. "It's that bloody garden. I'm not fit for it any more. All that digging and bending about. It's young man's work. And I hate seeing it in such a mess. I've been thinking, how about we sell up here and get back into the west end. A nice wee flat would do us fine, wouldn't it? We were happy there, weren't we? And no more gardening! We don't need one now. More sensible too for travelling when I retire. We could hardly leave this place empty for weeks, far too vulnerable for break-ins and the garden would be a mess, a sheer giveaway that we weren't at home. A flat's safer and warmer in the winter too. Eh? How d'ye fancy going back to Hyndland?"

Lily was taken aback at first. It seemed like a great upheaval but she came round to the idea. It was sensible. She made only one proviso. It must be a ground floor flat.

"I'm out of the way of climbing stairs, James, and bringing in groceries would be..."

"Oh, when I'm retired, I'll be doing all that heavy lifting."

"But what about your back?"

"It's gardening that's the problem there. Mark my words, a few bits of shopping'll be neither here nor there. No, no, I'll deal with the messages. Anyway didn't they used to deliver in Hyndland? Surely I remember your fruit and veg arriving in a big cardboard box. But we'll easily get a ground floor flat all right."

In his usual decisive way, James put the bungalow on the market immediately and very soon they received a price they could not refuse.

However there was not a ground floor flat available in Hyndland. There were very few flats available anywhere in the west end, for they sold quickly and at astonishingly high prices.

They looked at a flat in Dowanhill which was large and splendid. Though it was expensive, James was enthusiastic.

"I'm not taking on such a palace at my time of life." Lily laughed, but her tone was determined, for she saw her husband liked it. And she stuck to her guns.

They looked at a ground floor flat in Hillhead which was charming and just the right size.

"Bit near the University maybe, too many students around. Might be noisy at night." James pondered and Lily rejected it with no regrets for it was situated on a steep hill high above Byres Road and twenty rather broken steps climbed from the pavement to the close-mouth.

They looked at a garden or basement flat, in the splendid Greek Thomson Terrace of town-houses in Hyndland Road. It had a special atmosphere with low ceilings, quite large rooms and access to a small pleasant garden. It required a lot of basic improvement as well as decoration and there were rather steep stairs to deal with and James declared,

"This place needs a fortune spent on it and no more gardening for me, thank you."

Only two weeks were left before they must vacate their old home when a first floor flat in Clarence Drive came on the market, right size, right price and newly decorated throughout. Lily did not think the stairs, three short flights between each floor, would be a problem as long as James kept his promise about the shopping. In fact stairs would be good exercise, for she had put on a few unwanted pounds in the last ten years. She found the colour scheme bland and unexciting, but James said that was the fashion nowadays and they could soon brighten it up. They bought the flat at once.

Sons and daughters made themselves very useful with the removal and soon the couple were once more established in Hyndland.

Though the flat was entirely different from their previous one in Novar Drive, Lily was astonished at how familiar it seemed. The high ceilings and tall windows made her feel as if she had 'come home'. Lily enjoyed adding little touches of decoration to the flat and shopping locally, although that had changed a lot. No more early rising on a Sunday to catch the dairy before it closed at ten thirty, no problem with half day closing or rushing to buy something before the shops closed nowadays, for many stayed open until 8pm, and a large delicatessen was bright and busy until midnight. There were several coffee shops and a restaurant which advertised breakfast.

"My goodness! Do people actually go out to eat breakfast?" Lily exclaimed. It had been a quiet, unsophisticated life in Milngavie.

When out shopping one day, Lily was accosted by Margaret, a neighbour who remembered her from forty years ago. Margaret still lived in the same flat in Novar Drive. Lily would never have recognised her old neighbour and truthfully had never liked her very much. She thought those intervening years had been unkind to the poor old soul. Later she laughed to herself because probably Margaret thought exactly the same about her. It was such a long time.

One morning at breakfast, after they had been settled in for a month, Lily said,

"James, those folk upstairs must have moved in recently too and they don't seem to have got their carpets down yet. I can hear every foorstep. Sometimes it's like living in a building site."

"No, my dear, you've just forgotten what it's like to hear neighbours overhead. Anyway bare floors are the fashion nowadays You'll get used to it."

"No, James, I remember what it was like very well. I quite liked hearing sounds, knowing other people were around me. This is different. The floors vibrate and they are such busy people too. I'm sure I can hear the woman running around in an anxious sort of way. I think she has three sons, so I suppose she's busy. Sometimes there are strange loud noises that make me jump and my curiosity is aroused as well for I just *cannot* think what they're doing to make such peculiar sounds."

"Really, Lily, you're letting your imagination run away with you. You'll get used to it. Ignore it in the meantime. Be glad they're not practising the bagpipes or banging on a drum kit."

Just at that moment there was an incredibly loud clatter of several heavy objects dropped on the floor immediately above their heads.

"*Just listen to that*, James, that's exactly the sort of thing I mean. What on earth can they be doing?"

James was laughing,

"I do see what you mean. It sounds like a sack of boulders emptied out on the kitchen floor, but surely that can't happen very often. I've never heard anything before."

"Your hearing's not as good as it used to be and anyway you're at work all day. Just wait till you retire next year."

"I know you'll get used to it in time, my dear." And he returned to his Herald.

After a few minutes, some heavy piece of furniture was dragged noisily across the floor upstairs, there was a bang, then an even louder bang followed by quick clumping footsteps which traced and re-traced a path across the floor several times. Lily looked at her husband with compressed lips and raised eyebrows, but he was deeply involved in his newspaper.

"I think she's wearing those awful ugly plastic clogs."

James remained engrossed.

Lily heard sounds from other neighbours that she found much more charming. Ralph, the young man who lived across the landing from them left for work at exactly the same time each morning. Lily often checked her clock when she heard him shouting a cheerful good-bye to his wife.

"Cheerio, darling. See ya later!"

Then he glided down the stairs in a special way, hardly seeming to touch each individual step, although there was a faint rhythm of a light tip-tap if she listened carefully. How wonderful to be so young and muscular.

The teenage girl on the top floor was noisier, coming down two steps at a time. As each flight had an uneven number of steps, she would leap the last three and her descent could be heard from any part of the flat, 'bang, bang, *thump,*

bang, bang, bang *thump*, bang, bang, *thump* for three floors
but Lily liked her energy and Barbara was a very pretty girl.
Her older sister Ursula favoured little high heels which
clickety-clacked sharply on each stair, sounding to Lily as
though she had not complete control of those shoes. Perhaps
they were rather large for her. Ursula could be heard going
out very late at night and returning at some unearthly hour
in the morning, then off to work again at 8am. How did she
manage with so little sleep, Lily would wonder. But her own
daughters had been the same, starting their evening revelry at
the time that Lily would have been expected to return home.
She did think a pair of quieter shoes would have been
sensible for that regular 4am return, but Ursula was also a
pleasant and pretty girl.

Lily's favourite neighourly noise was Jasper, the little boy
downstairs. He was nine and had just started the violin. Lily
was making up the beds in the spare room, which must have
been above his bedroom, when she first heard the unmelo-
dious scrapings. She smiled then started to laugh because it
really was too terrible for words. His diligent practice could
be heard each day from four thirty until five-thirty and Lily
was impressed by his exact time-keeping. He was as clock
conscious as Ralph and Ursula. His playing was only audible
to Lily if she was in the spare room and if she was at home
and noticed the time, she would go and listen to him. It
always made her smile for it was so bad. After six weeks,
however, a ghost of a tune started to emerge. She thought it
wonderful that he should persevere when even he must know
how bad he was. Perhaps there was a parental bribe urging
him on. She remembered the box of chocolates which had
finally encouraged her to dive into the swimming pool.
Nowadays it was likely to be a more expensive bribe, probably electronic.

When Jasper had wrestled with his violin for three
months he had a sudden breakthrough. Lily could not believe
her ears. A pure little tune, uncomplicated but beautifully
executed, floated up to her spare room. Jasper never looked
back after that and started to play fiddle music as well as
simple classical pieces, obviously playing for pleasure as well
as practice. Before the end of the year, he added another

hour's practice after dinner and was picking out popular tunes and Lily was sure he was composing little pieces of his own.

"James, I'm sure we have a young genius living below us. You've no idea how well he has come on with his music and he's so keen, too. I think we have another Nigel Kennedy in the close."

"Nigel *who?*"

James was not a Classic FM listener.

"You know! The little lad downstairs, that plays the violin. Jasper. He's terribly musical and talented."

"He's a rare wee footballer too, I saw him across in the Lauderdale pitch the other night."

"I hope he's careful of his hands."

But James had turned to the financial section of the Guardian.

In spite of the curious sounds and hurried footfalls of her upstairs neighbours, Lily found they were very nice kindly people. She must just learn to live with their noisy clumsiness.

Lily would never regret her return to Hyndland. There may have been just as interesting folk in Milngavie, but somehow she had not met them.

Yes, she was happy here. Hyndland was home.

ALCOHOL

We'll never know who was the first
   discoverer of this cure for thirst.

But there's been alcoholic cordial
   since ancient times primordial.

And man has always kept his vessels filled
   with liquor which has been distilled

From grapes, grain, flowers, fruits and trees,
   herbs and honey from the bees.

These strange concoctions ease his lot
   in winter cold or when too hot,

And raise his spirits when he's sad,
   help joyfulness when he is glad.

Even ritual matters, spiritual,
   involve this fiery liquid fuel.

In fact any old excuse will pass,
   to drink a well-fermented glass.

Now humans are but poor weak creatures
   and excess booze will mark their features.

For noses which are roseate
   denote a fondness, much too great,

And protruding bellies, I do fear,
   show fellows very fond of beer,

Though strangely, people who drink gin,
   are often dangerously thin,

While rich and creamy Advocaat
   just generally makes folk fat.

Sadly, quaffing Croft Original,
   produces hips steatopiginal.

And tragically, you will find
   a few who'd leave the world behind.

Who indulge in such excess,
   that they achieve forgetfulness.

But in G12 we're moderate
　　and know just how to celebrate,

Eating lunch or dinner fine,
　　enjoying French or Spanish wine,

Bought from Peckhams or Oddbins,
　　not counting these amongst our sins.

My very favourite drink of all,
　　comes in a bottle heavy, tall,

That fluid of the highest rating,
　　created just for celebrating,

Encouraging the crowd to laughter,
　　with no fears for morning after.

A delightful sip which brings no trouble,
　　joy generated in each bubble.

Yes! Fill my glass yet once again,
　　For I adore sparkling Champagne.

SPIDER

I assure you I have little to do with gossip. Honestly, I am just not interested. If people want to confide in me or ask for my advce, that is fine and I am there for them, but generally I am far, far too busy with my own demanding existence to wish to delve into the secrets of others. I cannot even remember the names of the ex-spouses or ex-lovers that regularly crop up, almost always bitterly, in a normal G12 conversation.

Besides I have a poor memory for names and relationships. I am always so impressed when I visit my cousin Isobel, who has lived all her life in a small east coast fishing village. She quite puts me to shame, for her mindset is entirely different from mine. She has the complicated family relationships of the *whole town*, population fifteen hundred, at her fingertips. Honestly, the different families and all the different generations, from great-grandparents to the latest infant, are quite clearly defined in her head. She can reel off their phone numbers, their car registration numbers, even the names of their pets. She knows almost as much about those who have been dead for years. Not only that, Isobel has a working knowledge of the dynasties in the adjacent villages and in the outlying farms. This comprehensive database is kept firmly in her head and can be sourced at any time. She is a wonder. She should have been a detective!

And although Isobel may be supreme, she is not unique in that little town, for every conversation that takes place there depends, to a certain extent, on this exact knowledge. Village life demands that you know your company in order to avoid touching on any shocking scandal which might involve or insult a close relative of someone who is present, a gaffe which might easily lead to a life-long feud and add even more complications to daily social interaction.

No, I could never deal with such a mine-field in ordinary day-to-day chatter. It is not the way in the city. We may enjoy a little bit of spicy gossip now and again but only a proportion of any group will know the parties concerned personally. And after all, that is where the true excitement lies; so much more enjoyable to know that shocking behaviour has been perpetrated by friends.

Many, many years ago, without even trying, I found myself the recipient of various pieces of information which added up to a west end scandal of Hollywood proportions. It was a *multi* love affair, far more advanced geometrically than the traditional triangle. I knew all the people involved although not one of the individuals was aware of the fact that I had such knowledge. Without being in any way a part of the scenario, I seemed to be at the centre of it, like the spider who watches a group of flies fluttering about her web and sees them finally alighting and sticking helplessly.

Oh dear! That gives entirely the wrong impression, for it was not a role that I sought or relished. I had no intention of benefitting from their plight, I spun no web, nor did I gain anything from those long ago sexual antics. Quite the reverse in fact. I said nothing. Not a whisper. But without any effort on my part, the clues and facts continued to come to my notice.

It all happened so very long ago, before shopping became a compulsive hobby, before mobile phones and the internet became de rigueur for every inhabitant of Hyndland, before bare bellies and intimate piercings affronted the modest observer. It happened in the seventies, when women had long flowing hair and wore ankle length skirts and the smart man about town wore a sheepskin overcoat.

What is perhaps saddest of all is that all the protagonists who were then in their mid to late thirties, now have their bus passes.

First, I should explain exactly why I was in a situation to see the drama unfold before my eyes and thus come to hold the thread attached to each actor.

In 1975 my husband, Jim, was made redundant and our lives were changed overnight. He had earned an excellent salary as a design engineer in a long-established Glasgow firm. Sadly, that firm, like so many others, was closing, never to reopen. It looked as though there might be no financially comparable situations available again in his lifetime. He found another job but his earnings were inadequate to deal with the rising costs which started to escalate just as our bank balance started to dwindle.

Although I had not worked since the three boys were born, we had led a comfortable life in Glasgow's elegant west end. Our large flat was bought in the sixties before the property values started to soar and we had no mortgage to worry us. Our three boys were happy and successful at Hyndland School and those modern financial demands of teenagers for over-priced trainers and electronic toys were as yet unknown to parents. It is depressing to think that at the time we did not even know how lucky we were.

I had lived in France as a child, so in order to swell the family coffers, I started to give private lessons in conversational French. The westenders have a hunger for self-improvement and it is a good place to give private classes in practically anything. Almost immediately, I was rather successful. With three adult classes, a children's class and even a song-singing toddler group, I very quickly became a fixture in Hyndland. Sometimes I would tutor a schoolchild for an exam or perhaps give a short crash course to a family contemplating a holiday. It was such a pleasant way to earn money and all my pupils seemed delighted.

As you can imagine, our weekly meetings were a perfect opportunity to exchange the news of the neighbourhood, i.e gossip. Only French was spoken in the advanced class, but as it is the perfect language for the meaningful and suggestive remark, the trend of the conversation often veered towards dangerous ground. I want to impress upon you *thoroughly* that I have no real interest in talking of the private affairs of my neighbours and I assure you that in spite of the many innuendoes, chuckles, nudges and eye-rollings of those evenings, I was never part of that scandal-hungry conversation. In fact I would try, usually unsuccessfully I am afraid, to steer the group to a different subject. I am happy to say that at the time I had no inkling of the dramas which I am about to unfold.

I was a rather naïve spider.

One of the first couples to join my advanced class were Gerty and Derek. They were English with an excellent command of French grammar, though their accents were less successful and would always betray their nationality. I wonder if that long history of enmity between France and England makes it impossible for our southern cousins to relinquish their dipthongs or to pronounce the letter R.

Derek seemed a warm friendly fellow. There were six in the class and Derek kept the conversational ball rolling. I felt he asked too many personal questions but he asked them in such a kindly, caring way that people often told him the most amazing, even intimate things. I do not know how sincere he was in his quest for information, or even if he remembered all the facts which came to light, though I am sure the rest of us did. Perhaps it was his training that made him such a compulsive interrogator. Might he have been a psychiatrist? A detective? An anthropologist? I cannot remember. Certainly a questioner and seeker after facts about the human condition. I would soon find out that he was also a womaniser of the first order.

Gerty was much more subdued, repressed almost. She was a pretty woman, with fair curling hair and an attractive pink and white complexion, a typical English rose and would have been very attractive if she had seemed more cheerful. No doubt she was clever and her written work was excellent, but she found it difficult to respond and spoke only when forced. I suspected from the beginning that she was unhappy, though Derek always treated her affectionately. The years are not kind to that particular type of beauty and her cheeks would become a little over-flushed if we were enjoying a bottle of wine. I feared for future broken veins. We often did drink wine at my classes and where more suitable to drink it than in a French class? It relaxed their inhibitions and I suppose most further educational evenings are as much social as educational. At that time, wine was just starting to become a popular daily indulgence and I expect that in the intervening years more wine has been drunk per capita in G12 than in any other postal code you might care to mention.

Now I must introduce Elizabeth, an old school fellow of mine and another dedicated wine-drinker, almost too dedicated I might suggest. Though not a pupil nor a west-ender, she plays an important part in my story. It was she who suggested that Fiona, a junior partner in her legal firm, might join my class. More importantly it was Elizabeth who revealed the sexual secrets of my study group to my innocent eyes, and let us put young Fiona aside for a moment, for this is a complicated tale.

I might tell you that, compared to the rest of my friends, Elizabeth had lived a 'less respectable' life but in view of what will unfold, I will change that to 'a less apparently domestic' one. She was a woman who would probably be overlooked in most situations. Small and slender, she dressed in a strangely sedate and unimaginative way, her style hardly having changed from her university days of twenty years ago. It always struck me that it could not be easy to find such self-effacing clothes in the flamboyant 70s. Elizabeth spoke in a quiet, somewhat affected accent and was strangely pleased if mistaken for an Englishwoman rather than a Scot. She had never married, but surprisingly for such a pedantic, conventional, colourless woman, she had indulged in a series of love affairs, almost always with married men. Sadly they seemed to have brought her little happiness. Our friendship was intermittent rather than close and eventually I realised that our meetings coincided with a dramatic moment in one of her ever-changing affairs. I would be invited to her house in Pollokshields and the evening would consist of Elizabeth bewailing the perfidy of her latest lover and drinking too much wine. Perhaps she saw me as a shoulder to cry on, but I cannot think I was helpful in that role as my sympathies always lay with the wronged wife. Perhaps, masochistically, she enjoyed the disapproval that I obviously felt. Perhaps she required me as an audience to her tragic misery in order to enhance her own importance. Who knows? In spite of appearances, she was a very complex character and I was sorry for her clients.

Elizabeth had pursued a stormy on-off relationship with Timothy for several years at this time and one night she burst out,

"I know you think me wrong but his wife has a lover too. That's the sort of relationship they have. The marriage was finished long ago and she doesn't care a damn for Timothy any more, so you needn't look so severe."

I had never met the man, but I understood him only too
well. In spite of repeated promises, Timothy obviously found
it impossible, or inconvenient, to leave his wife. Elizabeth
longed for this to happen and spoke naïvely of the marital joy
of two pairs of slippers warming before the fire. As she
poured herself another glass of wine, I wondered wryly which
women's magazine she had been reading. She hiccupped
slightly and continued,
"What's more, you know the wife's lover. It's that Derek
whatisname that comes to your class."
Derek! My inquisitive pupil! I was absolutely astonished.
Apart from the affection he displayed towards Gerty, it
seemed such a coincidence that someone from the south side
should have an affair with a west ender. Glasgow is divided
by the River Clyde and in spite of a proliferation of large and
small bridges, the north side and the south are much further
apart than the modest breadth of a river should warrant.
Difficult to pinpoint just why this separation is so manifest or
why it has occurred, but there is no doubt that Glasgow is a
double town. Southsiders are apt to express fears about
getting lost in the west end, which is ridiculous as it is a
much smaller area than their own sprawling and mainly
affluent suburbs. I admit millionaires generally choose to live
on the south side. Westenders? We tend to ignore the south
side.
I brought different eyes and ears to my advanced class the
following week.
No wonder Gerty was morose, poor girl. I wondered if
anyone else in the group guessed that she had an errant
husband.
I now listened more carefully to Derek's questions and it
seemed clear that he was trying to ferret out the secrets of
other spouses who might be misbehaving. I was shocked.
What was his motive? Was he trying to justify his own bad
behaviour? Was it just a cruel game? I was not clever enough
to deduce the truth from his interrogations.
Innocent as I was, it had never occurred to me that adul-
tery might be rife in the west end!
Jim and I had led a comfortable, if slightly unexciting life
for nearly sixteen years. We had laughed as we discussed and

dismissed the possibility that either of us might ever be unfaithful. With Jim's demanding job, three romping sons and a large house to maintain, we agreed there was not time or energy for an affair in *our* marriage.

As I glanced around the room that night, it was as though the scales had fallen from my eyes.

It was young Fiona's first lesson and Derek, the philanderer, was obviously very taken and was plying her with lots of questions. I was often forced to interrupt him for he lacked the grammar or vocabulary to frame his complex inquiries. I could see Fiona was impressed. Gerty looked glum, took notes and said nothing.

Beside them sat Dora, a handsome woman, tall, thin and always wonderfully and exotically dressed. Was she obssessed by clothes? I never saw her wear the same outfit twice and I knew that she had three wardrobes and visited the shops in town every single day after driving her husband, Dick, to his office. Dick was an estate agent and too busy with clients in the evening to come to class. Now, when I looked more carefully at Dora, her eyes were unmistakably fixed on Jake, an architect and the only bachelor in the group. When it was Dora's turn to speak, her remarks, in impeccable French, were always addressed to Jake and her large beautiful eyes often rested on him while others were speaking. I further noticed that her blouse was immodestly low cut, although her extreme thinness ruled out the possibility of any alluring cleavage.

Jake was a pleasant, jolly fellow, tall, bluff and bearded, with not enough skills for that class. Unable to follow Dora's subtle and complicated language, he made halting and inadequate replies and seemed oblivious to the predatory glow in her dark pupils. He sat close to the new girl Fiona, and I noticed with disapproval that some of their whispered conversation was *not* in French. It is always a difficult task to know how much discipline should be imposed by the private teacher. Her pupils have chosen to attend classes in order to learn but they also want to enjoy themselves. She is torn between the desire to fulfil the contract properly and the need to keep the pupil happy and retain the income.

Next to Jake sat Brian, a tall, dedicated town planner.

Although he was unobtrusive and said little in French, he was
apt to take hold of the conversation in English and rather
forget to let go. He would speak seriously and continuously
about what the town council needed to build or demolish and
what he personally would build or demolish if given the
chance. His French always lapsed when it came to technicali-
ties and I could seldom help him out. I constantly attempted
to shut him up kindly and let others have a chance. Some
people have suggested that my husband Jim talks too much
about engineering, but compared to Brian's relentless spiel,
Jim is witty and brief. Brian showed not a scrap of humour
and was a crashing bore, particularly in bad French. I found it
hard to understand how an attractive girl like Freda had
married him.

Freda was on the couch at the other side of the room and
my blood ran cold as I saw how closely Gregor was snuggled
to her side on the couch, though I could not say she looked
unhappy at his proximity. She was always a very polite girl.

Gregor and his wife Martha were older than the rest of us.
Fifty was in sight for them and she had not worn well, over-
weight and unfit and with hair that had suffered too many
attempts to disguise the grey. Gregor had not much hair left
on top but what he had was wildly thick and curly around the
sides, rather like a medieval monk and strangely attractive.
Their abilities were too elementary for the group but they did
not seem to realise this and I did not point it out to them for
they were keen and could not come on any other evening.

Martha sat rather apart from the group, on a high hard
chair and was answering one of Derek's innumerable questions with a very sweet helpfulness and excruciating
grammar. Her unusually pale skin made her look tired and
drew unfortunate attention to a small hole in the knee of her
black tights. She was the only female wearing a short skirt
and I wondered if others were as mesmerised by that shining
nacreous circle as I was?

I never liked her very much.

I suddenly felt very tired of Derek and his constant
"*pourquoi?*" and "*qu'est que c'est?*". My eyes had been
opened and I was exhausted by the hidden glances and
underlying emotions that I had not recognised before.

I excused myself, claiming a headache and urging the class to finish the last half hour without me.

Jim was in the other room watching television. He had no interest in learning French.

"Why bark yourself when you keep a dog?" he always said on our continental holidays. And though coarsely put, I suppose that is a sensible philosophy.

I thought he looked rather disconsolate sitting there with the wine-driven laughter echoing from the next room.

"Are you all right in here, dear?" I asked.

"Have you finished early? Why are they not away yet?"

"I just felt a bit tired."

He grunted and said no more.

"Like a cup of tea, Jim?"

He grunted again, so I left him.

Since he had started the new job, which was so much less interesting and less well-paid, he had been discontented. The fact that I could double our income with my successful classes should have cheered him up. It meant that my students took over the sittingroom for three evenings each week, but Jim would only be watching TV anyway. Jim usually golfed on Saturday mornings when the toddler group was there and luckily missed out on the infantine warblings of *Frère Jacques*.

My unclouded vision of the class had left me less than content and Jim was certainly disgruntled.

Ten weeks later, the same group was assembled. It would be good to report that their grammar and accents were greatly improved but it would be untrue. The articulate still held the floor, I hardly got a word in edgeways myself and the unskilled said practically nothing. The ideal of mixed ability classes is all very well but the reality is terribly difficult and the dynamics of that class had been wrong from the beginning.

The emotional dynamics of the group were even more unbalanced and we were missing some faces.

Poor boring Brian had been deserted by Freda. Perhaps he had discussed one planning project too many. Perhaps the unknown someone could make her laugh. Brian bravely continued to attend but said less, which was a blessing.

Gerty had gone to South America!

"Gone tramping in the Andes with an old school fellow." Derek informed us casually and he seemed almost too nonchalant.

Derek himself had forsaken his previous lover for pretty Fiona. Their closeness was obvious in the class but I learned the details from Elizabeth when I was summoned to Pollokshields to listen to another night of sad wailing. Her lover, Timothy, had been so affected by the break-up of his wife's extramarital love-affair with Derek and her consequent misery that he thought he must say goodbye to Elizabeth and return to the arms of his wife.

"It's just not *fair.*" She kept repeating, until I, impatiently and perhaps unkindly, pointed out that as a mistress, she had no rights. I left early.

Meanwhile in my classes, the erotic allure of Dora's garments had escalated and was quite embarrassing. Jake now made sure that he sat in a seat behind her, putting himself out of the line of vision of those dangerous eyes, so longing and inviting.

Poor Martha had sensibly realised her inability to learn a foreign tongue and now watched TV with my husband in the room next door.

She had asked me,

"Would you mind? I find it terribly lonely at home when Gregor is out and he does love your class so much, I'd hate to stop him." Jim was quite amenable and provided her with cups of tea which she said she much preferred to wine.

I wondered if the class had as much fascination for Gregor since Freda had left, but he continued to attend and seemed cheerful. His lack of grammar made him heavy going but he had charm and I admit I liked to let my eyes rest on his tonsure and thick grey curls. He had started to take extra tuition with me, which swelled the coffers and was fun too.

Blatant Derek delved more deeply than ever into private thoughts and motivations, asking questions of Brian and Dora which seemed particularly tactless in the circumstances.

It was a relief when the summer holidays came along. I decided to take a few days in Paris to relax but Jim was not all that keen.

"Why don't you just go yourself, dear? You know you like all that froggy stuff much better than I do."

We laughed, but I feel hurt when someone speaks derogatively of such a wonderful culture. Also, I was surprised that he would let me go off on my own. I put it down to misplaced pride as I was financing the trip.

The truth was much simpler.

He used my absence to organise the removal of all that he considered his own possessions from the flat and also his elopement with poor, plump, dowdy Martha.

They were running away to Naples!

Jim was always fond of pasta, but I know for certain that he does not understand *one word* of Italian.

INVADERS

Though there are many gardens and hundreds of beautiful mature trees, the west end could not be more urban in character. Continuous traffic travels the main roads from early morning until midnight, with a flurry of taxis around 3am, while side roads have wall-to-wall parking day and night. Hyndland is served by several bus routes, each on a ten or twenty minute schedule. Local shops have constant deliveries from all sizes of vans. The large ones have hydraulic equipment to speed unloading. Incredibly gigantic pantechnicons bring fresh flowers from Holland and, because of their weightless fairy-like load, are bigger than many a house. I cannot approve of such monstrous vehicles on the road, yet if you are lucky enough to find one parked with its door open, you should pop your head inside and breathe the heady aroma. It is the atmosphere of heaven. Much more threatening are the articulated lorries delivering cars from the manufacturers. These can transport eight, ten or more saloons, and must represent a terrible weight. A few years ago, one misjudged the corner at Clarence Drive and Hyndland road and collided with a two-storey high lampost. Fortunately the standard did not quite fall over or it would have smashed into and demolished at least one set of bay windows. These monstrous lorries should be banned from a residential district. Strange to remember that long before they existed, it was once an envied job for a young man to drive a car north from the factories in the south, never exceeding 40mph in order to cosset the new engine.

Throughout the day we also hear the regular warning sounds of approaching police cars as they hurry to some crime, ambulances rush to one or other of the two hospitals in the west end and sometimes a flotilla of fire engines, heaviest and most blood-curdling of all vehicles, will hurtle down the hill on a practice run.

How overpoweringly busy and noisy it sounds!

Nevertheless unstoppable Nature flourishes in spite of the

furious noise, the pavements and the pollution. The west end is leafy and green. Trees and shrubs, with birds of all kinds to inhabit them, decorate every street. I can count twelve mature trees from my kitchen window, some of them clothed in pink or white blossom at the moment. The back gardens are full of flowers in the Spring and even front patches can grow wonderfully healthy hydrangeas, rhododendrons, pieris and clematis as well as shrubs and evergreens. In summer, it seems particularly miraculous to me that, in spite of buses and lorries passing only yards away, crowds of bees are toiling amongst my plants until darkness falls. I have few flowers but bees seem to favour the smallest most insignificant blooms. I wonder what sort of honey is produced from the nectar in my garden? I know of at least two beekeepers in G12.

Our family has a little house on the east coast with a tiny garden where the bees are the noisiest things around. Overlooking the sea, that little patch is as quiet and remote as my Glasgow frontage is noisy and busy. The Fife garden is surrounded by old walls built of the various beautiful cream and ochre stones that are found in that area. They make a charming background for the plants. Unfortunately the nooks and crevices in the walls offer attractive homes to snails. Snails are my enemy in Fife. Sometimes I wage war against them, going out on a rainy evening with heavy shoes and a hard heart to commit snail massacre. At other times I resignedly discard the sad small stalks, all that remains of yesterday's new plants and... shrug and accept no French marigolds, no delphiniums, no lupins, for snails find these specially delectable. But this story is about Glasgow and never have I seen a snail or a slug in my Clarence Drive garden. They must be there, for I have noticed a nibbled leaf or two, but they are invisible. Are these surreptitious city snails? Where do they live? Red sandstone has few crevices to offer. Two years ago I noticed another sign that these mysterious creatures enjoyed a life around my tenement. On the damp ground just inside my gate, was a definite clue that they existed and I burst out laughing. Surely it must be the aftermath of a Snail's Ball for the design of the little silvery trails really made it seem as if several of the species had gone

through the complicated figures of an eightsome reel. It put
me in a good mood for the day and somewhat softened my
harsh feelings towards snails. But that was not the end of the
story for within a few weeks, I found trails on my front step
and doormat. Perhaps only two this time, they had climbed
the seven stairs from pavement level, obviously curious to
investigate my porch. I felt this was overstepping the limit.
Worse was to come. Quite soon I found a wandering snail
trail *on the rug in my front hall.* Unacceptable! I could not
work out how it, or they, could have gained access, for the
front door has a bristled draught excluder which would be
unpleasant if not impossible for a small slimy thing to
bypass. Perhaps it had been brought in with the greengro-
ceries? Or with some of my gardening equipment? As the trail
did not appear to exit from the front door, the snail must still
in the house. I had been invaded! Did my invader wear a
shell? Or was it a *slug*? And I shuddered at this thought.

I have a habit of wandering in bare feet at bedtime. What
if I should tramp on it in the dark? That would be nasty for
both of us.

I searched thoroughly amongst the various objects that
accumulate near my front door, but could find nothing. Each
morning I looked around very carefully but no snail was to be
seen though obviously it had been out walking through the
night, for there was always a fresh trail, sometimes simple but
often quite complicated. Though scientifically ignorant about
garden molluscs, I did not understand how it could survive.
Surely it required moisture to create that glistening trail.
Where was the wee thing getting a drink? Did it know of a
secret portal where it might nip out for a snack of greenery,
then return to practise its enchainements on my rug? That
made it sound like that favourite story of my childhood about
seven dancing princesses. I searched all around my doorway
but found nothing.

It continued for many days and was a mystery and a
nuisance and I will reveal something of my character when I
say it was also a responsibility. I intended going off for a fortnight's holiday quite soon. What could I do about the snail? If
I had come across it in different circumstances, I might easily
have ended its existence with a quick stamp, but the idea of

the creature miserably dying of thirst in my house seemed
horrible. I could imagine it in its endless perambulations,
suffering the agonies of someone lost in the desert, faltering,
stumbling, changing direction, perhaps even hallucinating...
going more and more slowly, though how much more slowly
can a snail go?

On the day I left, and I blush to admit it, I put out a saucer
of water and a lettuce leaf on the floor.

When I returned, the leaf was untouched. Had it
succumbed? But soon, I realised that the snail was still with
me and it stayed for weeks. Then suddenly, one morning there
was no trail to brush away. It had gone and I was snail-free
and able to tread my floors unwarily once again.

Was there a secret entrance? Perhaps there was, because
one morning last week, shortly after treating myself to a new
rug for the hall, I stood motionless and incredulous gazing at
the square silver design which decorated its thick pile. It
looked very like the instruction plan for some old dance,
perhaps the Lancers?

THE BLUE TWEED CAPE

I wakened to a beautiful morning. My wife Jean is always up unnecessarily early on a Saturday and she had pulled the curtains back. I could hear her laughing with the children in the kitchen.

I felt too comfortable to get up, yet not relaxed enough to go back to sleep.

I was disgruntled and that's a rotten way to feel first thing in the morning.

Just above the red sandstone tenements on the other side of Falkland Street I could see a small piece of blue sky. It seemed to beckon me. I regarded those flats piled one on top of another with extreme dislike, just like so many enormous prison cells. I wanted to escape.

Don't get me wrong. We're not talking about the typical idea of a Glasgow tenement with its cramped two rooms, only a single room in many cases. Oh no, these tenements were built, as in so many European cities, for the wealthy middle classes. They were built when fuel and servants were cheap and available. These are wonderful flats, luxury flats. Ours has six rooms, all very spacious, with soaring ceilings, stained glass windows and beautiful woodwork. Not so much Victorian as Art Nouveau in style. There is even a fireplace in the hall. You could hold a small dance in the hall and our guests usually drift out there at parties, not that I'm keen on entertaining. That's Jean's department.

There was a time, forty years ago, when these flats did not sell. They were too large, too difficult to heat and too expensive to maintain on an ordinary salary, but those who bought at that time were making a very clever investment. My wife's parents bought this flat in 1966 for £5,000. At the time that was rather more than the salary than my father-in-law would earn in five years. He was a lecturer at Glasgow University, as I am myself. I don't know how they afforded it. Perhaps they had a windfall from an elderly relative.

You could easily add a couple of noughts to that price

now. And the rest. Quite scary to think you live in a property worth more than half a million. If we had to start from scratch, we could hardly afford a much smaller flat in Hyndland nowaday.

in 1997, my wife's parents very considerately popped off and left the house to their only daughter, Jean. I should not be flippant about it for it was a terrible time. Jean was pregnant with our second kid and I thought she might lose it when we got word of the car crash. Her parents were just reaching sixty, thinking of retirement. I hardly thought our marriage would survive the tragedy.

As I said, when I wakened this morning, I felt I needed to escape those heavy stone walls and mullioned windows and especially the streets crowded with parked cars.

I needed to get into the country and feel the wind on my face.

I suppose you would describe me as a romantic. I never have lived in the country proper, but it has always been my ambition.

Last night I was reading, yet again, Tolstoy's stories of the Cossacks. These intoxicating tales describe the drinking, gambling, womanising young army officers from Moscow, who, owing money to everyone, escape the sophisticated city and travel the incredible distance south to the Caucasus. There, where immense mountains dominate the landscape, these dissipated young men fall in love with the free open-air life which the Cossacks lead. How my heart beat with pleasure as I read,

> *"The morning was crystal clear. Suddenly he saw, at what seemed to him at first glance to be about twenty paces away, gigantic pure white masses with gentle curves and fantastical airy summits minutely outlined against the distant sky. When he realised the distance... he gave himself a shake but the mountains were still there.*
>
> *"What's that? What is it?" he asked the driver.*
>
> *"Why, the mountains," answered the Tartar indifferently.*
>
> *With the swift movement of the troika over the smooth road the mountains appeared to run along the*

horizon, their rose-coloured crests glittering in the
light of the rising sun.

Yes, Tolstoy's tale was certainly to blame for my dissatis-
faction. I would go into the country today and go alone. Not
in a troika, unfortunately. The old Toyota must suffice.

Jean was in the kitchen writing her shopping list. I kissed
her and said,

"'Morning, darling. Really think it's a day for the country
today. Get some fresh air in my old city lungs."

She smiled brightly and put down her pencil.

"What a great idea! The kids will love that and I can
easily shop tomor..."

I interrupted her hurriedly,

"No, no, I'll go myself today, I think."

That soldier of Tolstoy had no encumbrances such as a
wife and three kids. He rode through the forest on his small
trusty Kabarda horse alone or accompanied by a wily Tartar,
a magnificent hunter, dressed in tightly belted, ragged sheepskin coat. That night in the small dark over-heated izba, they
would drink chikhir and joke with the beautiful Cossack girls
who sat on top of the stove in their simple revealing smocks,
so much more charming than the armour of corset and crino-
lines worn by the Moscow ladies.

I could see surprise, disappointment then anger chase
each other in quick succession across Jean's face and I left
the kitchen before she could say a word. She has often
suggested that we should go out to Mugdock Park on a
Saturday but I generally have a student to see or some work
to do. In fact there was plenty that I should do today, but I
ignored it.

The trees were just turning and there might be mushrooms
in the woods. That was a great Russian delight, to gather
mushrooms. Truthfully I have never cared for mushrooms,
always leave them at the side of my plate in fact and I have
certainly never gathered any wild ones, but the idea is so
charming that I hoped I might find some today.

I grabbed my anorak and a big woollen scarf. The weather
might easily change in October. These articles seemed very
pedestrian compared to the furs and sheepskin of Tolstoy's

stories. I opened the wardrobe and looked through the clothes hanging there. Many were now seldom used in these informal times of jeans and t-shirts.

Right at the end of the rail there was an unfamiliar garment. I felt sure that I had never seen it before. It was large and made of pale blue tweed with a darker overcheck. The lining was a rich red, the colour of blood. I brought it out. It was a lady's cape, but Jean had never worn anything like it in her life. Nor had her mother, who was a frilly floral sort of person. Whose cape could this be?

I took it anyway. No idea what I might do with it, but it was warm and had a touch of the exotic.

As I left the bedroom, I heard Jean calling,

"Take out the rubbish and the re-cycling before you go, will you?"

She may have added 'please' but it sounded more like 'at least'.

Tolstóy's young officers had servants to perform those mundane tasks for them, lucky devils. However, as I gathered the re-cycling together I noticed a Guardian special pamphlet giving all the info about mushrooms. How fortuitous, I thought and shoved it in my pocket.

I drove off with no plans. I thought I might go as far as Glencoe. The grandeur of the scenery enticed me. Unfortunately, without breakfast my empty stomach drained my ambition and I found myself heading towards Drymen where I knew I could find an early lunch.

Loch Lomond seemed the best place after that and I passed Balmaha and climbed up and on towards Rowardennan. It was really busy and not at all as I had imagined my adventure. I should have set off earlier. I found my favourite beach and took almost the last parking place. I walked along beside the loch but it was not as I had imagined. People were everywhere. Children were shouting and throwing balls, dogs were dashing up and down. A small group of dedicated artists were sketching on the shore. They looked elderly and chilly. Several boats were on the loch and others were being unloaded from 4x4s driven right on to the beach. There was not one iota of romance. I left the loch and tried to cross the road but that was as busy as Clarence Drive.

The whole area was reminiscent of Hyndland on a Saturday morning.

I had made a foolish mistake in not leaving earlier and heading much further north. Risking life and limb I crossed the road and walked up the side of a stubble field in search of that wild freedom that I had been reading about with such pleasure. The ground rose steeply and I climbed towards a small group of trees. It wasn't the fathomless forest of Tolstoy's story but perhaps I could find some solitude there. So far there had always been vociferous family groups and determined walkers within earshot. Perhaps the trees would cut off the sound of humanity. Perhaps I would find some mushrooms.

The wood was deeper than I had thought and there was a strange mysterious stillness about it. Quite spooky in fact. The trees did cut off all noise from the outside and quite suddenly, I found myself very much alone. Well that was what I had wanted, I told myself. Though a little horse or a Tartar huntsman would have been company. A wind seemed to have arisen and the leaves made a sad shirring sound all around me. I ventured further into the trees and found that in the middle there was a hollow with old branches in it. It looked as though there would be plenty of wildlife around. Suppose I was quite pleased not to have a huntsman with me for I'm not a bloodthirsty sort of guy. The idea of popping off a rifle at some small creature suddenly made me feel a bit queasy. I sat down under a tree and took out the mushroom book.

By jove, what a lot of poisonous mushrooms there are. I had never realised. The writer was a chef and wanted us to enjoy all the marvellous edible fungi, but obviously did not want any of his readers to succumb! He carefully pointed out the dangerous and the extremely dangerous and how some edible ones looked not unlike the dangerous. Mistakes were possible and his caution for his readers' safety exceeded his enthusiasm for a delicious mushroom feast. At least that's how it seemed to me. It was horrifying! Gathering wild mushrooms seemed far too much of a gamble, a Russian roulette sort of gamble and I considered my philosophy of non-fungus eating safest and best.

You know how reading can make you tired? Well, I started to feel sleepy.

I rolled up my scarf for a pillow, then wrapped the tweed
cape around me and lay down under the tree. It was then that
I started to feel the magic suggested by the Tolstoy stories.
The sound of the leaves above me became musical and
soothing, the dry leaves and twigs underneath me gave off a
pungent earthy smell that conjured some other time and
place. The birds started to make a louder chirping and I
relaxed and felt very content. The cape was warm and
comforting and seemed to enfold me in a safe, almost
maternal way. I lay on my right side with my right hand
under my cheek and my left hand clasping my right wrist.
Yes, this is what I had been searching for. This was perfection.
I would not fall asleep but I would just lie and *think*. So
seldom that one gets a chance just to think in this busy life.

What would I think about? Something academic? The
chaos theory?

Too difficult.

Tolstoy and his strange tortured life? Too upsetting.

What I would cook for the couple that were coming to
dinner next week?

I knew that Jean would rather do it herself, but we had
enjoyed a very splendid barbeque at their house with the
husband in charge, and I wanted to show that I too could
produce a fabulous meal. I would probably need some advice
from Jean, for so far pancakes are my only culinary achievement. They are very good pancakes but I realise a meal will
be a bit more complicated.

I looked down at the tweed cape and suddenly I realised
its history. How could it have escaped my memory so
completely?

Serena, a schoolfellow of Jean's had married an American
fellow when she was twenty-one and gone off across the
Atlantic. She kept in touch with her old friends and visited
Scotland every two years or so. One time she had come in
October and unexpectedly encountered bitterly cold weather
without the correct clothes to deal with it. Determined not to
be caught out on her next visit, she came laden with too
many heavy clothes, for it was a particularly mild November.
Such are the vagaries of our climate. As she was visiting
other parts of Scotland, she left the tweed cape with us. And

although she had returned once or twice since then, somehow the cape was always forgotten.

Jean was sure that Serena did not really like the cape and wanted rid of it. I advised her to give it to Oxfam, but she said she couldn't do that in case Serena ever asked for it again. It was a typical female mix-up.

Well anyway, I was thoroughly enjoying the cape. I felt deliciously relaxed. Momentarily, I wondered if anyone walking through the wood and seeing a tall man wrapped in a feminine blue cape, with his hiking boots sticking out inelegantly might have thought it peculiar. But I seemed to have escaped all those other people and I was just so comfortable, so terribly comfortable, I did not care.

With the solving of the ownership of the cape I drifted off to sleep.

I awakened with a sudden jerk. I have no idea how long I had been asleep.

My eyes opened and immediately shut again. Directly in my line of vision and only a few feet away from me was a small rabbit. It was watching me as it nibbled a leaf. I peered through my eyelashes for it would realise I was an enemy if I opened my eyes wide. I'm not sure where that theory came from but certainly the rabbit stopped looking at me and continued to eat with great enjoyment. There is nothing as endearing as a rabbit stuffing its little face. Its nose wiggles as it chews faster than your eyes can believe. I suspect this particular rabbit was quite young and sometimes, as it chewed, it looked around as though it might be reprimanded for eating whatever it was cating. It was very cute. It was Walt Disney cute and I was charmed and also terrified that my slightest movement might scare it away.

That cunning huntsman of Tolstoy's usually had a dead rabbit or pheasant dangling from his belt and I realised, not for the first time, that I was much more the sort of chap to watch animals rather than shoot them.

My right leg started to cramp but I was unwilling to stretch it. Any movement might put an end to this woodland repast, this unique experience.

What was the little blighter eating now? The leaf was demolished and the rabbit now sat on its haunches holding a small chunk of something between its forepaws. For all the world, it looked like a child with a piece of melon. It would take a bite of whatever it was, then, with its little jaws going like miniature pistons, stretch its neck and ears and look into the distance or to the right or left. Sometimes it looked straight at me but I might as well have been a fallen log.

The rabbit turned his back on me and continued eating.

What delicacy had he found? There was little greenery on the ground.

Suddenly it struck me. Mushrooms. He had been successful where I had failed but of course he was closer to the ground with sharper sense of sight and smell. The clever little devil! He was certainly enjoying his find.

Suddenly I had a terrible idea. You will think I am an idiot but my blood ran cold at the thought that this small creature might be eating *poisonous* mushrooms *while I was happily watching him!*

My rational side suggested that surely a wild creature would know what was good or bad for him.

My emotional side insisted he was just a baby still. These were possibly the first mushrooms he had ever seen and he was filling his little stomach with deadly poison. Those busy little jaws might never munch another leaf!

I considered those two possibilities for a few moments until the emotional side triumphed and I jumped to my feet. The rabbit jumped ten inches in the air then scuttled off along the path, showing, as all rabbits do, a clean pair of heels and a white tuft.

My legs were very stiff as I disentangled myself from the cape and I stamped my feet to rid them of pins and needles.

I stepped over to the spot where the rabbit had been eating. I'm no woodsman or botanist and I could not even tell if the few broken fragments on the ground were the remains of fungi, never mind whether they were poisonous or not.

And what was I going to do, if they were poisonous? Chase after that rabbit, cleverly distinguishing from its fellows, and give it an emetic?

I was cold and stiff and quite hungry. It was after three and the warmth of the day had faded.

Jane would wonder where I had gone. Would she be worried?

As I tramped back down the hill to the car park, the familiar feelings of inadequacy and ineffectuality oppressed me. What had I hoped this day would bring me?

The drive home was slow and boring, as everyone else had felt the afternoon coming to a chilly end and left at the same time.

When I reached home, the house looked spick and span and there was a good smell of cooking. I had an excellent appetite for just about anything but hoped there were no mushroms or rabbit involved.

Jean was sitting at the kitchen table and the children were playing quietly in their bedroom. She looked up at me and I could see she had been crying.

"Where on earth have you been all this time?" she asked and started to weep.

I wondered if her tears were because of worry for my absence and I felt a bit guilty.

"Have I been gone long? I... I didn't realise the time. I just popped down to Loch Lomond and it was busy... but very pleasant. The roads were impossible coming home and I... you didn't think anything had happened to me did..."

She interrupted me,

"I have had some dreadful news. Serena is dead!"

"Serena!"

"Yes, you must know who I mean. Remember! Serena! My old school friend that went to America."

Her sadness had changed to irritation. Perhaps she thought I had forgotten who Serena was but at that moment no person was more vivid to me. Serena's cape had wrapped me in a cocoon of bliss that day,

"Of course I remember Serena. What has happened to her?"

"She's dead. In a car crash just like Mummy and Daddy..."

And laying her head on the table, Jean burst into uncontrollable sobbing.

I stood there, unsure of what to do or say.

What terrible news, with its echoes of her parents' accident.

Suddenly I thought of the children in the other room and grabbed the door handle to go and see if they were all right.

A fresh outburst of grief stopped me and I suddenly remembered something the bereavement counsellor had said to me in that terrible dark time in 1997. She was a small, energetic grey-haired woman and she had taken me aside after the session,

"I hope you won't mind me making a suggestion" she said and she seemed rather embarrassed, "But I notice that often when your wife is particularly sad, you look away from her, often turn your body right away. Try to turn towards her then and take her in your arms. She specially needs your love and support in those moments of extreme misery."

I resented the woman's implied criticism at the time. Did she mean I was running away from my wife's sorrow? However I noticed that very often I *did* tend to look away when Jean was crying bitterly. It worried me. Perhaps I *was* hard-hearted but when I thought about it, I realised it was the difference between male and female, for if I had been shedding such uninhibited tears, I should have preferred not to be noticed. My masculine pride would have baulked at appearing so vulnerable.

Now here I was once more turning away from her in her sadness, about to leave the room, unnecessarily, for of course the kids would be fine.

I went over to Jean and knelt in front of her. When I cradled her in my arms, her hysterical tears calmed almost immediately.

"I want you to do something for me, darling," she was still sobbing.

"Anything, sweetheart."

"I know it seems silly but in our wardrobe, right at the end, there is a blue cape that belonged to Serena. I just can't bear to see it ever again. I would be imagining poor Serena in it... and she'll never wear it again now. Please, will you give it in to a charity shop? Not the one in Hyndland Road, they might put it in the window. Will you do that for me, darling."

I nodded vehemently and held her tighter.

"Yes, of course I will. I promise you'll never see it again"

I could make that promise easily, for the cape still lay under a tree, on the hill near Loch Lomond.

❖◆❖